Soldier of the Cross
A novel by
John Oliver Mason

2

I wish to give my greatest possible thanks to all my friends who have guided me and encouraged me in this work-Harry Hyde, Harold Ash, Nancy Forrest, David Gracie, Ken Collier, and Fred Stefon. I thank them for their advice and encouragement while I was writing this book.

I want to also give a special thanks to my fellow writers-Walter Snow, Bob Sadler, Ivo Giomi, Tim Sheard, Joy Stocke, Fran Metzman, Sandy Crimmins, Denise Larrebee, and all the gang at the Sedgwick Cultural Center, Philadelphia, PA. Thanks also to Arthenia Hall, and to the Moonstone Arts Center and its beloved founder, Larry Robin.

I thank Andres Cruciani for his great editing work.

May the memory of Ivo, Sandy, Harry, Harold, and David continue to be a blessing.

3

In my life I have known many fine people in the religious field. It is not my intention to insult sincere religious faith, but to analyze religious bigotry and intolerance.

John Oliver Mason

4

I dedicate this book to the brothers and sisters in Leyv Ha-Ir Reconstructionist Congregation.

5

1

The Chamber of Commerce of Midland County held its monthly meeting for January 1978 in Salon 2 of the Dorita Hotel in Erno, New Jersey. The leading business and political figures of the county–real estate developers and construction company owners grumbling about building trades unions, oil and gas investors complaining about environmental laws, restaurant owners upset about equal opportunity rules and complaints about sexual harassment by their female employees, and politicians sympathetic to their plight–dined on roast chicken, rice pilaf, mixed vegetables, vanilla ice cream, and coffee, muttering among themselves about minorities and unions amid the bluish carpet with the odd black patterns and drab-red curtains.

At the podium, the chamber's President, Richard Corbett–like many of the members, in his late-fifties, with whitish-grey hair, in a fine but dull suit–concluded his report:

"In spite of the socialistic ideas stemming from Washington, whereby the government is to control *our* lives supposedly for *our* sake–" a moan from the audience–

"we continue to operate our economy under the free-enterprise system, which men have found to be worth fighting for, as they have done in Chile, where they overthrew the Communist regime and continue to undo its damage, and where that system of freedom continues its success in South Africa...

"Recently," continued Corbett, "we have seen the rise of radical factions– *women's liberation! the homosexuals!–demanding* their alleged rights!" (More moans from the audience.) "We who are assembled here this evening are really the most significant members of this community–the entrepreneurs, the builders of factories, the employers, whose decisions benefit everyone. It is only *fitting,* therefore, that *we* take the lead in the decision-making in the halls of government, and insist that the government do *nothing,* except allow us to make our investments and create jobs for workers, so that everyone join in our prosperity."

On the far-right side of the head table sat the Reverend David Lucas, pastor of Wingate Memorial Baptist Church, and son-in-law of Richard Corbett. Lucas listened to every word his father-in-law said; Corbett owned the Corbett Broadcasting Company, which owned several radio stations around Philadelphia and Southern New Jersey, and had investments in other businesses in Central and Southern New Jersey.

Corbett ended with, "And now, let us have our closing benediction by the Reverend David Lucas."

Lucas rose, smiled, mounted the podium and proclaimed:

"Truly, Richard is right. It's through living a clean, industrious life that success is attained. I learned that the hard way, through trials and tribulations, that faith in God, through his son Jesus Christ, and following His laws, is the way to live. You men here are proof of that, and I commend you. Now let us pray."

Everyone closed their eyes and Lucas intoned: "Lord, guard us and guide us as we depart this company of ours. As the old blessing says, 'May the Lord watch over me and thee, as we are absent one from another.' Ah-men."

"Ah-men" murmured through the group.

Lucas descended from the stage, and he heard a voice state, "Reverend?"

Lucas saw a tall, thin-faced man in a navy-blue suit extending his hand: "I'm John

Thomas Guthrie, the state senator."

Lucas smiled and said, "Nice meeting you, sir," shaking his hand.

Corbett, standing behind Lucas, said, "John is keen to support free-enterprise in Trenton. He had a real-estate business on Culver Street downtown, before getting elected."

Lucas stepped aside to let Corbett pass, and Corbett added, "John also helps other local businesses deal with government interference in their performance. Right, John?"

The senator smiled, "For sure, Richard." (Corbett was always "Richard," never "Dick," "Rich," or "Rick.") "I believe the companies know what they're doing, let 'em alone."

All three men moved to the exit. "You know, Reverend," said Guthrie, "I heard a lot of good stuff about you from Richard and your radio program on Sunday," started Guthrie.

"Thank you, Senator," replied Lucas.

"Uh, it's John, okay?" smiled Guthrie. "Have you followed the movement in

Miami, you know, the campaign against homosexuals."

"Oh, sure have–John," said Lucas. "It was great to stop the homos like that. I wish they'd learn what a terrible sin it is. Civil Rights have nothing to do with it."

"Well, I can help you about that," assured Guthrie, as they said good-bye to men passing to the coat-check and the exits. "I can help block bills that would give them more privileges."

"It would be great if you could," said Lucas, his mouth a straight line.

There was a pause, then Guthrie continued, "In fact, I could sponsor legislation that would make their rights, you know, would make the state civil rights laws not apply to them." Guthrie's eyes widened as he added, "No, not just a law, but a constitutional amendment!"

Lucas smiled, "Senator, uh, John, that would be great but"–he sighed and said, "I'm sorry, but I don't like to deal with politics. I mean, I care about what goes on in the world, I try to keep up with the news, but, I'm sorry, but, it's all so dirty."

"Yeah, I understand," nodded Guthrie, recalling the magazine article calling him one of the ten most corrupt members of the legislature. "But please, think it over, okay,

Dave, can I call you Dave?"

    "Oh, sure, all my friends call me Dave," smiled Lucas, and they shook hands.

2

Richard Corbett and the Reverend Lucas strode to the parking lot beside the Dorita,

through the bitter January night air. They heard laughter and disco music and lifted their

heads——a block down was Waldo's, the county's gay bar.

"They make me so *sick!*" muttered Lucas, hissing air in. "Homos, right out in the

open!" Corbett nodded and hummed "Um-hum."

They climbed inside Corbett's Cadillac, and Lucas asked "Just got this, Richard?"

"Yes, a week ago," said Corbett. "Why not, I can afford it. I'm a successful man,

so why *shouldn't* I?"

Corbett started the car, and looked at Lucas's face pulled downwards. "Dave,

what's the matter?" he asked.

"The fags, those guys at Waldo's" moaned Lucas, as Corbett steered the car into

the road. "I keep preaching and yelling, I keep *telling* people to stay away from the porn

and the booze, and they still go at it." A second's quiet, and Lucas asked, "Richard, what

more can I do?"

Oh, you're doing fine," assured Corbett, patting Lucas' knee. "Just keep going about your business. Oh," he added, "you going to consider what John talked about?"

"About the–what he said?"

"*Yeees,*" drawled Corbett, as he eased the car through the wet snow, "campaigning against the homos."

"Well, like I told him, I don't like politics," stumbled Lucas, "Everyone seems so, like, all the corruption."

"Yes, I understand," agreed Corbett. "But think about what John said, okay?"

"Okay," nodded Lucas.

"You going to tell Christine what went on?"

"Naw," said Lucas, "this kind'a stuff, women should stay out of it, for their sake. It's not for them."

"Yes, that's true," agreed Corbett. "Also, Helen and I've been wondering when we'll see grandchildren."

"Working on it," assured Lucas, although he did not like the work involved. Then he thought out loud, "Having a kid would be nice, I know. It would be something to take that young life and make something good out of it. My kid'll learn about Jesus from the start, and he'll never do what his dad did, when I was younger and stupider. Oh, man, what a character I was."

"Raising children's tough, even if you're affluent like I am," recalled Corbett, navigating the Cadillac through the two-lane road leading to his own house. "After Christine was born, Helen's been complaining about these chest pains and weaknesses. For twenty years, she's done nothing but eat very little and go into her room. I shell out a hundred dollars a week for that girl to clean the house up. The girl does alright. Helen complains about her all the time, though. Helen complains about everying. Oh, I'm sorry, you have to go home now."

"'S'alright," forgave Lucas. It took another ten minutes, but they were at the parsonage, a two-story house, half red brick at the bottom, white at the top, behind a brief lawn.

Lucas went in and entered the living room, where he found Christine sitting on the cushioned floral-printed chair–longish blond hair brushed back, pinkish-whitish complexion, blue eyes, prominent but modest bosom, wearing a turtleneck blouse and floral skirt. "Oh, hi, honey," she said, "how was the meeting?"

"Alright," shrugged Lucas.

"What did you all talk about?" she asked.

"It's *not* for women, okay?" he stated, smiling like at a little kid. "Your father did fine, as always, is you're wondering." His eyes grazed the couch, and he asked, "What's that you're reading?"

"Uh, *Hamlet*, Shakespeare," confessed Christine, her voice shaking–did she do something wrong? "You know I studied English Lit–"

Lucas snatched the book from Christine's hand. "Study the Bible, that's all you need," decided Lucas, then he smirked, "All that college, for what? All you are is my wife."

Her voice and head lowered as she said, "I still would like to be an English teacher–"

"Never mind that," grunted Lucas, still smirking. "You're my wife, period. That's that women's lib stuff, you don't get into that, do you?"

"Uh, no," said Christine, her head down.

"Good girl." Then, he turned and went up the stairs, grunting, "Gotta check to see what I gotta do."

Christine let out a moan and a twitch.

Lucas turned, "Something wrong?"

"I don't know, honey, I'm not–my stomach's upset."

"Well, see," smiled Lucas again, "if you're home all day, you can just lie down when you feel like it. In fact, you should get to bed, I'll join you later."

"All right, honey." She followed Lucas up the stairs.

I just remembered," said Lucas, "you want your allowance, I guess."

"Uh, yes, David," muttered Christine, her head bent down.

"I'll get it to you in the morning," said Lucas as he went up the stairs, "just don't buy anything stupid."

Lucas went into the den and sat behind the polished plank desk, the Olivetti typewriter on his right side. He gathered the notes for her Sunday Sermon, and then leaned back, the chair creaking. He surveyed the three pictures on the eggshell beige walls:

Jesus, done on black velvet, in the center; on the left, Lucas' mentor, the Reverend Doctor RT Garfield, founder of the Garfield Bible Institute, in Gillyville, Pennsylvania, where he learned the ministry, how to preach the Gospel; and on the right, Billy Sunday, the great "Baseball Evangelist," the champion of the simple, plain unvarnished Gospel, a manly man for Jesus; Billy Sunday was the role model that Doctor Garfield wanted his students, like David Lucas, to emulate. The chaplain at Fort Hood, Texas, where he got into trouble, also mentioned Billy Sunday.

Lucas next remembered Mrs. Dewey, the retired English teachers who taught English composition at the Institute. In the first semester at the Institute, Mrs. Dewey gave a writing assignment–"How did you come to Jesus?"

Lucas pulled the essay out of his top desk drawer–he kept it all this time. He wrote of how, when he was in the Army early in the 'sixties, he got drunk on whiskey and smoked marijuana behind the barracks; how, as he staggered towards nowhere in particular, an Duty Officer yelled at him, "Soldier, you're drunk and disgusting!"–and Lucas slammed his fist into the Duty Officer's face; how another officer ran towards him and proclaimed, "You're under arrest, mister!"–and Lucas slugged him also; how he screamed a number of profanities before the MPs came, and Lucas punched the younger one in the nose, and the sergeant struck Lucas.

Lucas' essay also told of his time in the stockade, where a chaplain-Daniel Briggs, a Major- told them of Jesus and how Jesus could save them from sin; how Lucas read and re-read his copy of the New Testament the chaplain's assistant handed out to the inmates; how Chaplain Briggs also spoke of Billy Sunday as a role model to follow on being a Christian man; and how, at Chapel, hearing Chaplain Briggs preach, Lucas started crying–and then and there, David Lucas gave himself over to Jesus.

Now, he, David Lucas, who bullied a fat and brainy kid in school from first to twelfth grades, who couldn't care less about learning–he scanned stories about Julies

Caesar, and recited Shakespeare's *Julius Caesar*, and forgot about them the next second–
was a Minister of the Gospel of Jesus Christ; he wrote articles in Christian newspapers
and magazines; and his sermons at Wingate were broadcast over Corbett's stations. Only
Jesus could enable him to do that.

Lucas looked at the pictures of Jesus, Doctor Garfield, and Billy Sunday–what
would they think about homosexuals out in the open and other forms of immorality? He
thought of what Guthrie said–the crowd at Waldo's–Corbett asking about grandchildren–
In the Army, Lucas was punished for his sins–smoking grass, drinking, whoring–he knew
America would be punished for its sins.

Lucas went to the bathroom to undress to his underwear. He scanned his six-foot
frame in the mirror: the carefully pushed-back brown hair; the hot-pink cheeks and the
trimmed, thick brown mustache; and the lean, muscled, baseball-player's body.

And then–his penis. Luas recalled Doctor Garfield calling the penis "the Devil's
Doornail," and Garfield gave talks to young men warning them about "the Devil's Itch"
and how women would lead them to destruction. The young ministers-to-be came from

small towns in rural areas, coming to the Institute just out of high school, knowing little about the world or women.

"Don't scratch the Devil's Itch, boys," Garfield warned, his voice like a siren. "If you scratch the Devil's Itch. it'll lead you to all other kids of sins! It'll pass when you get on your knees and pray that it goes away!"

At that, the young men, Lucas included, knelt and beseeched God, "Oh, Lord, take this demon spirit of Satan away from us!"

Lucas thought of his talk with Corbett about having grandchildren, and that meant–sex. It was what got him in trouble in the Army, what got good men into trouble–that dirty sin–which brought life into the world. Lucas reminded himself what Paul said, that it was acceptable in marriage: "It is better to marry than to burn."

Lucas did burn; his groin and his stomach churned, his throat clogged, his breath was shorter–he had to do it. He hated himself for his lust, but–for children–his children–

He scrapped his feet as he walked from the bathroom to the bed; he knew what he had to do. He looked at his wife–her hair, her eyes, her skin–

"Christine," he moaned, "we're going to do it."

Christine's mouth and eyes widened as she pleaded, "Please, don't–"

"Christine, *please*," urged Lucas, "I don't like this either, but your parents want grandchildren!"

She moaned, her arms clutching her chest, as Lucas yanked off the blanket, pulled off her panties…

3

The following Saturday, Lucas arrived at Veterans' Square, to preach to the gay men who hung out there. Snow covered the ground, but the air was not as cold.

Lucas recalled Doctor Garfield speaking about when, as a young minister, he preached outside of "road houses" and brothels as men went inside; "Take the fight for the Gospel to the enemy!" Garfield told the new pastors, like Lucas, "Confront the sinners with their sins! Tell them to their face what lies in store for them in Hell!"

Lucas wore the black overcoat with the extra-heavy lining–he could take the cold, but Christine fussed about him catching a cold–and he had his Bible with him–one of several he acquired over his time as a Christian. He got on a bench, let out a smirk, and proclaimed:

"You homosexuals, you act like the laws of God don't apply to you, but they *do!* You're engaged in a *sin*, the worst, most terrible sin imaginable!"

"What about murder?" called a male voice.

A heckler–Lucas had them before, but he ignored them. "You don't like me coming here, telling you you're on your way to Hell! But it's the truth, whether you like it or not! God doesn't want to leave you in your sins! He wants you to accept Jesus as your Savior! The sin of homosexuality, like all the other sins, will be forgiven of you if you accept Jesus! He died on the Cross in Calvary to take your sins upon himself, then He rose on the Third Day from the grave, and He ascended into Heaven to be with the Father, to prepare a place in Heaven for you! Are your sins so wonderful, that you want to spend eternity in Hell?"

He kept at it for an hour; there weren't that many people in the Square. People said to each other, "That guy again?" What did Doctor Garfield say about this? "NO matter how many people, or how few, you have to preach the Gospel! It's not about numbers in the pews, it's about bringing the Gospel to the *masses*, no matter where they are!"

He got down from the bench; a park worker walked up to Lucas and said, "Hey, why do you bother, you know they won't listen to you."

Lucas turned, smiled, and declared, "I hate homosexuality, it's a terrible sin! I'm dedicated to spreading the Gospel wherever I go, in the face of the enemy! For that I give my life!"

The worker walked away.

Lucas would keep at it; maybe he could preach at Waldo's? Wednesday he would be at the parking lot of the nearby shopping mall.

Lucas arrived home, undoing his coat, rubbing the cold from his arms and shivering. Christine stepped forward and whispered, "David, aren't you afraid you'll get hurt?"

""Not at all," he proclaimed, 'a real man isn't afraid of pain. I'm ready to die for Jesus, Christine, so get used to that!"

4

On Sunday; Lucas woke up at six AM, got into a set of yellow sweat clothes, attached his pedometer, and then got into his daily two-mile run. Christine was still sleeping when he got out. His run took him toward the municipal building, close to a mile, then back to the house again.

As he ran, Lucas reviewed the day's work. After his run, he would lift weights at one of the basement, shower, and then get ready for the morning service. Running down the road in the chill January air, Lucas kept up a steady, strong pace, a regular beat on the pavement-*plap-plap-plap.* Lucas inhaled deeply and exhaled firmly, following the advice of the guys at the gym.

Lucas' nose was clogged and runny, and the sweat chilled his forehead. He considered giving it up for the time being, going to the gym instead, but – something told him that such would be weak. Jogging like this in the cold weather was somehow manlier; it built strength of spirit. Doctor Garfield preached this constantly–"Be a man for Christ! Endure what you must for Christ!" He kept jogging – his feet pounding the sidewalks – his arms churning at his sides, back and forth – the wind whining at his ears…

Christine has been just sitting around the house sick all week. *Women!* thought Lucas, *Spoiled children! And Christine brought up so rich!* But Lucas loved Christine so much; an old-fashioned girl, one who believed in and followed old-fashioned rules for men and women. And what a great mother she'd make! Her parents have been on them about that–"When will we see some grandchildren?" But there will be children, great Christian kids who wouldn't go through what their dad went through to find Jesus.

Lucas jogged down the street towards the municipal building, turned around and jogged back towards the parsonage, breathing deep and slow, until he got back inside the house; it all took sixteen minutes and three seconds.

It was the morning service at Wingate Memorial Baptist Church. The church building was in a tree-crowded area of Wingate Road. People filed in through the huge front door leading into the sanctuary, and the little kids were guided downstairs for their Sunday School. The church was made from large gray-brown limestone, with a small front lawn. Rose bushes edged the building, and an announcement board stood facing the road – WINGATE MEMORIAL BAPTIST CHURCH-with the title of the morning's sermon, and the words "The Reverend David Lucas, Pastor" below.

Sitting behind the pulpit, the Reverend David Lucas looked over the congregants, along with checking the notes for his sermon, seeing his wife and his in-laws below in the first center pew. The congregation was around Lucas' age or older, mid to late 'thirties; for many of them, their social life was the church, the place where their friends were.

The congregation finished the hymn "Faith Of Our Fathers," then sat down. Lucas rose and looked on the congregants, his notes in his hand, both confident, not nervous but alert, smiling at the people he ministered to for so long. He began:

"Welcome, brothers and sisters, again, to Wingate Memorial Baptist Church, where we strive to live and act according to the Word of God, as proclaimed through His Son Jesus. In this age of sin and depravity, where the most decent person can be corrupted and let down the path to nowhere, like I was for a long time before I came to Jesus, that's not always easy. But God as they say gives His mightiest battles to His strongest soldiers–" He heard that line somewhere, he thought it was good- "and so the rewards of Heaven will be greater for those who stay strong in the faith."

There was another hymn, muttered throughout, and everyone sat down again, then announcements of the church's activities–Boy Scout troop, Cub Scout pack, women's club, men's bible class, the need for volunteers to mail out the monthly newsletter. Then, Lucas gave the sermon:

"We Christians live in the world, but we are not of the world. We make our livings, our jobs, in the world, and we go about our business in the world, and maybe we have worldly success, but our focus is on the word and world of Jesus, and preparing ourselves for when we see the Father in Heaven.

"To get truly ready for the time we meet Jesus," added Lucas, "we have to keep ourselves separate from the world, even though we live in it. I agree it's not an easy trick. But see what the world tell you, and what the word of God tells you. Lately, I don't know why, the world says it's okay to cheat on your spouse, to have sexual affairs with people who aren't married to, and would never be seen with, and with–sorry to tell you–the same gender."

There were some soft moans; Lucas said what they felt, and several nodded and said, "Yes, so true." Lucas went on:

"Also the world is now telling us that there's no difference between a man or a woman, that women have to do men's jobs or dress and act like men. The Bible tells us in Genesis, 'Man and Woman he created them,' and the world is starting to say there is no such thing as gender, or a man or a woman. That is *so wrong!* The Christian knows the Bible ordains the roles that man and woman live by."

Lucas railed against feminism and gay rights, and added, "Nowadays, we're expected to go along with that, to be hip and trendy! A Christian separates himself from that! A Christian knows the world is corrupted, and he doesn't let himself be corrupted with it.

"You know the Books of Ezra and Nehemiah," added Lucas, "how they went to rebuild the walls of Jerusalem, and there were those who wanted to keep the walls from going up. Why, to be 'open to new ideas'? To hear 'both sides of the story'? Remember the hymn, 'A Mighty Fortress Is Our God,' and we must enter that fortress when we are attacked! A Christian conducts himself according to the Bible whether the world likes it or not. He honors God, His Son Jesus, and the Holy Bible. He doesn't hang out in bars or strip clubs, he doesn't read pornography, he reads the Holy Word of God and he honors the woman who he married and has his children from. The company he keeps is with other Christians, who strengthen his faith. He doesn't have any shame about telling people how much God and Jesus mean to him."

As he preached, Lucas' mind rambled through the events at the Chamber of Commerce dinner-Senator Guthrie's proposed amendment, his chat with Corbett about having children, the crowd outside Waldo's-standing up to the fags—

The organ sounded "Just As I am," and Lucas declared, "Now is the time for you to come to Jesus, and accept him as Lord and Savior. Now is the time, who knows what might happen later on? Accept Him now, He'll take from you the burden of sin that's weighting you down, and give you a new start for the rest of your life. He loved you so much, He died on the cross to take your sins upon Himself. There is no other hope you have, except in Jesus." A couple dozen people trickled down the aisle and knelt in front of the alter, and Lucas prayed with each one of them.

5

Guthrie's bill, which he titled "the State Civil Rights Clarification Act of 1978,"
entered the Senate. As Guthrie promised Lucas, the bill stated the state's civil rights laws
would not apply to homosexuals, which meant that they could be discriminated against to
one's desire.

The hearings on the "Guthrie bill" were big news every evening for about two weeks.
Starting out the hearings was a professor of constitutional law from the University of
Pennsylvania, who warned that the bill was possibly unconstitutional and would not stand
a chance in the Supreme Court.

Another senator pointed that out to Guthrie, who said, "So what, I wanna get the
religious folks on my side, this'll play great with them"

The Reverend David Lucas sat at his desk in the office of Wingate Memorial
Baptist Church, reading the news of the bill. Good, thought Lucas–a strike against the
fags and their sin. Lucas put the paper down, and leaned over the desk to see the bills of

the church–electric, heating oil (getting more each month, he thought), water, and food for the Sunday social hour. He would pass these on to the secretary, who would cut the checks and send them out.

In Lucas' office, a small alcove with windows curved the wall behind him. Right in front of him was another picture of Jesus, with bright glossy paints, done of a canvas of black velvet. By the picture stood a bookcase filled with bibles, some with concordances and all King James. There was a separate concordance and a dictionary of the Bible. There was a set of encyclopedias and annual updates, a present for their anniversary. (Lucas did not think Christine would be interested; he did not ask her.) There was an edition of *Bartlett's Quotations*, which Lucas bought second-hand after his instructor in public speaking at Garfield Bible Institute told the class that such quotes would make a good garnish for any sermon, provided the quotes were relevant and from a certified Christian.

The one that the Institute made the most use of, besides the Bible itself, was *The Fundamentals,* a series of essays written in the 1920's by ministers against such new ideas as "Modernism" and "Higher Criticism", which they did not understand and so believed them to be evil.

Lucas looked at the King James Bible on the desk, and pulled it open. He stopped at the third chapter of the second letter of Paul to Timothy, where Paul warned that tough times for the new Christian sect would come, where people would become bad and turn away from God; the chapter ended with, "All scripture is given by inspiration from God, and is profitable for doctrine, for reproof, for correction, for instruction in righteousness, that the man of God may be perfect, thoroughly furnished unto all good works."

Lucas read it, and thought it would be great for Sunday afternoon bible study, sometime. He jotted the passage onto a notepad, then continued through chapter four.

He read what Paul said about "Preach the word; be instant in season, out of season; reprove, rebuke, exhort with all longsuffering and doctrine; but after their own lusts shall they heap to themselves teachers, having itching ears. And they shall turn away their ears from the truth, and shall be turned unto fables..." And Paul went on about his impending martyrdom.

False teaching—homosexuality accepted as okay—Guthrie's bill—martyrdom— this buzzed within Lucas' mind as he sat at his desk; *what can I do?*

The secretary, Sylvia Duncan– a sharply efficient woman whom nobody asked if she was a Christian–walked in and said, "Reverend, Senator John Guthrie on the line," and walked out.

Lucas picked up the phone and said, "Hello, Senator–John."

"Hello, Dave," said Guthrie, "did you see the news, my amendment was introduced."

"That's great," Lucas said, "best of luck."

"One favor, Dave," said Guthrie, "next month they'll hold hearings on the amendment, and I was wondering–"

What could he want me for? thought Lucas?

"–if you would testify to the committee about the need for such an amendment. The fact that you're a minister of the Gospel would add weight to support it."

"Sure, I'll do it," spouted Lucas, "no problem."

"Great," Guthrie's voice had a smile, "I'll let you know the date and time. Thanks a lot, Dave."

"No problem, John," said Lucas, and they hung up.

Then–Lucas sat, a quiver in him, staring forward, and thought, *What did I just do? I'm a preacher, not a politician!*

Lucas never thought about politics; Doctor Garfield always emphasized to his students, "You must NEVER get into politics! Politics is corrupt and dirty! If you're not a crook when you get in, you're a crook when you get out of it! Separate yourselves from that forever! You are to be Ministers of the Gospel, and the Gospel is your authority! It's the issues of the Spirit you work on!"

Doctor Garfield spoke these words in the 'sixties, whenever the Civil Rights movement came up on the campus. Lucas always acted on this; he has never even voted, in any election.

But–he inhaled, bent his head down, and lifted it up; he gave his word; whenever he was to testify to the committee, he would do so.

6

In mid-February 1975, Lucas went back to his home town-Fieldstone Township, New Jersey-to visit his family and any of his old buddies who would still talk to him. The snow lay thin on the ground, and the sky was gray with no clouds. He kept his six-year-old Plymouth in good order–no junk in the seats, the road dirt cleaned off–but his Bible sat on the passenger side.

He drove past Carl Bertram's Esso station where he worked part-time—the lights were off and the lot was empty; did it close? "Bert" was a great guy to work for-always talking about his time in the Army during *the* war. The sign was still on the window-"I fight poverty, I work!" Lucas always heard Bert talk about the day's issues, like the Viet Nam War ("We ought'a get in there and win this god-damned thing, like we won double-yuh double-yuh two!"), and Civil Rights ("I didn't get this from stompin' around and burnin' shit, I worked for ever' God-damn thing I got! Oh, yeah, I did get a small

business loan from the VA, and the highway the feds build brought more business in, but

I did it all by myself!")

He also remembered the guys he hung out with-entering the Jackpot Inn with fake

IDs to see the "live entertainment," finding girls to have carnal fun with, and harassing

and terrorizing Peter Mullen, who was fat, dully dressed, and was a math genius.

Whatever happened to them-? Hank Pringle? Joe Ostroff? Chuck Denning? Tim

Kaminsky, who entertained everyone with his father's Polish jokes?

Lucas was glad his old life was gone, but he missed those guys. They weren't bad

guys at all, merely young and foolish; every time he came up, he would try to find them—

sometimes he did–and start some pleasant chat, steering it to Jesus–and then they would

say something like, "Great seein' you, Dave, gotta go." If he could only find them…

He drove into the parking lot of the Hilltop Diner; maybe he could find some of them there? Entering the diner, Lucas saw Peter Mullen, waiting for his taxi. Peter looked up and saw Lucas; Peter Mullen–the heavy, brainy kid Lucas and gang others harassed, bullied, and teased to no end at Fieldstone High–faced his former tormentor.

"Hey, Pete," smiled Lucas hopefully as he strode to an empty stool next to Peter.

"Lucas," Peter grunted in response, shifting his shoulder away from him. "I hear you're a preacher in Midland County, that true?"

"Yeah, it's true," Lucas said joyfully, "I love my work, and I married a great Christian girl. How're you these days, Pete?"

"I'm a chemical engineer for Union Carbide, in Camden," returned Peter, a lift in his voice. "I married a good woman, an' I'm doin' a great job. You really cleaned up your act?"

"Yeah, Pete, I really am a Christian," Lucas gravely nodded. "Pete, I can tell you hate me for what me and the guys did to you, but I asked forgiveness from, God, and His

Son Jesus Christ came into me and –"

The waitress at the counter – blond and full-figured – stood at where Lucas and Peter sat and asked, "What'll y' have, sweetheart?"

"Just coffee, for me, thanks," replied Lucas.

She stepped away, and Peter snickered, "Y'know your ol' buddy Hank Pringle? He lost his job at the brewery, kept getting into fights with the Black guys. He punched a woman cop, an' now he's in Rahway. You might've ended up like him, Lucas."

"Still, bitter, huh, Pete?" stated Lucas. "Y'know, it might be a good idea for you if you became a Christian yourself."

"Know something, Lucas?" grunted Peter after he bolted down the last drop of his coffee. "You never, after all your born-again talk, you never once said you were sorry for what you did to me. That was a sin, too, y'know."

"Yeah, it was," agreed Lucas, "an' now I'd like t' apologize."

"Okay," he replied softly, and the waitress brought Lucas his coffee.

"Can we be friends now, Pete?" asked Lucas.

"Maybe someday, not right now."

"Pete," said Lucas, "I'd really like you to take Jesus as your Lord and Savior –"

"I already have a religion," Peter snapped. "I'm doin' great at my job, an' the better I do there, the better I feel when I think about what happened t' your buddy Pringle!"

"You shouldn't enjoy people's suffering like that, Pete," Lucas said. "You might lose your job, your home –"

"You'd like that, huh, Lucas?" sneered Peter, as he moved to pay for his coffee. Outside, tires ground out front, as a car horn beeped.

Peter left a five on the counter and called "My taxi, thanks for the service."

"Bye, hon," she called.

Lucas stood and stared at the blur of movement. He could not talk to Peter about Jesus. If Pete could forgive him, just a little bit...

Lucas arrived at his parents' home–a two-story Sears kit house, with aluminum siding and a small front yard. He entered and hugged his mother, Grace, while his father,

Charlie, curled up on the couch watching the football game on TV.

"Hey, Ma," cheered Lucas as he hugged Grace. He then shrugged off his coat and said to his father, "Hey, Dad–"

"Shuttup, stupid," barked Charlie, "I'm watching the god-damned game!"

Lucas glared at his father; he could never satisfy Charlie, who always griped about his son's misbehavior, his mediocre grades, his time with girls; after Lucas became a Christian, Charlie complained about his son becoming a "creep" and "crazy," and didn't attend his ordination ceremony, saying, "Naw, the game is on."

Lucas hung up his coat, and Grace said, "Wanna help me put the food on the table?"

Lucas took the plate of roasted chicken on the dining-room table, and Charlie snapped, "That's women's work, are you a woman?"

Lucas stomped towards Charlie and griped, "What's the matter with you, Dad, Mom needs help, why don't you help her?"

David heard footsteps and saw his mother carry in the mashed potatoes, then went back to the kitchen and carried in the gravy.

When the food was all on the table, Grace called, "Well, c'mon an' eat!"

"I'm watching the fuckin' game, can't anybody shut up so I can hear?" howled Charlie.

"Y' wanna let it get cold?" griped Grace.

"Heat it up later," called out Charlie.

"I will *not,*" returned Grace as she pulled out her chair. Lucas watched; Dad always talked tough, saying he'd smack anyone standing up to him–then he eased into his seat.

"Dear Lord," prayed David, "We thank thee for this food, and the gift of Thy Son Jesus, for the redemption of our sins, ah-men."

The two of them ate without talking. Half-time came, and Charlie quickly strode to the table to plow into the mashed potatoes, creamed corn, chicken leg and breast, and stuffing.

"So, Ma," David tried to start conversation, "The high school's about to have its game soon, right?"

"Yeah, they're playing a home game against Holy Rosary," Grace answered, referring to Fieldstone's parochial school and longtime rival.

"I think I'll go see it," decided David.

"It's on tomorrow night," said Grace.

"Bunch'a niggers took over the union last month," grumbled Charlie through the food in his mouth. "Use' to be that meetings were fun, now it's just talk, talk, talk."

David and Grace sat silently through Charlie's outburst.

Later that night, Charlie followed his habit of stomping down the stairs into the basement, sat at the dusty old kitchen table and chair, and pulled from the cabinet the bottle of Four Roses. David stepped downstairs and faced him.

"Dad, what's with you?" David asked. "I'm now cleaned up, I'm a Minister living a decent life with a good woman, and every time I come here you complain about something. What more do you want from me, Dad?"

Charlie turned his head, glanced at David, and muttered, "Y' could'a been a great baseball player. Lookit how much they make! Too fuckin' lazy!"

David Lucas turned and walked back upstairs, his head and chest heavy. This was his father–his own father–a man he wanted to please, but he could never please–everything he did was bad or wrong or stupid. Charlie didn't show David how to be a good man–he learned that from Jesus, Doctor Garfield, and Billy Sunday.

Lucas went to the basketball game against Holy Rosary; he might see some of his old buddies there. At the ticket counter, he came upon Edmund Casey, long the high-school's vice-principal, who was still vice-principal, and never would be principal.

Casey made a good impression on the parents who came to the school, and anyone else who didn't know him personally. His full head of grey hair, the dull-checked jackets and suits, told everyone that this man had nothing of the passions, lusts, and bad habits of mere mortals. It was as if he had no part of the regular world, of getting the car fixed, paying bills, and buying groceries. He was so aloof and strict with the kids he wasn't afraid of, so superior, that no student could imagine that Edmund Casey was really ignorant, cowardly, and self-centered, as well as owing his position to political connections.

As Casey saw Lucas at the concession stand buying a hot dog and soda, Casey stated, "Well, is this the David Lucas I remember?"

Lucas recognized Casey and smiled, "Well, Mister Casey, I *am* David Lucas, but not the one you remember."

They strolled away from the stand, and Casey said, "Yes, I can tell you've become very successful. Are you in some sort of business?"

"I'm a minister of a church down in Erno."

"I see," said Casey. "And what sort of church would have *you,* of all the people in the world, for a pastor?"

"I pastor a big Baptist church," Lucas stated innocently – then realizing what Casey was getting to.

"How *did* you become a minister, if you don't mind my asking?"

"I became a Christian when I was in the Army," replied Lucas. "I went to bible school in Pennsylvania, and I got out, an' now I'm a minister, an' I got married."

"So you're a Christian, and a minister," said Casey. *"I* wanted to be a minister, so I got into teaching to pay my way, but I forgot about it." He bent down his head and muttered, "I could've been a *great* preacher. Things never go right in the world!"

"You know, I met Pete Mullen, the kid we always picked on, an' he still doesn't forgive me for what we did t' him."

"Oh, never mind him!" grumbled Casey. "I could never stand his whining! He wasn't any better than any of you! And now he's getting rich!"

Lucas recalled how Casey, who also taught math, never forgave Pete Mullen for getting straight A's in tests, and Casey kept trying to prove he cheated; Pete's father, a better auto mechanic than Lucas could ever be, bawled Casey out.

Lucas sat at the bleachers, and the game started. Lucas enjoyed the narrow victory that Fieldstone had over Holy Rosary; but Lucas felt like a spectator, an observer. Usually the crowd, through the players their school represented, took part in the game, screaming, groaning, and howling through the entire thing. Now, Lucas frowned when Fieldstone missed a shot, and smiled when it made a basket; there was no vicarious participation for him.

As he gazed out his Plymouth going back to Erno, David Lucas could see again the sights and sounds of his past. There were the guys about his age hanging around the Jackpot Inn; and the older guys at the smaller McAdam Inn, which was just a bar, and had no entertainment besides a pinball machine and a juke box. The gas stations and diners were still there, though his favorite pizza place was torn down and a Burger King put in its place. He saw the workers at the toy factory and the textile mill hang around at the front gate – it was quitting time, and there was just one shift anymore.

For all his bad grades, his bullying, his whoring, Lucas wanted more–something better–but he never knew what. At senior year, the guidance counsellor asked him, "David, what would you like to do with your life?"

He ticked his shoulders up and grunted, "I dunno, somethin'"

Lucas thought about these people he grew up with. They seemed trapped in this place, this cycle – get out of school, get a job, and that was it until you died – with no way of escaping. He grew up with these people; but David Lucas got out of it. Then he

50

realized - Fieldstone, New Jersey, and the people in it, were no longer his.

7

Lucas leaned back at the chair of the desk in his den the following Monday. A tapping sounded at the door, and Lucas said, "C'mon in."

Christine peeked in and said, "David, Sheila Tomlinson's here."

Sheila's husband was Chet Tomlinson, manager of the Footwise Shoe Store in the Devon Heights Shopping Mall. "What's she doin' here?" asked Lucas.

"Chet hit her," Christine answered.

"Chet hit his *wife?*" murmured Lucas as he bounded from the desk and into the living room.

Sheila Tomlinson (nee Meeker) sat in the living room, two inches taller than Christine, sobbing heartily. Her brown hair was parted down the middle, draped over her shoulders.

"David's here," announced Christine.

When Sheila raised her head to look at Lucas, he found a large purple bruise on the upper right side of her face. Lucas asked, "Now, what's going on?"

Sheila blurted, "Chet – he hit me – we had a fight –"

Lucas sat down on the couch; Sheila sniffled, "We can't get along anymore. Everything I say and do is wrong. The house isn't clean enough, the food's bad, nowadays he's so mean, he never was like that before!"

"Something wrong at work?" asked Lucas.

"He doesn't tell me," replied Sheila, "He doesn't tell me anything! Each day, I hope it would pass and he'd be better."

"How long this been going on?" asked Lucas.

Sheila paused, breathed deeply, and said, "Oh, about a year. And sometimes the kids would be in the room! This is the last straw! I'm taking the kids to my sister's, and I'm getting a divorce!"

"Hey, whoa, hold on," warned Lucas, "Don't do that! Remember what Jesus said, what God has joined, let no man put asunder." He walked to the closet, pulling on his jacket. "I'm gonna talk to Chet, see what he has to say."

"Don't you believe me?" begged Sheila, "I'm telling the *truth! Look* at this!" she pleaded, pointing to the bruise on her face.

"I just wanna patch things up," assured Lucas. "Sheila, you don't want to divorce Chet, you just want him to treat you better."

"But I'm *scared!"* pleaded Sheila, "for myself and the kids!"

Lucas held his right hand up in a sign of assurance. "Give me some time with him," he stated, "I'll settle things."

Lucas arrived at the Devon Heights Shopping Center and entered the Footwise shore, located between the McDonald's and the Wilder Jewelry store. Walking into the store, he could see the women's shoes on the left side, men's shows on the right, and tables with sneakers on sale in the middle. Chet Tomlinson–thin with pushed back brown hair, church usher, and a basketball aficionado– strode over to Lucas with a handshake and a "Hey, Dave, what brings you here?"

Lucas did not smile; he looked like he was at a funeral.

"It's Sheila, right?" asked Tomlinson.

"Yeah," nodded Lucas. "Can we go into your office?"

"Let's have lunch," returned Tomlinson, who turned and called to an employee, "Bill, I'm going to lunch."

The two men strode to Big Joe's Pizza Parlor.

"Dave, I'm not a bad guy, really," pleaded Tomlinson.

"Sure, I know that, Chet," agreed Lucas, "but what's wrong between you and Sheila? She has a bruise of her face."

"It's the store!"

"What's wrong with the store, it looks like it's doing real good."

"It is, *real* great!" said Tomlinson, "I just want it to *stay* great!"

"Anybody pressure on you for this, Chet?" wondered Lucas out loud.

"Just me," stated Tomlinson. "I'm always like this. I push myself hard. Always have been like this. Plus there might be an opening for district manager, and I want that *so* bad."

"I understand, Chet, really," agreed Lucas. "But Sheila's your wife, you're supposed t' take care'a her, but *this.* "

Tomlinson bent his head down over the counter, and murmured, "If you want me to be ashamed of myself, Dave, I am."

"Sheila says this' been going on for about a year," said Lucas, "True?"

"Yeah," nodded Tomlinson. "In plain English, Dave, I'm driven. I just have to be numero uno, the best store in the mall, the best in the company, I want it *bad,* Dave. Like

I said, I'm putting pressure on myself."

"Y'know, Sheila's been talking divorce?"

Tomlinson nodded, and said, "I guess that's what it all boils down to."

"It's wrong, man, *very* wrong," warned Lucas. "God doesn't *want* divorce! Tell you what, Chet, you and Sheila come to my place for dinner and we can talk it over."

"She won't go near me," Tomlinson complained, his head bent down in guilt. "She wants the divorce, I can't stop her."

"Do *you* want the divorce?"

"No," Tomlinson replied dully.

"So it'll be work to save your marriage," Lucas said. "We have dinner at six on the dot."

Tomlinson nodded.

The only sound heard at the table of the Lucas dining room, twenty-five minutes after six, was the clatter of plates and forks as they dined on baked chicken and mashed potatoes. Chet and Sheila could not look at each other. Lucas he tried to break the ice:

"Say, you know, there's movements going on, against the homos going for their rights so-called."

Chet said, "Yeah, I hear," and he kept eating, his head over his plate.

When the dinner was finished, Lucas proclaimed, "Hey, let's go into the living room with the dessert."

Christine sat on a chair beside the couch near Sheila; Chet sat at the other end. Lucas opened the bible which lay on the coffee table.

"About this time," began Christine, "David and I have a little bit of bible reading, except when it's Wednesday, then we go to the bible study in church. Isn't that right, honey?"

"Yeah, it's true," agreed Lucas. "Chet, you believe in the Bible, right? You know it's the inerrant word of God."

"Yeah, Dave, I do," droned Chet.

Lucas said, "Let's have a prayer, okay, to take care of all this."

All bowed their heads in prayer: "Dear Lord," prayed Lucas, "as we enter this prayer in all reverence, let us all keep our hearts and minds on Your son Jesus, and your word the Holy Bible. In thy name, we pray, ah-men."

They raised their heads and opened their eyes. Lucas pulled open the bible and stated, "Here's some verses you may all be interested in."

He turned to a passage marked by an index card, the fifth chapter of Ephesians. He started with the twenty-second and twenty-third verses: "Wives, submit yourselves unto your own husbands, as unto the Lord. For the husband is the head of the wife, even as Christ is the head of the church: and he is the savior of the body."

Lucas stopped there and said, "That's *your* part, Sheila, to submit to Chet as the church submits to Christ. But here's *your* part of the bargain, Chet."

Lucas reopened the bible and read the twenty-fifth, twenty-sixth, and twenty-seventh verses: "Husbands, love your wives, even as Christ also loved the church, and gave himself for it; That he may sanctify and cleanse it with the washing of water by the word...For no man ever yet hated his own flesh; but norisheth and cherisheth, even as the Lord the church."

Lucas laid his bible down on the coffee table, and explained, "That's the relationship between the husband and his wife. Chet, you and Sheila are one unit, ever since you got married. If you hurt Sheila, you hurt yourself. God doesn't want you arguing and hitting each other. He wants you to care for each other, to love one another. The husband's to love his wife, just as Christ loves the church. What d' y' say t' that?" He punctuated the sentence with a smile of peace and bliss.

Chet raised his head and agreed, "I know that married couples ought'a get along, Dave."

"So do I" cheerfully admonished Lucas. "How would that look to the kids, the parents punching each other out? Jesus is the needed ingredient for any person and group of people. My advice to you guys is more family bible study, more prayer, and no arguing, and remember what I just read to both'a you, and follow accordingly."

The Tomlinsons looked at each other. "Well, we *do* wanna follow God's rules for a happy life," agreed Chet. "I've always enjoyed the church, especially with you, Dave. You're a friend."

"So you know I won't steer you wrong," continued Lucas.

"Maybe it would be nice if you and Sheila moved in closer?" suggested Christine.

The Tomlinsons looked at each other, then edged closer to one another until their bodies brushed close to each other.

"Now, is everything alright?" smiled Lucas.

The Tomlinsons said "Yeah" together.

From that time of, the Tomlinsons remained married, they had family prayers like Lucas suggested, and they never quarreled again. And they slept in separate bedrooms.

8

On the way to the Corbetts for dinner later that week – the sun was bright, but the temperature was fifty-five degrees – Lucas, with Christine on the passenger side, played the Corbett station. Corbett's editorial, in part, proclaimed, "In this election year, the party who wins will be the one that *undoes* the New Deal, the New Frontier, and the Great Society, and *every other* Communistic, Socialistic scheme that the liberals have smuggled into this nation, a nation whose glory and supremacy came from the Free-Enterprise system and a belief in *God!* The party who takes over for the next four years will be dedicated to *winning* wars when they arise, and in rolling back the Communist wave! Such work has been done by the great Chilean army, liberating their country from Soviet-Cuban hegemony and reversing the red flood..."

Hegemony, thought Lucas, great word to learn and use.

The main parts of the dinner were glazed ham with pineapple chunks, and sweet potatoes. As Christine and the maid Bridget worked on the dinner under Helen Corbett's supervision–she just stood and stared–Richard Corbett, his son Jim, and Lucas huddled together in the living room.

"Carter has shown his incompetence as President," proclaimed Corbett, "and so, if the nation lasts that long, the next election will be ours."

"That's right, Dad," agreed Jim. His two-hundred pound body, his six feet of muscle, and his tidy hair and beard made him look almost like a biker–except for the dark-blue Dior suit trousers, the pointed shoes, and the Cardin tie and shirt. He then bent forward and murmured, "How's Mom doin', how's she been feelin?"

"Alright," returned Corbett, "But let's not change the subject, this is important."

"She's my mother, can't I be worried about her?" shrugged Jim.

"David, how do *you* stand?" Corbett queried Lucas.

Lucas stood by, worriedly as they argued, and he was a bit flustered. "Uh, well, I'm not so sure," he began. "I really don't deal with politics, as you know, but I'll trust your judgment, Richard."

Corbett wheeled towards the dining room, and Lucas quietly asked Jim, "Jim, is there something wrong with you an' y'dad?"

"My mother," began Jim sadly, "Ma's been dying since I knew what was going on here. Her heart, Dave, somethin' wrong with her heart." Jim paused and added, "Dad keeps diving into the politics, it's his, like, I dunno, his passion. Aside from the business, he has nothing else."

Jim turned to the window and grumbled, "Where is she?"

"Who?" puzzled Lucas.

"Fran!" Jim snapped, "She's always late!"

Lucas looked at his watch and said, "It's just ten of."

As he spoke, the sound of tires grinding on gravel sounded on the driveway. Then Fran–Francine, the middle child of the Corbetts–flew into the house proclaiming, "Greetings, family mine!" in a voice like a clarinet. She shook off her light brown jacket, pulled off her hat freeing her long brown ponytailed hair, and picked a thread from her trousers.

"You sure took your time getting here," griped Jim.

"I'm in no hurry to be insulted."

When they sat down at the table, Christine piped, "Fran, how's your job doing?"

"Pretty good," smiled Fran. "I been commissioned to do the design for a new set of senior citizen's apartments. None's shocked anymore about a woman architect."

"Me, I'm gettin' into local real estate lately," Jim stated.

"The best investment, always," agreed Corbett, "what is it?"

"The Orchard Heights development project –"

"Oh, no, a housing project, *here!*" moaned Helen, her hands on her forehead, her face curled up like she would cry.

"No, not *that,* Ma," laughed Jim, "It'll be for middle-income people!" (Everyone knew who he meant.)

"I remember that area," recalled Corbett, "used to be fields of apple orchards, now nothing."

"Not going to be nothing *anymore*," smiled Jim, "the ground's getting dug up, trucks and backhoes all over."

"You did say there'll be a lot of people moving from the city to here," amiably recalled Lucas.

"Sure, and industry," continued Jim on the same vein. "I just got on the ground floor for investment in the Red Valley Industrial Center."

"Good, Jim, real good," agreed Lucas.

At the end of dinner, the men moved to the living room, while Fran and Christine worked with Bridget in washing the dishes, while Helen sulked in the dining room. The dishes were finished, and Bridget went to ask for her salary, so Fran and Christine were alone.

"Nobody seems to excited about my project," noted Fran, leaning on the counter.

"I am," said Christine, squeezing Fran's arm, "I think you'll do well."

"Nobody has any confidence in me because I'm a woman," said Fran, shaking her head." The vice-president of the firm that asked for the project is a woman, but she likes t' think she's one of the guys."

"Fran," started Christine, "The folks have been hard on you because you won't get married like they want. They want an old-fashioned upbringing for you, like me. I want you to know, Fran; I love you, no matter what they say.'

"Thanks, sweetie," smiled Fran.

Helen burst into the kitchen demanding, "What're you two doing in here?"

"Just talking, Mom," replied Christine cautiously.

"Ma, we're mature women, not little girls," declared Fran, "Do you have to butt watch everything we do?"

"Yes, it's my right, as your mother," returned Helen.

Fran took two steps to her mother and stated plainly, "Mom, the guys can be by themselves if they want, like now. So Chris and I can be by ourselves in we want. We're not gonna steal the silverware."

Helen stomped out, and Christine sputtered a giggle, saying, "Steal the silverware, that's funny!" then she got serious and said, "I feel safe when you're around, Frannie, Mom scares me sometimes."

Helen's footsteps tromped up the carpeted stairs. Jim, recognizing his mother's steps, strode over and asked, "Ma, everything okay?"

"No, everything's *not* okay!" returned Helen, "*nothing's* okay!" and she moved into her room.

Jim stepped sadly towards Lucas and murmured, "All the time I known her, she's always sore about something. Nothing makes her happy."

"Women have their moods," sighed Corbett, then he announced, "Excuse me," as he rose and climbed the stairs to the bathroom.

"The dinner's hit him pretty quick, didn't it?" wondered Lucas.

"He's always had bowel problems," recalled Jim, "but he's too cheap to get surgery for it. Money and politics, that's all he knows. All he cares about. Never had any fun, never took me out to games and stuff. He was always at the station or the county committee."

"I respect what you say, Jim," returned Lucas. "I've seen him get caught up in his work and his ideas. Still, he's your father, so you ought to respect him."

At that point, the toilet flushed, and Corbett tromped down the stairs.

As Corbett settled into his seat, Jim stated, "Say, Dad, I been hearing the station lately, are all the stations like that?"

"Jim, you know the stations all follow the same format," stated Corbett. "The music in all of them are about the same – big band, easy-listening, the stuff I grew up with. Now that was some *real* music"

"Well, Dad," explained Jim, "you know there's a lot of people in management positions who grew up on rock –"

"I don't want to hear about that junk!" declared Corbett.

"Let me finish!" demanded Jim. "At least the one near Philly could play rock! There's an audience that buys from sponsors, and that's the music of this time, Dad, like it or not. You got an older audience for the music you play now, Dad, but they won't last forever.'

"I play the music of good, clean people," stated Corbett, 'and not the music of young hoodlums who go to college to rebel against their country!"

"Aw, Dad, those days are over!" moaned Jim. "Have you forgot the Beatle are broke up? It's not that old change-the-world stuff, now it's have-a-good-time. The people who do that stuff now are in it for the money, see? And when people listen to their favorite music on the radio –"

"You call that junk music?" snorted Corbett.

"They'll buy from advertisers who'll pay for the air time from the station. You know that, Dad, so c'mon, at least the Philly station–"

Corbett raised his hand and proclaimed, "I'll think about it," in the majesty of his favorite chair.

"Dave, help me out here," pleaded Jim. Lucas watched the argument, sitting with crossed legs.

"I have to look at it as a minister," decided Lucas. "I don't believe in compromise in anything you stand for. Like me, I don't like to accommodate the Gospel of Jesus with the world. I always hear, times change, so change with them. No, Jim, I don't like any compromise, so I'm going to go with your dad on this one."

"Dave, this is about the survival of the business," moaned Jim.

"Don't matter," insisted Lucas. "Just because it's popular don't make it right."

Corbett smiled at this support. Jim bowed his head, accepting defeat, and asked, "You still my pal, Dave"

"Sure," smiled Lucas.

Meanwhile, Fran and Christine were still chatting in the kitchen; a small pan of hot water boiled for Christine's tea. Christine poured it into a cup with the tea bag.

"I have t' tell you, hon," sighed Fran, settling on a stool, "being in the man's world of architecture's no fun for a woman. Either you're a sissy, some dainty little thing without a deep thought in your head, or else you're acting like a man, all tough, all serious, not a real woman. Sometimes, you start believing it yourself, an' you wonder what role you want to play."

"I always accepted whatever Mon and Dad said," shrugged Christine, "It seemed simpler. Women did this and this, men did that, that's what I was told. Complicated things, why, I could never handle them. If something was simple, I accept it. Do you think I'm wrong, Frannie?"

"You're just being you, Chris," returned Fran.

"Sometimes, I admire you, Frannie," sighed Christine as she tapped on the linoleum floor. "You don't seem scared of Mom and Dad, yet David – I never know how to answer him when he gets angry, even though I don't think he has the right to."

Christine sipped her tea, and said, "But he's still my husband, and I have to go along with him."

Fran said, "I never could take anybody giving me orders, talking to me like I wasn't human! That's why I haven't seriously considered marriage yet, and why I couldn't get along with the ROTC guy they fixed me up with back in college. He just sat there bragging" about being in control of everyone –"

Fran got up from the stool and said, "I'm going now," pecking Christine's cheek. "I want to avoid another scene with the folks."

Christine kissed back and returned, "'Bye, Frannie."

As Fran gathered her coat and handbag, she called, "'Bye, Dad," to her father, who was too busy orating to notice his elder daughter.

Corbett proclaimed:

"South Africa and South America are spots on the map where our strength of will and military might are now being tested. The reds come into a friendly country and call themselves 'forces of national liberation,' and they take advantage of the minor flaws in that country's political system –" At that point, Fran went ahead and left – "to gain sympathy from the mushy-headed liberals, who fall for such rhetoric. Oppression, denial of rights, who the greatest guarantee of rights in any country, is the right to make and keep a profit, and to do with it what you want. All the other rights are not important. If the right to Free Enterprise is in danger, just what good are the other rights, what value are they? And also –"

He looked at Lucas – "The right to worship is important as well. The Communists don't care for that either, David, so the Christian churches have a rooting interest in the anti-Communist struggle around the world."

Lucas nodded.

9

Later in March, in Trenton, the state senate committee on the judiciary held hearings on the Guthrie bill. A number of gay activists took the stand against the bill; they stated plainly that they were citizens of the country, and were entitled to the rights of other citizens.

The Reverend David Lucas was the last witness of the day's hearings. He waited out in the hall, resting on the couch next to the door to the hearing room, and he looked at the gay lobbyists seated at and near a couch. He reflected at how right his father-in-law was about this idea of rights – what were rights but excuses for wrong behavior, if not outright sin? *For the past years*, Lucas thought, *we had to put up with the faggots out in the open because they had "rights". Not any more....*

The Sergeant-At-Arms came out and announced, "The Reverend David Lucas." It was Lucas' time to testify before the committee.

Lucas glanced at the gay activists on the couch, and entered the committee room, hugging the bible close to his chest. The pale-white camera lights beamed at him as he strode down the aisle through the seats packed with people from one end of the room to the other. He quivered inside; he was to speak on an important issue. *What should he say?* He thought, *how will this turn out?* But he had to do this.

The chairman of the committee–Paul Hamblin, from Hunterdon County– raised his right hand and asked Lucas, "Do you solemnly swear that the testimony you will present before this committee will be the truth, and whole truth, and nothing but the truth, so help you God?"

"I, uh, do," returned Lucas, and he sat down.

"State your full name and occupation," asked Hamblin.

"The Reverend David Lucas, and I am the pastor of Wingate Memorial Baptist Church, Erno, New Jersey."

"Would you please, Reverend, make your comments about the bill in question?"

"Certainly," agreed Lucas. Settling in to the chair, and inhaling, pulling out his notes from his jacket pocket, he intoned:

"I have come to state my opinion about the bill in question, that is, the State Civil

Rights Clarification Act of 1978. I am a Christian, a minister of the gospel, and not a lawyer or a politician. In my faith, my Christian faith, I believe that homosexuality is wrong, what is called a sin. The homosexuals believe that it is their right to espouse their activities, to tell the entire world that they – they do what they do. I don't believe that is so.

"Homosexuality is wrong, it is evil," continued Lucas. "You should no more accept homosexuality as a lifestyle than you should accept robbery and murder as a lifestyle. I believe that when you begin to tolerate the homosexual lifestyle, you do not stop tolerating other deviate lifestyles and activities."

One black member of the committee–Senator Alvin Drake, formerly a police officer in Atlantic City–asked Lucas, "Reverend, what you are asking us to do is to act on this legislation according to your personal religious beliefs. You are aware, I assume, that not everyone shares them?"

Lucas replied, "Sir, I know that not everyone is a Christian like me. Yet, I am convinced that Jesus is indeed the one true way to follow. Before I became a Christian, I chased women, I drank and I took drugs. Not anymore, now that I am a Christian, I no longer do those things. I am a completely respectable person. Jesus did that for me, and He could do that for the entire nation. And that is why I cannot accept homosexuality."

Drake asked, "As a former police officer, I know how it in almost impossible to enforce a moral code as an ideal legally. How can you be certain, Reverend, that homosexuals in the closet would be weeded out if an employer does not want them, and that they would not lie about their sexual orientation to keep their jobs?"

"Sir," politely returned Lucas, "I know that some persons would deny their sins, because they are rightly ashamed of their sins. If our society states that homosexuality is tolerable, they would be brazen about it. If it is *not* tolerated, they would either be secretive about it, or give it up. That is, if they are denied jobs and education because they are homosexual, that would show that this is one sin not to be accepted."

"I believe, Reverend Lucas," continued Drake, "that the purpose of the law is to keep people from robbing and killing each other. My work as a police officer has taught me that. However, if a person does no harm to another, no matter how much I disagree with it, I cannot say nor do anything about that. What about that?"

"Well, Senator," started Lucas, "I don't agree with that idea one bit. There is right, and there is wrong. Right must be encouraged, and wrong must be discouraged. As a Christian, I believe that the state's function is to develop ideals for the public to follow and aim for." He left it there.

John Thomas Guthrie, from his seat in the back and left, said, "Gentlemen of the committee, this gentleman we have been listening to is well-known in his community as an advocate of righteous living. For too long, the political stage has been cluttered up with drug-crazed hippies, foul-mouthed feminists, radicals in colleges who know nothing of the real world, and homosexuals. Now we have here a minister, a veteran of our Armed Forces, and one of the Silent Majority that President Richard Nixon spoke about, now finally speaking up. The time has come to listen to men like Reverend Lucas, who believe in the simple values of God, Country, and Family, and not the fancy foreign imported ideas of Marxism."

As Guthrie spoke his name, Lucas bowed his head, moved that such an important man as Mister Guthrie would praise him.

There was one more week of debate over the Guthrie bill, and the legislature, finding no safe agreement – one was either a champion of civil liberties and rights of privacy, or a defender of moral values and decency – made a firm decision: they made it a statewide referendum for November, to let the people decide. Both sides claimed victory, and the legislators were proud of themselves for pleasing everybody.

10

The men of Wingate Church met in the assembly room in the basement of Wingate church early in April. They sat lined up on metal folding chairs, on top of a floor of linoleum tiles, facing a stage with a dull-blue curtain; a piano stood at the stairs leading to the stage.

At seven o'clock PM, Lucas sprung to the podium in front of the stage:

"Brothers in Christ, how many'a you know about the Guthrie bill that's up for referendum?"

A cloud of applause rose from the men. Lucas continued:

"*Right here* in Jersey, we have a chance to stop the fags and their so-called rights!"

"Uh-huh, right, let's get 'em," sounded from the men with enthusiasm.

"Let's decide to forget about what our enemies say about us," decided Lucas. "They'll call us bigots and religious nuts, but we'll *win,* because God's with us!"

The men applauded, and Lucas proclaimed, "We'll defend our Christian beliefs *to the last!"* thumping the podium with his fist.

George Emerson, a senior partner in a Manhattan advertising agency, stood and said, "I know I can get my firm to help. We can handle the public relations and the ads."

"You're hired, George," declared Lucas with a smile as the men applauded.

"This'll take money," warned Emerson, which is why he brought up the firm in the first place.

"Are we gonna put it up?" barked Lucas.

"Yeaaaaauh!" howled the men.

"I can get my father-in-law to help," continued Lucas, "He has connections, I know he'll be willing to help. Now, we better get ourselves organized. How about this for a name, 'Alliance of Christian Voters'?"

"Good, good!" agreed the men.

Emerson stood and said, "Fine, Dave, but it would be good to alter the name a little, so it comes out smoother, something like 'Christian Voters Alliance.'"

"I like it," nodded Lucas with a smile. So the men accepted it, if Lucas did.

Emerson still stood and continued, "My agency can make slogans and logos, we can set up press kits for the media, we can play them like a violin."

"'Vote Christian,'" announced Lucas, "How's that for a slogan?"

"It's good for a start," agreed Emerson. "It's so new, so novel."

"Okay, now what we need is a president, vice-president, secretary, and treasurer," declared Lucas.

Steve Gates, a realtor, rose to his feet and said, "You're President, Dave."

"Ah, naw, naw, naw," merrily moaned Lucas, waving his hands. "I'm a *church pastor*, not a politician."

"We don't *need* politicians, Dave," proclaimed Carl Ogden, a stereo-TV appliance dealer. "We're sick of politicians! What we need are men of God! You can *do it,* Dave, we'll be right behind you!"

The men applauded.

Lucas stood and thought; all his life he wanted to do something big, something great—as a minister, he wanted to do the upmost for Christ. Is this *it*, the big thing to do?

Could this be his mission? Could God be using him in this campaign? A plain minister like him? He looked at the men in front of him...

"I *never* backed away from my duty as a Christian and as a minister of the Gospel," Lucas decided. "I *never* wanted anything for myself, but everything for Jesus. Since this is so important, *I'll be* President."

The men applauded.

Lucas walked home, thinking, *What have a gotten myself into?* Then he thought, *This is for the Lord, for Jesus. Billy Sunday-Doctor Garfield-the preaching in the park-the crowd at Waldo's- Stand up for Jesus.* He had to make a stand, no matter what happens. He would go through with it.

When Lucas arrived home, Christine trotted towards him, smiled and flushed, as if in the sun, and asked happily, "David, guess what?"

"What?" he replied, expecting bad news, and irritated by her guessing game.

"I'm preg –" she couldn't use that word– "uh, I'm going to have a baby!"

The news registered in Lucas' mind, and he smiled. He scooped Christine up in his arms and laughed, "That's the *greatest!* How'd you find out?"

"Well, I wasn't feeling well lately," explained Christine with a smile, "And Mom told me to go to the doctor, and he ran some tests – oh, I'm so happy!" she concluded – and she could see that David was happy also, which made her more happy.

They moved to the couch and sat down together. Lucas held her small hand in both his large hands, and told her quietly, "Chris, I know that sometimes I've been – I haven't given you – uh, the attention you deserve. But see, I have a duty to do what I can for Jesus. Now, I'm starting a campaign to fight the fags, I have to do it, for Jesus. You don't mind staying sometimes with your folks, do you?"

"Of course not, honey," assured Christine. "Whatever would make you happy, I'll do." She wrapped her arms around his neck, and he wrapped his arms around her waist, and she announced happily, "Oh, David, things will be so good from now on!"

11

Two weeks later, Lucas worked at the Christian Voters Alliance office at the Coventry Towers, at Market Street in Erno, on the referendum– officially put on the ballot as "Referendum Question Number Nine", or "Q9" as the media called it for short, but it was commonly called "the Guthrie Amendment." A map of the state was tacked on the wall, the counties' borders lined in red. Volunteer workers sat at long tables stuffing envelopes with flyers printed by George Emerson's agency.

Lucas had his office in a large glass-cubicle space on the far side of the room where the volunteers worked. He put out an ad for an Executive Director–Emerson advised hiring one, to run the office and handle the finances while Lucas toured the state for the amendment. One man answered.

Lucas hovered over the desk of the office, strewn with newspapers and press releases, the muttering from the volunteers in the background, his jacket off. A young man, in his early thirties, with hair thinning at the edges, looked inside and said, "Brother Lucas?"

Lucas looked up and said, "Uh, yes."

"I'm Gary Hennessy," he replied, "I answered the ad for an Executive Director?"

Lucas strode around the desk and shook Hennessey's hand, saying, "Hello, Brother Hennessy, come on and sit." Lucas shut the door.

They sat, Hennessy saying, "Brother Lucas, I hope to, that you could hire me for the position. See I have a lot of administrative experience."

"Such as?"

"I was a plant manager at DuPont," Hennessy replied," and I won commendation letters from my, uh, higher-ups, I've been really great at administering the plant."

"Um-hum."

"I was proud of my work, my record," added Hennessy, "but, I felt-like, I needed something more. Still, I needed a guide in my life."

"Okay?"

"I walked around my neighborhood, and I went inside a church–nothing fancy, just a local church in a nice suburb. Fortunately the minister was there, and I had a chat with him, and–"

"Right, go on."

"I felt like this is what I need, and a month later I declared myself a Christian," proclaimed Hennessy.

"Well, praise the Lord," smiled Lucas.

"I want to get–well, as much for Jesus as I can, and so I'm in a theological school, I'll complete my third year next year."

"That's great, Brother Hennessy," cheered Lucas, "I see you serving the Lord well. Oh, can I call you Gary, and you call me Dave."

"Okay, *Dave*," smiled Hennessy. His tone lowered as he added, "Plus, I have to admit–"

"What?" coaxed Lucas.

"The plant has been closed for six days," warned Hennessy, "they don't get back to me if I'll be in another position. I ask, they don't respond. My wife is pregnant—" He inhaled, then let it out, then, head down, "Dave, I'm worried."

Luas bent his head, then, "Gary, so far you're the only one who's answered the ad. You got the job."

Hennessy beamed, his body loosened, and shouted, "*Thank* you, Dave!" clasping Lucas' hand with both of his.

"How soon can you start?"

"Tomorrow!"

Lucas conferred with Hennessy about organizing efforts, mainly by sympathetic fundamentalist ministers throughout the state. Lucas and Hennessy discussed with George Emerson the advertising campaign for the amendment:

"The entire campaign's gained national attention, Dave," intoned Emerson as he opened his briefcase, "So you should expect the networks and major magazines doing articles on you."

"I don't need any attention for myself," Lucas insisted – but the thought: *All this attention for me...*

Emerson pulled out of the briefcase a trifold pamphlet and a cassette tape, then said, "What we plan to do, Dave, is play up the most bizarre and perverse aspects of the gay lifestyle, like sadomasochism, cross-dressing, that sort of thing." He handed Lucas the pamphlet and added, "I'm afraid the tone of the campaign could be very negative."

Lucas scanned the pamphlet, which was loaded with references to child molesting, photos of men in drag and in leather, and it concluded, "Do you want THESE teaching your children? Do you want THESE living in your building? Do you want THESE serving your customers?"

Returning the pamphlet, Lucas smiled, "It's just like we talked about!"

"Here's our radio ad, more will come soon," continued Emerson as he put the cassette into the player:

A vaguely male voice squeaked, "I'd like to be a school teacher because I *looooove* children!" Then a deeper voice intoned, "Isn't it time to call a halt to immorality that has run so rampant it is now accepted and tolerated? Homosexuality is wrong. Vote for high moral standards. Vote yes for the Guthrie Amendment. This message paid for by the Christian Voters Alliance."

"I like it," smiled Lucas again. "Make sure every station gets a copy."

12

The most spectacular propaganda effort of the CVA was the street preaching. Young bible school students, recruited by CVA, would rent a van or a pickup, attach a loudspeaker to it, and preach against the sin of homosexuality, not mentioning the Guthrie amendment, but the vehicle was paid for by CVA.

At a special meeting for the street preachers in the CVA office, Lucas told them, "You guys are warriors on the front lines of Jesus to the streets, to confront the homosexuals with their sinfulness. Remember, this is not just another political campaign, it's a holy cause, for Jesus and His true church."

At that, the young men shot to their feet, applauded, screamed, cheered, and concluded with the singing of, "Stand Up, Stand Up For Jesus, Ye Soldiers Of The Cross," which became the fight song for the campaign.

Much of the CVA street preaching would deliberately take place in areas where gays congregated – bars, bookstores, and entire neighborhoods. Because they dared this, the media were out in force. The news crews thought the preachers were asking for trouble, and they were right – like their hero David Lucas told them, they were to challenge the sinners on their own turf; if they were attacked, they would become martyrs for Jesus, and could hit the attackers with a good lawsuit.

One incident occurred in Erno itself. From the bed of a red Ford pickup, a young man brayed through the loudspeakers, while two colleagues stood by:

"There will come a *time* when men will have *unnatural affections* with one another, and sin *will run rampant* throughout the land! With our prayers to *God*, let us *resist* the sin of homosexuality, oh, Lord, let us like *true Christian men* take out stand against sin, let us turn our nation back to God, for if we turn to Him and beg His forgiveness for our sins, He will graciously forgive us! Praise the name of the Lord!"

After hearing that oration, several true Christian men ran down the street, chanting "Fuck the queers! Fuck the queers!" and attacked anyone they thought looked gay, and ramming a trashcan through the window of Waldo's.

At Princeton, a young man going for his MBA degree was doing great business selling "Fag Hunting Licenses" which limited the bearer to a quota of five "homos," and sold for five dollars, along with bumper stickers ($1.59 each) and T-shirts ($10.00 each) that read, "Kill a queer for Christ."

At the start of May, David Lucas took Christine to dinner at her parents' home. (Christine was just starting to show her pregnancy.) Fran did not come, but Jim did arrive from Atlantic City. Christine sat in the living room along with Lucas, Jim, and her father.

"How's the campaign coming, along, Dave?" asked Jim.

"Great," replied Lucas. "They guys your dad contacted are a big help with money."

Then Lucas' smile faded, and he sank back on the sofa. "All this," he thought out loud, "I never thought this could happen. I'm in the middle of – all this! This campaign – the whole nation's looking at this!" A pause, then, "I had dreams as a kid I'd be famous," sighed Lucas, "but now, it's being real, and –"

"You're going to be a great man, David," smiled Corbett, patting Lucas' leg, "You *are* a great man!"

David Lucas, a great man – after all he did before becoming a Christian – what was the Lord planning for him? Then he looked at his wife – he was going to have *his*

child – He smiled; Things are going so well for David Lucas, praise be to God.

13

In May, in a classroom at Rutgers, forty gay activists met to form an *ad hoc* coalition against the amendment, calling it the Committee for Human and Civil Rights; the president of the group was Mike Durkin, owner of the Apollo Health Club, Inc.

Durkin was as broad and tough as a safe, strong enough to flatten any assailant (which he had to do often, and he recommended that others do the same), and just one inch shorter than the Reverend David Lucas. His Apollo Health Club was one of the landmarks of the Gay community in Atlantic City, with a weight room, sauna, basketball court, Jacuzzi, heated swimming pool, and classes in martial arts.

CHCR's first act was to call a press conference, where Durkin announced, "I hereby challenge the Reverend Lucas to debate with me on the issue of the Guthrie amendment, and his attitude towards Gay people in general. I believe that I can show the public that his fears about Gay people are very mistaken and foolish. This is the challenge I offer Reverend Lucas."

Back in the CVA office, George Emerson sat with Lucas and brought this up

Durkin's challenge: "This is a real two-edge sword, Dave," started Emerson. "This is free publicity for them, plus a chance for the voters to compare and contrast the two sides. Dave, if you make a slip-up, it could cost the campaign. You could blurt out something that sounds bad, and it'll make you look bad."

Lucas tilted back in his chair, his eyes aimed at Emerson, and he grunted, "What're you talking about? People are gonna take a minister before they take a pervert *any* day." He rose, smiled widely, patted Emerson's forearm and said, "Don't worry, George, things'll turn out oaky. I know it. So go tell the faggot I'll take his challenge."

When Lucas got to the parsonage, he realized he was tired – his arms, legs and stomach weighed heavily. As he entered the living room, Christine rose from the couch and exclaimed, "Honey, look at this!" as she showed a *People* magazine to Lucas.

Lucas' irritation at Christine was overcome by his curiosity, and then his joy – the *People* carried the article about Lucas and the anti-gay movement he led, with the title, "A Loser Turned Minister Leads New Jersey's Fight Against Gays." As Lucas scanned the article, he found pictures of himself at the pulpit, Lucas leading at the front entrance of the parsonage, and Lucas in the CVA office, standing over the desk staring at papers on his desk.

Lucas smiled and returned the magazine to Christine. "Not bad," he grunted happily. "How's your day?"

"Oh, Fran called," began Christine eagerly, "she was telling me –"

The phone rang, and Christine fell silent.

"Hell-low," Lucas answered.

"Hey, Dave," said the voice of George Emerson on the other end. "Listen, I got arranged a couple of press conferences, an' the date of the debate's set for October first. Is that okay?"

"Great, perfect," happily agreed Lucas. "Anything else?"

"Yeah, the debate's sponsored by the public broadcasting system, and it'll be held in Trenton, at the public station there."

"Okay," concluded Lucas, "See y' tomorrow," and they hung up.

While he was looking at the magazine and talking to Emerson, Lucas forgot the tiredness of his body, and everything became lighter. Now, the tiredness returned, weighing everything down. "Let's get t' bed," he said to Christine, who forgot what she wanted to say about Fran.

14

The night of the debate came. That morning, Lucas stood at the steps of the Midland County courthouse, facing two hundred journalists in the first of the press conferences arranged by Emerson. With the courthouse in the background, Lucas looked judicial and dignified on TV – which was how Emerson planned it.

Lucas said to the journalists, "As we all can see, the public has become sick and disgusted with immorality that has been renamed freedom! This is *not-at-all* what our Founding Fathers worked for and died for, in founding our great country! We will win this campaign, and we will take this victory throughout the entire nation with a national crusade against homosexuality, so help us God! Thank you!" At that, he turned to his left side and walked off, followed by Emerson and the gaze of the TV cameras, into rented cars parked on the curb.

Lucas and Emerson ended up in the back seat of the rented Ford, Hennessy in the front right side, and a volunteer at the wheel. "Shouldn't have done that, Dave," worried Emerson.

"What?" Lucas said.

"The press conference," replied Emerson. "What you did back there, just walking away from the reporters before they can ask questions, that looked pretty rude. The press could turn against us."

Did Lucas make a mistake? He wondered. He twitched his shoulders in a shrug and sighed, "Well, it's done."

"Y' ready for tonight, Dave?" asked Hennessy.

"Yeah, I'm ready for the faggot," grunted Lucas merrily.

When they got to the office, Lucas closed his office door, then he realized – he wasn't prepared for the debate! A cold chill ran through his brain, and he struck his thigh with his fist, grinding his teeth.

Then he thought of God; he sank to his knees on the red-carpeted floor, gathered his hands together, and prayed in a mutter, "Please, God help me, forgive my unreadiness, please, Lord, don't let me fail, not in this Holy cause."

He felt calmer; he would let God put the words into his mouth.

That evening, when the time approached seven, Christine was at her parent's home, sitting at the couch while Helen sat at the matching chair nearby. "Remember to sit up straight," Helen warned Christine, "you need good posture for the baby."

"Yes, mom," Christine replied.

Bridget came in with a tray of food – sandwiches and small bowls of salad – on the coffee table in front of the couch. Richard Corbett strode in and eased himself into the big easy chair, on the other end of the couch. Jim entered with a bowl of potato chips and a smaller bowl of dip, asking, "Why ain't the TV on?"

"Jim Corbett, watch you grammar," admonished Helen, enjoying barking orders to her grown children. Jim respectfully ignored this.

At the station in Trenton, David Lucas paced up and down backstage, inhaling, then exhaling. A bible lay on a nearby table, for Lucas to take on stage with him.

"Nervous, Dave?" asked Emerson.

"Naw," said Lucas, "just wanna get this over with. Yeah, I guess I am, a little."

The audience in the studio was made up of broadcasting and journalism majors from colleges and universities throughout the state. The moderator was Don Prager, a heavy, white-haired man who recently retired from news casting in Perth Amboy and was considered the godfather of journalists in the state, having been in reporting since radio. The debate would be broadcast throughout the public radio and TV stations of the state.

The time came, and the debaters stepped on stage – Lucas from stage right, Durkin from stage left, Prager sitting at a desk in the middle – to the applause of the audience. Durkin extended his hand for shaking, but Lucas kept his arms down, his eyes wide with fearful uncertainty. They then took to their seats, each with a small table beside it.

Both men were dressed conservatively – Lucas in three piece suit, silver-looking watch, blue shirt and red tie; Durkin in a black two-piece suit, white shirt, and grey tie. Lucas thought, *this guy didn't look like a faggot, he looks tough.*

Prager introduced the two men and opened with, "Reverend Lucas has won the toss of the coin and may begin."

Lucas stepped to the podium, griping the sides, inhaled, and began:

"I would like to thank the public broadcasting stations for this opportunity for a debate. It gives me the opportunity to express my opinion that the entire trend of toleration of immoral conduct has got to come to an end. Homosexuality is definitely a perversion, it is wrong, and we, the American people, have to put a stop to it." He could think of nothing else, and he sat down.

Prager said, "Mister Durkin?"

Durkin walked to the podium, and in a voice like a trombone, replied: "I also wish to thank the public broadcasting stations of this state for the opportunity to answer the lies and slanders that have been aimed at gay people during this campaign. In this debate I will try to proclaim the rights of gay people to be full, active citizens of this country, this country that has been founded on the rights of individuals." He sat back down.

"At this point," announced Prager, "we begin the debate, in which each of the participants makes a statement and the other person replied. Mister Durkin, would you begin please?"

(*Why did the faggot get to speak first*, thought Lucas.)

"Thank you," replied Durkin as he leaned forward and asked Lucas:

"Reverend Lucas, I've been reading some of the literature and press releases your group puts out about gay people. You have us all connected with all kinds of strange sexual activity, like sadomasochism and pedophilia. What you are doing, Reverend, is slandering us, lumping us all together with all this bad stuff to make it easier to attack us. For one thing, Reverend, gay people are a pretty diverse bunch of people, and they include radical Marxists and businessmen like me. Second, and this is most important, your slanders against us would make it easier for us to be attacked. It's as if we're less than human, evil, not deserving of justice or even life. Can you imagine the flack you got if you said the same things against Black people? Even during the campaign period, Reverend, assaults against Gay people have risen enormously, and some have been killed. Our campaign proves that we're not going to accept assault and slander, that we'll stand up for our rights to live the American dream, or at least to live. Reverend, right now, all I want from you is an apology for these slanders and your word that it won't continue."

Gay bars and households throughout the state sounded with cheers and the clink of glasses. Christine Lucas did not understand what Durkin talked about. Lucas sat and stared at Durkin: *this faggot would dare stand up to him!*

"Your reply, Reverend Lucas?" asked Prager.

"As I have said," Lucas said quickly, "homosexuality is definitely a perversion, what we Christians call a sin! Homosexuality naturally goes along with all the other sexual deviations, like pedophilia and sadomasochism. You start with one, and soon all the others follow, and that's a fact! But in the past few years, we thought that we had to accept immorality as a sign of a free society! It is *not* a sign of freedom, *Mister* Durkin, it is a sign of *degeneration!"*

His voice was getting emotional, passionate, angry, as he continued, "Mister Durkin, I'm one of the many millions of Americans who have been disgusted with the moral downslide of this country, not only homosexuality, but pornography and the degradation of the traditional family. I don't need any scientist or sociologist to tell me what's right and wrong! I *won't* alter the ads we put out, just because it hurts your delicate feelings, not *one bit!* We will *defeat* you in this campaign, *here* and *throughout* the nation, and with God's help you *will* give up your perversion! In the name of *God,* Mister Durkin, *give up* your lifestyle!" He sat down, heavy with anger.

"Mister Durkin," said Prager, "your response?"

Durkin frowned, strode to the podium, and replied, "Reverend, your *real* complaint about gay people is that we do something differently from you, but otherwise we're just the *same* as you! We work, we pay taxes, we take our garbage out and drive cars, just like you do! You want us to conform to a pattern that *you* set, and you want everybody to fit into it! But you see, Reverend, it comes under the heading of freedom, the right to be different! There's always going to be people that're different from you! This is no *communist* society, where people have to conform to an ideology set by a certain group of people for the rest of us to follow! This is *America,* land of the free! Do you want it like a *communist* system, Reverend, all things fitting into a set dogma?"

As he sat back, howls of joy rang among the gays; Christine and her family were puzzled; and Lucas frowned: *Call me a communist, how dare he?* Without waiting for Prager, he replied from his seat:

"*Mister* Durkin, as a Christian and as an American, I *hate* Communism! However, I must point out that such Communist societies as the Soviet Union are dedicated to personal morality as the strength of a society! Moral discipline is what all societies need to survive, and even the *Soviet Union knows* that! There's *no* homosexuality, *no* pornography, *no* drugs, *no* prostitution, and criminals are *punished,* not protected, Mister Durkin, *pun-ished!* That's a society that's morally disciplined, *Mister* Durkin, and we have to be like that if we're to survive and prosper once more!"

Corbett was puzzled; *was his own son-in-law endorsing the Communist system?* Christine was also bewildered; and the gays throughout the state laughed their heads off. Lucas rested in his chair and exhaled.

Durkin pounced, "Reverend Lucas, it disturbs me that you would say *anything* good about a communist society. As for myself, Reverend, I was a Marine in the Korean War – landed in Inchon, fought my way up to the Yalu River an' back down again. *And,* pardon my French, Reverend, but I'm *damn* proud to have done my part there, and I'm *damn* proud to be an American, I'm *damn* proud to be in a land where I know I'm oppressed, but I can legally and peaceably fight against it! And it's not a narrow official dogma or control or dictatorship that makes a nation great, Reverend, it's *freedom,* and any nation that's big enough to allow all kinds of opinions an' lifestyles to be expressed is in my mind a *great* country, one worth fighting for!"

A spattering of applause came from the audience; the gay community let out a cheer wherever they were; Durkin was relieved that he said what he said. Prager said, "Please refrain from applauding until after the debate."

Lucas just sat there, glaring at Durkin, and then retorted, "All this talk about rights and freedom! Why are we even having this debate? It should be evident to every sensible American with a sense of morality that homosexuality is wrong and must be discouraged! We've always known that, and that's never going to change, I don't care how many laws you pass, how many marches and riots you have!"

"Reverend," snapped Durkin, "you've been talking a lot about morality, and that's fine, but what statistics, what evidence, what data do you bring to the debate? Or are you being just emotional?"

Lucas looked at Durkin, then Prager, then the audience, then declared, "I don't need statistics or any dumb four years wasted at some college, I have common sense and the Bible!" Swiveling his head, he brayed, "I believe we need to get back to those things, and stop arguing about what's right and wrong! We already know what's right and wrong!"

He stopped, inhaled and thought; *don't get excited, that's what the fags do.* He calmed down, ready for ore debate.

Prager announced, "It is now time for question from the audience."

A young man in a black blazer, red tie, and blue trousers appeared at the microphone in the center aisle and asked, "Reverend Lucas, why do you call your organization the *Christian* Voters Alliance? Can only born-again Christians be members?"

Lucas told the young man, "The Christian Voters Alliance is an organization of

Christians who want to vote according to their faith in the Lord Jesus. We're non-partisan, and, *well,* this campaign for the Guthrie amendment is just one part of the nationwide movement to legalize morality, not immorality." (Lucas thought of those words "Legalize Morality," and thought that would make a great bumper sticker.)

A young woman in a plaid skirt and long brown hair walked to the mike and asked, "Mister Durkin, may I ask, how did you become homosexual?"

Durkin smiled and answered, "Well, miss, I didn't become gay, I just *am,* and always *have* been. I realized that something was different about me when I was a kid. That's the story of just about every gay man."

The young woman made a quick "Thank you," and went back to her seat.

Another young man, thin-faced, with a stylish haircut and suit, declared, "Mister Durkin, what you're asking the public to do is accept the homosexual lifestyle as legitimate. For these many years, Mister Durkin, homosexuality has always been considered a sin and a disease. Won't the acceptance of homosexuality lead to acceptance of other vices?"

Lucas sneaked a smile into his face; someone else cares about morality. He thought; *let's see the faggot get out of this!*

Durkin's face stiffened, his voice grew deeper as he declared, "Lissen, young man, I, along with the other gay people in the world do not appreciate being considered evil or bad just because we're gay! Isn't attacking people because they're somehow different evil?

"Let me tell a story," Durkin began, "After I was discharged from the Corps, I moved to Philly and studied Physical Education at Temple, and I found a lot of guys just like me, and this was before Stonewall. So many times we had to put up with assaults, from the cops and plain thugs, and I'd see a kid jacked up, and we were expected to take it. But I took up boxing, and I passed my training on to other gay men.

"One evening," he continued, "a gang of punks came at me, and I duked it out with them, and they ran, and *they* called the cops on *me*! But I don't regret it at all! It's time that *you, buddy,* and *you,* Reverend Lucas, learned to accept us gay people as your fellow citizens, with rights and feelings like everybody else!"

Again, gays throughout the state cheered, but Lucas fumed; *this faggot has nothing to say to me,* he thought. *Maybe if he gave up his sin, he would have any trouble.*

Prager then proclaimed, "We're coming to the end of the program, so if you gentlemen would care to make closing statements, we will begin with Mister Durkin."

How come he got to speak first, thought Lucas.

Durkin folded his arms on his massive chest, smiled, and concluded, "I have truly enjoyed this debate, and especially the opportunity to give our side a hearing. It's important we air our views, to show who we really are as people, that we're free to tell our stories, and even just live our lives. If it's okay with the Reverend Lucas, I'd like t' have another one before the election."

Prager nodded to Durkin. Lucas saw this; *is there something going on between them?* Prager said, "Reverend Lucas?"

Lucas jolted–he had to reply, and he stated, "I have made myself plain about how I feel about the issue of homosexuality. I believe I speak for the majority of Americans who say it's not acceptable. I've always known it to be wrong, even before I became a

Christian, and I don't see the need to surrender that belief. It is wrong, now and forever, and no amount of debate will change that!"

Prager ended the debate, "This brings the debate to a close. I would like to thank the audience for joining us, and for the participants for being here. I'm Don Prager, good evening." The audience applauded, and the house lights dimmed.

The two debaters moved back to their sides off stage. Lucas' aides joined him in grabbing their coats and dashing to the front door of the building, where their cars were located. When Durkin reached his side offstage, he was greeted by grins, slaps on the back, and cries of "Great, Mike, that was terrific!" from his own aides. At this time, the Lucas party strode through the lobby to the front entrance, as if they were trying to get away from something.

Some news people found Durkin, and they needed an interview to cap the evening. They moved in a body toward Durkin and his team, asking "Mister Durkin, do you think this debate's made any difference in the campaign?"

"Sure I do," smiled Durkin, "just fighting back is an accomplishment." He and his staff kept moving, the media with them.

Lucas and his team got to their cars in the parking lot, and one man asked, "Dave, you okay?"

"I dunno," he grunted, "I keep telling them, what's right and wrong, what more do they want?"

Durkin's team spied the Lucas team, and Durkin called out, "Hey, Lucas!"

The news people saw this and muttered, "Something's gonna happen!"

Lucas turned and saw Durkin and his team, and thought, what does he want? He found a whole crowd coming to him, and he unconsciously raised his left arm as a shield. Durkin's asked, "Lucas, why the hell didn't you shake my hand?"

"Watch your dirty mouth!" snapped Lucas.

"Never mind my mouth!" barked Durkin, "Ain't I good enough to shake y' hand?"

"No! I consider you a degenerate and a sexual deviate!" proclaimed Lucas. "You're beneath contempt! You disgust me!"

"Durkin drawled, "So that's you opinion of me, is it? Well, you ever read your Bible about *love?*"

Lucas shouted, "Keep away from me, y' queer! Just don't come near me!"

Lucas thought, *this queer, this homo, a Marine, not weak like they all are, standing up to him and all decent people...*

Durkin's eyes widened, and he shouted, "What's the matter, Lucas, you scared'a me?"

"What do you want from me, Durkin, huh, *what?*" demanded Lucas.

"Just for you to know that we won't quit, and we want you to respect us!" declared Durkin, and then he turned his muscular form around and walked back to his aides. Lucas and his team got into their car.

As they drove away, Lucas grumbled, "He gets mad at me because I wouldn't hold his hand! That's faggots for you!" But he felt a twitch in his stomach. When he got home, his back ached, and it took a while for him to fall asleep.

14

Two days later, the metropolitan section of the *New York Times* was spread across Lucas' desk in the CVA office. The polls showed the two sides of the Guthrie amendment just about dead even.

"Look Dave, the media lies like a rug, you don't have to believe it!" snapped Gary Hennessy.

"Yeah, but Gary, you can't deny the fact that more people are coming out against the amendment," protested George Emerson. "And Dave, you can't just say to the other side, 'you're wrong, you're wrong, you're wrong,' you have to learn to debate."

Lucas sat at his desk, head resting on his hand. "How could we lose such a big lead?" he moaned, and then he let his arm land with a thump on the desk, again moaning, "This political stuff's too weird for me!"

The phone rang, and a secretary said, "Christian Voters Alliance."

"I'll handle this call," Hennessy said, and he stepped out.

"Mainly," continued Emerson, "the other side got the undecided vote."

"What d' y' mean?" puzzled Lucas.

"The way polltakers do it," explained Emerson, "is they phrase the question, 'Do you strongly favor, somewhat favor, somewhat oppose, or strongly oppose, or have no opinion on such-and-such an issue?' The way I see it, the 'no opinion' people have moved to 'somewhat opposed.'"

Lucas jumped to his feet and walked toward the window, glaring out – *Could he actually lose? What was wrong with people?*

"The best thing we can do now," said Emerson, "is to motivate our own people to get out and vote, make them see how urgent this is for them."

Hennessy stepped back into the office and said, "Dave, that was Durkin, he wants to know when you want another debate."

The three men looked at each other; Lucas tapped his hand on the window sill and grunted, "Naw, George, you're right, we got to get them out there! I'm going to get back to street preaching! Get off my butt and fight!"

"Maybe if you debate Durkin again," said Emerson, "I know a good debating coach–"

"Uh-uh, no more debates," snapped Lucas, I got nothing to say to the faggot!"

One day later, Lucas started his rallies, speaking at baseball fields and parking lots. At a tent in a shopping mall, Lucas proclaimed, "This is a fight to the death for Jesus and His true church! God doesn't care about *what* is fashionable at the time in Man's eyes! The Word of God says that Homosexuality is a *sin,* a *grave, terrible sin,* and we who call ourselves Christians have got to fight this sin with every ounce of our being! A true Christian must oppose homosexuality and vote for the Guthrie amendment! We must *vote* according to the *Will* of *God,* and strike a *blow* for moral values, to transform the world for Jesus Christ our Lord and Savior!" After these rallies, there were more assaults on gays.

Mike Durkin's Apollo Health Club was hit with a Molotov cocktail. The door and the front entrance were burned, but otherwise the damage was easy to repair. The next morning, Durkin stood in front of the club as repairs were being made, and told the media, "This just shows the world the kind of people we're up against! The closet's no place to go now, because it would mean a victory for our enemies! If the Reverend Lucas wants to separate himself from this act, he should come out now and say he's sorry the incident took place!"

Reporters asked Durkin, "Are you blaming Reverend Lucas for this act?"

"Well," began Durkin, still angry, "His rhetoric surely helps to incite the situation! That's the natural assumption, you know, and like I said, if he doesn't want any blame for this incident, he better apologize for it, and say out loud that he doesn't want any violence! I know *I* don't!"

The evening news broadcast Lucas' reply: *"They* sin, *they* commit the sin of homosexuality, and they blame *me* if they get punished for it! That's the way a sinner thinks! A Christian accepts authority! More punishment is sure to come for them!" The CHCR got a copy of that clip and put it in their ads.

One Saturday evening, Lucas was accompanied by five young men – ministers and other CVA activists – facing cameras and microphones while preaching from the bed of a Ford pickup parked in the parking lot of the Pink Flamingo Café, another of Atlantic

City's gay landmarks and Mike Durkin's favorite place for a drink.

Durkin was at the bar at that time with his boyfriend, Stephen Voss, who was a

Marine in Viet Nam and now was studying Law at Rutgers. Durkin sat at the bar, pleased

with the sight of the community coming together to fight the Guthrie amendment – The

bartenders and dancers donated their tips to the cause, and a graffiti wall was set up in the

back, for patrons to write, for a dollar, clever things about David Lucas – "Lucas is a

cross dresser," "Lucas says let us prey," "Jesus saves, Lucas hates," etc.

Voss saw that Durkin was unusually quiet, nursing his favorite drink, Irish

Coffee. Voss put his arm around Durkin and asked, "What's wrong, sweetie?"

"Aw, them old rich queens are getting on me," moaned Durkin. "Rickman, you

know, the famous lawyer, likes them young boys? He told me, he *ordered* me, to lay off,

not get so excited about what if the amendment passes, they can always declare in

unconstitutional in the Supreme Court! That's great, but in the meantime, kids are getting

beat up on the streets! Rickman thinks that all we have t' do is keep quiet, like he does, an' everyone'll love us!" Durkin rubbed his hand on his forehead and moaned, "I'm tired, Stevie, I'm pissed off!"

Voss hugged Durkin closer and whispered into Durkin's ear, then Durkin giggled and said, "Jesus Christ, bitch, don't you ever give up?"

"Hey, I love being your court jester, hon." smiled Voss.

A young man ran in and said, "Sorry, Steve! Mike, Lucas is outside preaching!"

"Oh, *shit!*" snapped Durkin as he ran outside.

From the back of the truck, Lucas declared, "No good can come from the life of a homosexual, only *evil* and *sin* and *death!* I call on all homosexuals, in the name of the Lord and Savior Jesus Christ, to abandon their sin and accept Jesus as their Savior..."

Patrons going into the Pink Flamingo stopped to watch, and some went outside from the bar to see. The words "What the fuck's *he* doing here?" mumbled through the crowd, and one tall man in leather took two steps towards Lucas and howled, "Get yer fuckin' ass out of here!", and more men came forward and yelled at Lucas – "Asshole, go fuck yourself, get fuckin' lost!" and began to throw beer bottles at Lucas.

The men around Lucas and the media scattered to the other side of the truck, but Lucas stayed on the truck – He was too contemptuous of the gays to fear them – and he kept preaching to them, "The Lord Jesus Christ can save you from all your sins, and homosexuality is a *sin!* Man says it's okay, but Man is lost in darkness! Jesus stands ready to enter your heart, and you must let him it! He died on the cross that you might be redeemed from you sins!"

Lucas knew there was some danger – he could see the mob of gay men yelling and throwing beer bottles at him – but he was facing sin, confronting sinners with their sin, and that thrilled him – and he wouldn't back down to a bunch of "fags." This was confronting the enemy, just like Doctor Garfield said, just like Billy Sunday would have done—be a manly man for Christ, facing danger.

The mob came closer as Lucas brayed, "The wages of sin is *death*, but Jesus offers you *life!* I'm *not afraid* of you, for I am comforted by the *Son* of *God!* I will never *stop* until you have *turned* from your *wicked sins* and *turned* towards *God* through His *Son Jesus Christ...*"

At this point, Durkin raced to between the mob and the pickup. He raised his arm high and yelled at the crowd, "Let him *alone*, for God's sake!" The crowd stopped and went quiet.

The crowd stopped moving, but Lucas kept preaching – "this nation is in ruin because of the easy tolerance for sin! We must return to the traditional gospel of Jesus Christ! If you love your country, give up your sins and accept Jesus, and God will be merciful to American again..."

"Don't stop us, Mike," warned a man in the crowd. "We're going show this asshole the fags're on the warpath!"

"That's *exactly* what the hell he wants you to do!" warned Durkin. "He'd *like* you guys attacking him, he'll go away feeling like a martyr, an' he'll *sue!* So let's just start chanting, GO! GO! GO!"

The crowd picked up the chant, "GO! GO! GO!..."

Lucas stopped preaching, letting his arms dangle. He got off the back of the truck, a sign for the young men around him that it was over for the evening. The crowd kept chanting "GO! GO! GO..."

Durkin walked over to Lucas and said, "I saved your life, Lucas, now you owe me. You gonna stop slandering gay people now?"

"Sick perverts all you guys are!" muttered Lucas as he entered the cab of the truck and slammed the door. The truck drove off, and the crowd cheered and moved back into the bar to celebrate. The media crews flocked around Durkin.

15

General Election Day, November 1978; the day came to vote on the referendum.

That morning, the Reverend David Lucas, Christine, and several supporters marched towards the neighborhood polling station, followed by a horde of reporters and camera crews. As they neared the voting station, Lucas had an idea: he bowed his head and intoned, "Dear Lord Our God, we acknowledge you as supreme King of Kings" —

Christine and the others around them also bowed their heads – "The almighty ruler of heaven and earth, and we accept Your Son Jesus as our Savior. We ask of you this day that we elect our public officials according to your will. In God's Name, we pray, ah-men."

The cameras and reporters followed Lucas into the voting station. It took place in the cafeteria of Erno Central High School, with older women seated at tables taking people's names in the register and directing them to the voting machines.

"What's your name, sir?" asked the election clerk, Marie Scalicie, a woman with a thin face and short gray hair.

"David C. Lucas," he replied, with dignity.

The woman flipped through the registration book and stated, "I'm sorry, Mr. Lucas, there is no such name in the register."

Lucas was dumbfounded, then he remembered – He didn't re-register after 1972—and he didn't even bother to vote since.

He turned away, Christine in his wake, the cameras and reporters taking this all in. As he got outside, he smiled earnestly and said, trying to be good-natured about it, "Well, I know I can't vote, but other Christians can, and I know this referendum will come through."

Lucas dropped Christine off at her parents' home, then drove off. *Will this amendment pass?* He thought about praying, but he had to keep his eyes open to drive.

Lucas got to the CVA office, with workers rushing for a last-minute push to get the vote out. The five o'clock news showed the gaffe at the voting station.

"Looks bad, Dave," warned George Emerson. "Makes you look dumb."

Lucas stepped to the window, leaned on the wall, and sat at the desk–then back to the window, then back to the desk; Gary Hennessy squeezed a pen in his hand off and on, inhaling shrilly; and Emerson brushed his gray-brown hair, tightening his eyes and lips. They kept watching the TV, listening to the anchormen say something about the Guthrie amendment being the hottest item in the election, and that it could go either way.

It could go either way – Lucas kept hearing that over and over for two weeks.

"I'm going to the Dorita," Lucas said, "the press'll be there, an' out supporters."

Salon 1 of the Dorita Hotel was loaded with television cameras and reporters. The two portable bars served sodas and fruit juices. The crowd applauded Lucas as he came in.

A young woman in a red suit, a microphone in her hand and a press card around her neck, asked Lucas, "Reverend Lucas, may I interview you for our viewers?"

"Sure," happily agreed Lucas.

They moved towards the cameras arrayed along the wall. A red light blinked on atop one of them and the woman said, "This is Karen McKenzie at the Hotel Dorita in Erno, where the campaign for the Guthrie amendment is coming to an end. With me now is the leader of the Guthrie campaign, Reverend David Lucas." (The crowd behind them roared a huge cheer.) "Reverend Lucas, What do you feel are your chances?"

"We're *going-to-win!*" proclaimed Lucas, as the crowd again yelled in joyous agreement.

"Are you at all concerned about the recent polls that show the referendum dead even?" asked Mackenzie.

"No, not at all," returned Lucas– the people and the atmosphere changed his mood.

"As you can see," McKenzie told her viewers, "there remains a strong hope among the Gutherie amendment's supporters for victory. This is Karen McKenzie, from the Dorita Hotel in Erno," she concluded. The red light on the camera went off, and she turned to Lucas and said, "Thank you, Reverend," and Lucas went off to mingle with the crowd.

He came upon Nick Pastorini, the funeral director, who asked, "Hey, Dave, how're you, where's Chris?"

"She didn't want to come," Lucas replied. (He never asked her.) "You know the baby's coming soon, an' she doesn't feel too great. She says she could hardly breathe this morning. She's at her parents' place."

More supporters came in as eight o'clock arrived. At eight, the early results came on the air. The chattering crowds went silent as the clustered around the TV sets located at each corner of the room.

Three precincts reported: 41 percent yes, 59 percent no.

A moan roared in the room. An eighty-year-old woman screamed at the media crews, "Liars! No-good liars! You never tell the truth!"

Lucas jumped to the podium located at the center of the ballroom, and announced, "Like the man said, only three percent of the precincts have come in–" He didn't know what that meant actually – "so the night's still young! So let's not worry, *okay?"*

The crowd cheered and applauded, their faith in victory renewed.

All through the night, two hundred people crowded the ballroom at any given time. As the night continued, more and more precincts reported the results, and the percentage of "yes" for the Guthrie amendment grew smaller. By ten o'clock, the vote was 74 percent "no," 26 percent "yes." The newscasters were all saying the same thing – "We project a victory for the anti-Guthrie forces..."

The crowd groaned. Lucas bent down his head and leaned on the bar, his guts sinking. He, and all the other diehards, had to admit it – they lost, and the fags won.

Lucas shoved his way out of the ballroom, past calls of "Hey, Dave," grabbed his coat from the rack, and disappeared, just as the reporters started to look for him.

Lucas strode through the lobby, out the front entrance, and into the street, as if escaping something. He went past Waldo's (the plywood slab still covering the broken window) where the local CHCR branch celebrated their victory. The street rocked with disco music, yells, and chants of "Free-dom! Free-dom!" and "Lucas sucks! Lucas sucks!"

Lucas arrived at the CVA office and saw Hennessy and Emerson slouched in front of the TV. The broadcast showed the scene at the Dorita salon, and the reporters announced, "There's a pall of defeat here..."

Emerson looked thoughtful, and said, "We'll have to go over what we did wrong." Hennessy looked on the verge of tears, and moaned, "We didn't even carry this county."

Lucas flopped into one of the metal folding chairs. He watched as he saw Mike Durkin, at the victory party at his club, proclaiming, "All of us, who worked like mad to win our freedom, should thank ourselves for this triumph over bigotry! Now, let us remember, that this is only *one* victory over our oppressors, and that we have to stay always ready to keep fighting and fighting to win our freedom and self-respect! Remember, they are *not* beaten, but they *are* beatable! *Thank you!"*

There was a yell of joy, and the band broke into the Marine Corps Hymn, with new lyrics:

From the Halls of Montezuma,

To the shores of New Jersey,

We have won a mighty battle

to preserve our liberty!

We have beaten back the forces

of hate and bigotry!

Through hard work and dedication,

we have saved our right to be!

Lucas said, "Let's pray," as the three men bent their heads forward, and Lucas prayed, "Lord God in heaven, all we ask is that you intervene to save our land. Than is all we ask. Ah-men."

The other two men repeated" Ah-men."

The phone rang. Lucas picked himself up and answered the phone with "Christian Voters Alliance."

"Dave, it's Jim," the voice on the other end said urgently, "Listen, get over to Crossland Memorial," a local hospital.

"What for?" asked Lucas.

"It's Chris," Jim answered, "something's wrong!"

Lucas slammed down the phone and sped off ignoring the "Dave, what's the matter?" from the two other men. When he got out the front door, he called and cab. One stopped, Lucas jumped in and barked, "Crossland Hospital!"

When he got to the hospital – being reminded by the cabbie to pay him – Lucas stepped through the front entrance and into the empty lobby to the information desk. The receptionist finished with one patient, then he gasped, "Where's my wife, Christine Lucas."

The receptionist looked at the sheet and said, "She's in surgery now, sir, you can wait in there," pointing with a pen at the waiting room.

Lucas went into the waiting room and flopped into one of the armchairs, wondering, *What could be wrong?* After ten minutes, he glanced through the glass door at the reception desk and saw a mature blond woman step over there. The clerk pointed, again with the pen, towards the waiting room. The blond woman stepped over to the room.

"Reverend Lucas?" she asked.

"Yes," Lucas said as he rose.

"I'm Doctor Grandy," the woman said as they daintily shook hands. "I have to tell you something, please sit down." Lucas fell back into the chair, and Grandy sat on the nearby couch.

"Your wife," started Grandy, "complained about chest pains and shortness of breath, and sweating. Those are symptoms of a heart attack, and it was. Pregnancy takes away many vital nutrients from the body to the developing fetus."

She inhaled and continued, "If the pregnancy continued, it would have been fatal for both your wife and the baby, so I had no choice but—" she inhaled—"to abort the fetus."

Lucas' lips and eyes widened and his head dipped back, then he jumped up and shouted, "You killed my baby! You killed it!" as he stamped his foot. He gained control of himself.

Grandy rose to her feet, not feeling too safe. "Please understand, Reverend," she added, "that this was a very difficult decision to make for me. I'm not very much in favor of abortion, as I'm a Catholic, but – I did what I felt was needed to save your wife's life."

Lucas heard Grandy's words, but he moaned, "But you killed my baby."

"Reverend," Grandy replied, "It was *her* baby in *her* womb! The choice was between your *wife* dying or both your wife *and* your baby dying. Would you want your wife to die?"

Lucas slammed his eyes shut and clenched his fist to his mouth. Christine dying–her and the baby dying–what could he say?

Grandy, seeing that Lucas had no answer, stated, "She's is room 367."

Lucas found the room and stepped in. Christine laid still, her skin pale and her eyes open. The eyes turned to Lucas and she said softly, "David?"

Lucas walked in and shut the door behind him. She raised her hand for him, but he just stared at her with a reddened face. She put her hand back down and said, "How are you feeling, honey?"

The election—the abortion–all this– at one time! He fell on the chair and cried, sobbing and screaming loudly. Christine was upset by this, her husband crying, and she reached over and stroked his hair.

16

The defeat of the Guthrie amendment was nationwide news for days. Durkin's slogan, "They're not beaten, but they're beatable," moved throughout gay communities from New York to San Francisco. The newest fashion statement was parts of the Marine uniform – fatigue caps and trousers, combat boots and overcoats. When word got out that Durkin's favorite drink was Irish Coffee, the bars had trouble filling the demand.

And David Lucas…The morning after the election, he stayed in bed until eleven AM. His face prickled with almost thirty hours of stubble, and his clothes felt stale. He showered and shaved, and put on a fresh shirt and suit. He then went into the den and pulled out a hand-held tape recorder and a cassette.

When he got to the office, things have remained as usual – the secretaries answered the phones and opened letters as if nothing had happened. He got to the door of his office and told them, "I'm going to tape some things for dictation. I want you to transcribe it later."

Lucas got behind his desk, turned in the recorder, and spoke into the built-in microphone:

"As long as I have been a Christian, I have wanted to live a clean, decent, righteous life, and I have urged others to do the same. I have never been a politician, never involved myself with politics. I have simply wanted to serve the Lord Jesus Christ, my Lord and Savior, and bring others to His fold."

"The recent failure of the Guthrie referendum shows how weak people are spiritually in this country. The so-called Christians have been taken in by such phrases as 'freedom of choice' and 'do your own thing,' and they show their tolerance for shacking-up without marriage, promiscuity, *and* homosexuality! Christians are expected to tolerate these moral cancers in our society."

"A Christian's life must be a rebuke of the world, to challenge the world's sinfulness, and not conform to it."

The phone rang, and the secretary picked it up. She came in and said, "Reverend, George Emerson on the line."

Lucas picked it up, expecting something bad, and sighed, "Hey, George, what's up?"

"Hey, Dave," said Emerson, "Durkin's going to be on, he going to be interviewed on PBS, you may want to watch it, this evening at six-thirty."

"Yeah, for what?" grunted Lucas.

"It's always good to know what the other side is doing," said Emerson. "Also, do you still want to keep CVA going, or do you want to disband it, and what do you want to do with the money raised?"

Lucas inhaled, let the air out of his lungs, and said, "I dunno. I'm thinking about making an evangelistic ministry out of it, I dunno. Oh, George," he brightened, "I decided to write a book about what I been through with this referendum thing. I think it'll be a hit in the Christian market. Do you think your agency would be interested – "

"In marketing it? Sure!" agreed Emerson, "The Christian market's hot right now, and you're famous! Just get it finished, okay?"

"Yeah, will do!" said Lucas – then he heard thumping noises in the outer office. "Gotta go, George, I'll be in touch!" and he hung up and went outside.

He saw four well-stuffed sacks of mail thumped down by postmen. All this mail, thought Lucas, for *him...* The secretaries look worried at all this mail to handle, then Lucas proclaimed, "Don't worry, call the temp agency, they'll send more girls here!"

When they pulled out some of the letters, they read something like:

"God bless you, Brother Lucas, for your brave stand for Jesus, Keep it up!"

"Keep it up, Dave, keep fighting the queers and dykes!"

"Run for some office, Dave, all the Christians will give you their money and prayers!"

Lucas went through these letters, wondering if the same thing went on in the CVA office. He called the office, and Gary Hennessy cheered, "They're coming in from all over the country, Dave! Letters and telegrams, some with money, *lots* of money! The letters say they admire what you've done!"

Lucas smiled. *This* was his revenge against the faggots who defeated him! He told his secretaries and Hennessy, "Get down the addresses for the file, and copy them!" He would get in touch with them in the future, and he would tell Emerson about it – his ad agency was just getting into direct-mail advertising.

When he went home, Lucas took off his coat and jacket and tossed them on the sofa, then strode into the kitchen to look for something to eat. He landed on a chair by the table; he was lonely, he wished Christine was here with him. He would check with the hospital to see when she would be discharged. His stomach had a twinge; order Chinese takeout?

6:30 was coming up; he remembered what Emerson said about Mike Durkin being interviewed. Lucas turned on the TV and waited for the interview. Durkin, looking unstoppable, appeared, and the anchorman asked him, "Mister Durkin, I assume you feel pretty good about the victory you had yesterday, where do you go from here, or do you know yet?"

"Well, for starters," said Durkin, "we're going to follow up our win with more campaigns like the ones we had, you know, educational programs, rallies and marches, throughout the country. They won't be about any particular issue confronting gay people, but they will establish our political presence in any given community, to show everyone that we're here and that we won't go back into the closet. And of course, to show that we're not just interested in our own narrow interests, we want to go into coalitions with other disadvantaged minority groups. A union of all the minorities, sharing problems and tactics, would be a pretty strong force to be reckoned with."

Lucas listened to this – the minority groups – like the Blacks and the Spanish – working with the fags and dykes?

"What do you have to day about the Reverend Lucas' campaign against gay rights in this election?" the anchorman asked Durkin.

"I don't like it when a person votes against my rights," asserted Durkin, "but I recognize that person's rights to think and vote as they see fit. But I have a challenge for the Reverend Lucas. I think a lot of bad feeling can be avoided if the gays and lesbians on one side, and the born-again people on the other side, got together and talk over our mutual problems and areas of disagreement, peaceably. It would not require any compromise in beliefs, but it would require a willingness to see the other side's point of view, like detente with the Soviet Union."

Sit down with – *them?* Thought Lucas. He turned off the TV and jumped to his feet, pacing around the living room. The thought of Durkin gloating and feeling confident angered him. Someday...He picked up the phone and called the Chinese take-out restaurant.

17

Two days later, Lucas drove to Crossland Hospital to pick up Christine. She felt weak and tired from the abortion, the heart attack, and from lying down for so long. She held on to Lucas, while walking to the door, and led her into the car.

"We're going to your parents; for dinner," Lucas told Christine.

"Okay" peeped out of her mouth. Lucas saw she was pale, her face and head down. They arrived at the Corbetts'; Fran hugged Christine and smiled, "Welcome home, sweetie," and Jim patted her shoulder.

Her father placed himself on the couch next to her and said, "You don't have to do anything, dear, just take it easy." Then he moved to Lucas and said, "That was a tough break you had, all that at one time. It'll get better." Corbettt turned to the dining room and called, "Is dinner ready?"

"Coming up, Mr. Corbett," Bridget said. Helen was already at the table, her eyes on Bridget. They all settled into their chairs.

At dinner–turkey with stuffing–Jim said, "So, what are the prospects for the future, Dave? Still hope for any little Lucases in the future?"

"Haven't thought about that," said Lucas, "I'm still upset with the whole–" He thumped his hand on the table.

"Maybe Christine should see a doctor before having any more babies," warned Fran.

"Why?" questioned Lucas.

"I was there, Dave, when she had the heart attack," recalled Fran.

Lucas inhaled, and ruminated–*Heart attack–Christine dying–That bitch of a doctor killed my baby–The fags beating me!*

"We can wait," agreed Christine," "I'll feel better and we'll see. There's no rush."

Lucas looked at Christine–*No rush to have a baby? Doesn't she want one?*

"Look," grunted Corbett. "I don't like abortion any more than you do, David, but I don't like my daughter to die before I do. So let it go until next time."

Lucas nodded, muttered "Yeah, you're right," and ate some more.

Jim asked, "What're you gonna do with the organization you started, CVA?"

"I decided to make it into an evangelistic group, a ministry," said Lucas, "to address some of the moral issues we have to deal with in this country.

The dinner broke up and the men went into the living room, and Fran and Christine stayed for a while in the dining room.

"How d' y' feel, kid?" asked Fran.

"Better," sighed Christine. "I *am* kind of lonely, even though the campaign's over. He sits in the den, with the door locked, and just talks into the tape recorder. I know he's busy with his work, but – I'm not being selfish, but – I wish he would spend some time with me."

"You *do* have the right to some attention from him," agreed Fran. "You've been a good wife to him, and he should treat you better than this."

In the car on the way home, Lucas asked Christine, "So what were you and Fran talking about?"

"Nothing much," returned Christine, nervous, wondering why he asked.

"Had to be be something," Lucas said, wanting to know what his wife was up to.

"About our marriage," Christine answered, hoping that would satisfy his curiosity.

"Yeah, when's *she* getting married?" sniffed Lucas, "Did she say?"

"No."

"Well, I wish she *would* settle down soon," proclaimed Lucas. "Women gotta learn that the old-fashioned ideas of morals and women's roles are the only right way."

They got to the parsonage, and before they got out of the car, Lucas moaned, "All this immorality, Christine! I'm sick of it!" They opened their doors, got out and Lucas muttered, "Sick of it."

18

The following Sunday morning, the Reverend David Lucas chatted with some of the men of the church in the hall leading to the back entrance to the sanctuary. They smiled at Lucas and told him, "Better luck next time."

Lucas would respond with "Yeah, it'll be better."

After the first hymn was sung, Lucas stepped to the pulpit, inhaled, and stated, "I have been very disappointed by the results of the past election. A law that would have promoted moral standards has been defeated by a public that has become foolish and spineless."

He inhaled again, and continued, "It is my prayer that the people of this state, and this nation, become aware of the state of things, the decline of moral values. After the defeat of the Guthrie referendum, and after consulting with attorneys, I have decided to dissolve the organization I headed for the campaign, Christian Voters Alliance, and form a new organization, the David Lucas Ministries, Incorporated. However, I will remain, full-time, the pastor of this church. I believe I can carry out both functions for I believe in

God, in Whom all things are possible, and I believe that being pastor of a congregation gives me the strength and authority to carry the message of Jesus to the nation. The evangelistic operation is designated to bring the American people back to God, back to righteousness, back to the principles that have brought America to greatness among the nations of the earth! I *ask* you, will you *help* me?"

At that, the congregation applauded, then rose to their feet, with whistles and cheers of "Ah-men" sounding.

There was another hymn, then announcements – a wedding that Lucas would officiate, meetings of the Boy Scout troop and the Cub Scout pack, and reminders to members to make their pledges for the year. Then, the collection, then Lucas' sermon:

"The overwhelming tendency of the professing Christian in this country is to somehow, someway, try to soften their witness for Jesus. Trying to be popular, accepted, 'with-it,' and in style, these alleged Christian are willing to give up solid doctrine, and willing to state that some parts of the Bible are not to be paid attention to at some times. That's wrong, very wrong. The Bible is for all times and all men, and its teachings are as true today as they were when the Bible was being written by men who were inspired by God. To deny that the Bible is applicable is to deny its being the eternal word of God, and to deny its very holiness.

"I'm sorry to say that the Christians as a group, and I'm not singling out individuals, have lost their guts. They don't want to tell the world that they accept Jesus as their Savior and Lord in their lives. They don't want to risk being ridiculed as fools and fanatics, or, the worst of all, *bigots!*"

This resounded in members of the congregation who didn't like being called prejudiced just because they didn't want to deal with minorities. Lucas went on:

"Call me a bigot if you want, but I believe that there's *nothing good* about anything that is *not* of God! God is the final arbiter of all that is just and good in the world, the founder of justice and righteousness! All that would go *against* God, or *deny* God, is nothing but *pure evil!* Atheism, Communism, feminism, humanism which would glorify weak, corrupt Man above God, *all* of these are evil and must be fought! As a Minister of the Holy Gospel of the Lord Jesus Christ, I have sworn to fight against *all* these evils! As Christians, our silence and complacency is the face of sin and evil and wickedness and immorality is a *sin* in itself!"

"Ah-*men!*" sounded, and Lucas kept at it:

"I put this challenge to *all* you who call yourselves Christians here, and all within the sound of my voice. Out in the street, at home, at our place of work, *where-ever,* I want you to *witness* for Jesus! Tell everyone, everywhere, that Jesus is your Lord and Savior, no matter *what* the risk. *Take* the risk, *take* all the suffering and ridicule the world dishes out to you, and you will be blessed by the Lord God! The suffering and ridicule you have to put up with will be brief because Jesus will rescue His True Church in the End Times. Besides, you may be saving somebody from sin if you tell that person about Jesus. If you tell that person the plan of salvation that only Jesus can give, you can save a person from a life of sin. So it's necessary for Christian to proclaim the message of Jesus to the world!

"Look at how we can change the world! On the one hand, there are the Christians, the born-again, Bible-believing Christians, who live their lives according to God's word, who live clean, decent lives, who care for their families! They don't steal, they don't drink and smoke or use drugs, they're wonderful, kind people! On the other hand, there are our enemies – the homosexuals, the pimps and prostitutes, the drug users and drunks, the whores and whoremongers, the pornographers, the radicals and revolutionaries and all other troublemakers! They respect *no* authority or law, they *do not know* about right and morality, just what's convenient for them, here and now on this earth! Yet, it's the *Christians* who are mocked and insulted and ridiculed, who are excluded from positions of authority and respect, who are *not* allowed to express their faith in God in school, while it's the *others* who are listened to in the media, and who are catered to by the politicians! If we reassert ourselves to the world, if we so dare to proclaim the message of Jesus to the world, no matter what it may cost us, the world will be transformed for the better! So let us dare to do as the old hymn says – take the name of Jesus with you!"

At that cue, the organ sounded, and the choir rose and sang the hymn "Take The Name Of Jesus With You." After the choir finished the first verse, Lucas resumed the pulpit and announced, "I want everyone, *everyone*, to sing the rest of the hymn with the choir." So the congregation also sang the hymn. At the end, everyone applauded, and Lucas remained on the pulpit and smiled.

"Now, let us pray," He announced, as a dull rumble sounded from the congregation. Lucas bowed his head and prayed, "Lord our God, and land which Thou hast blessed in the past is suffering from plagues of immorality. We have ceased to be a great nation because thy people have turned their backs from you. Give us the strength, oh Lord, to carry the Name of thy Son Jesus to the whole world. We ask in the Name of Jesus, ah-men."

19

The next morning, Lucas witnessed the sacks of mail coming in from the post office. He knew that some of the letters would include donations, and that would mean more money he wondered how to spend.

One of the temporary secretaries tapped on the door of his office and said, "Reverend, this letter came registered mail."

Lucas took the letter and unfolded it. He saw that the letterhead had the name of *Jimmy Wheeland,* America's leading television evangelist! He read:

Dear Brother Lucas:

A number of my fellow ministers and evangelists, including myself, have watched your campaign against the sin of homosexuality with keen interest. For a couple of years,, we have been discussing how we, as Christians, could somehow return the nation to traditional moral values, and how we could resist the growing dilemmas of homosexuality, abortion, and the erosion of the family, to name a few.

We have decided to form a political organization of born-again Christians to address these moral problems in the political arena, and to elect those persons who

would bring Christian principles to their offices. We will meet at the Wentworth Hotel in

Washington D.C. on January 17th. We would like you to give the keynote address at this

historic occasion. If you are interested, please let me know as soon as possible. I look

forward to meeting you soon. Thank you and God bless you.

Yours In Christ,

Jimmy Wheeland

A burden lifted from Lucas' guts. He told the secretary to call Wheeland's office and tell him he would come to Washington.

After dinner–he did not tell Christine a thing about the letter from Wheeland– Lucas moved right into the den and spoke into the cassette recorder:

"As a citizen, the first duty of a Christian is to obey the laws laid down by the state. Jesus told His followers to render unto Caesar that which was Caesar's, and to God that which is God's. The State is God's instrument to enforce His laws for man to follow.

"The Law of God is superior to the law of Man. If a law of Man is the same as the law of God, then the Christian obeys. But if the laws of Man violate the laws of God, then all Christians must be willing to suffer imprisonment, torture, even death to see that God's law in supreme once more."

20

January 1979; the National Christian Political Conference took place in the Wentworth Hotel, one of the most expensive in Washington – and it looked it. The Grand Ballroom, where the conference met, was the size of a basketball court, and it held crystal chandeliers, full wall-length mirrors, and a stage where the dais was held. On the request of the conference organizers, the bar was empty.

The chairman of the conference was the Reverend Jimmy Wheeland, pastor of Rose of Sharon Baptist Church in Roanoke, Virginia, and host of the "Jimmy Wheeland Revival Hour" on television. He was a massive and elegant man, six feet and two inches, with an aristocratic voice and a mane of light-brown hair trimmed with gray. On his program he spoke about his ancestors who were Confederate officers, but not about his father who made a fortune in real estate; nor of his opposition to the Civil Rights movement or his habit, up until seven years earlier, of referring to "Colored" people.

None of the thirteen-hundred ministers – like David Lucas – taking part in the conference had any political experience. The ministers were all male, none were

Catholic, and over half were under thirty-five.

As counselors and advisors, there were a variety of congressmen, a few US senators, and other veterans of various political campaigns – veterans of the Barry-Goldwater-for-President campaign in 1964 and of the George-Wallace-for-President effort in 1968; Birch Society organizers; oil and insurance company lobbyists; veterans of campaigns in support of the Viet Nam war and against the Civil Rights movement, of campaigns against gun control and for higher military expenditures.

David Lucas surveyed the scene from his seat at the head table. All this – the makeup of the ballroom – the crowd of people here, listening to him – the event – he was part of it. He felt both proud and nervous – could he do this? He turned to Jimmy Wheeland and said, "Brother Wheeland, I'm praying for the strength to be a part of this."

"You got the strength, Brother Lucas," smiled Wheeland, "you've proven it in the campaign." Lucas smiled.

Wheeland rose and opened the conference, declaring:

"Thank you, brothers in Christ, for coming to this assembly. Our purpose is to formulate a political strategy for the decade in which the political interests of born-again, Bible-believing Christians are advanced and protected. I know that together, we shall return America to those principles that have made it great among the nations of the earth.

"Now, I proudly turn the podium over to a young man, once a soldier for his country, and now a pioneer in this movement to bring about morality through law. In New Jersey, he headed the popular 'Vote Christian' campaign against so-called 'gay rights' which the liberal churches, the civil liberties fanatics, and the militant homosexuals were forcing upon the good people of New Jersey. Unfortunately, due to a campaign of misinformation and hysteria, the 'Vote Christian' effort failed. Still, we learn from our mistakes and failures, and this defeat in New Jersey will give birth to victories in the entire nation. He is the pastor of Wingate Memorial Baptist Church, in Erno, New Jersey, please welcome the Reverend David Lucas!"

The young ministers cheered the great warrior for Christ who was on the minds and lips of everybody. Lucas arrived at the podium, shook Wheeland's hand and smiled – and felt nervous, but that would not stop him. He turned to the conferees and spoke:

"My friends–brothers–I'm extremely happy and honored to be here, and that's a fact. Just like Brother Wheeland says, when we lost in New Jersey, I felt sad, angry, and just plain down with everything. Like Jesus on the Cross, I felt like, 'My God, my God, why hast thou forsaken me?' You've heard the expression, haven't you, that victory has a thousand fathers, defeat is an orphan? That was how I felt – and the homosexuals had a big party for their defeat of Christians. They *enjoyed* their victory over morality!

"The idea behind the Guthrie amendment, and all other laws like it, is to tell the homos and their allies that we *don't accept* homosexuality as a proper lifestyle, and we never, *ever,* will! Maybe we *can't* make them change their ways through the law, but we can remind them that homosexuality is as much a sin in *this* day, as it always has been! If we can make it hard for the homos to practice their sin, or to put it out into the open, they'll either give it up or go back into the closet, hiding their sin like all sinners do! We won't have to see them parading it around for everybody to see!"

"Yah, uh-huh, ah-men!" sounded throughout the audience with applause. Lucas smiled; he felt better, and he went on:

"No so-called 'gay rights!' No legal protection for homosexuality! If I have a queer working for me, I want the right to fire him if he doesn't straighten himself out! I don't want to be forced to keep him, or her, or whatever"– A giggle from the audience – "I *won't* do it, and I'll *fight* anybody who tries to *make* me!"

The audience applauded, and Lucas continued:

"Now we come to women. You know, I can't help but wonder if there's something wrong with the feminist crowd. They don't *like* men, and yet they *look* like men and they *talk* like men and they *act* like men, and they look like they want to *be* men! To me, a Christian, men and women are not the same, either physically or mentally! You *know* they crack under the strain of heavy weights and heavy decisions, especially those that deal with life and death!"

More chuckles and claps from the audience, and Lucas continued, "As a Christian man, I recognize my duty to support and protect my wife and children, to head my household, as God through His Holy Scriptures command! And I do these things in the name of the Lord Jesus Christ, in a manner befitting our Savior, so that my children will lead a Christian life and carry on our Christian heritage! And *any* man who would *abandon* these things to appease his foolish wife, to me, *is just not a man!"*

The all-male crowd of ministers applauded, especially the younger ones. Lucas went on:

"Women must *like* women, genuine Christian women! Feminine! Kind! Gentle! They should *assist* the husband in the family and *not* try to dominate him. Any women who won't do that, to me, *just is not a woman!"*

The audience nodded and mumbled their approval. Lucas went on:

"And now, let's talk about our children. Both the husband and the wife must work together to raise the children in the nurture and admonition of the Lord, no matter *what* goes on in the secular world! The secular world, with its corrupt values, its sexual perversions, its atheism and agnosticism, stands as a threat to our morals and values! Let us do *all* that we *can* to make sure out children inherit our faith, and continue it on to the generations after us!"

Lucas paused, catching his breath, while the attendees barked their agreement;

then he went on:

"In the schools, they say they try to be neutral on moral values, they don't want to impose a standard of morals on kids, as if that's something bad! Let me tell you something, wherever there's no Jesus, there can only be *Satan!* Let there be tax breaks for parents who send their kids to *religious* schools, whether they're Catholic parochial schools or private Christian schools! In *those* schools, you *know* that morals and values are taught along with the math and geometry! They have standards of personal conduct, like what is appropriate to say, do, act, wear, and they *en-force* the standards, and where have you heard of that in a *public* school?"

"Yeah," the young ministers brayed, as Lucas went on:

"Furthermore, I don't accept this idea of unisex and bisex or whatever – the confusing of male and female. I believe in maintaining the proper, God-given sexual roles laid down in the Bible! Before I became a Christian, I thought it was weird if I ever saw a boy play with a doll, or a girl play with a baseball glove! Now that I *am* a Christian, I know *why* I don't like it, because it *violates* the laws of nature, as God commands!"

"Ah-men," called the audience, especially the younger men, as Lucas continued:

"All of this is interrelated, homosexuality, women, and the upbringing of our children! Homosexuals distort the sexual roles, so that children don't know what a *man* is and what a *woman* is! Our secular humanist society doesn't guide them in a Christian way, but instead tells them that *homosexuality's* okay, that *fornication's* okay, and that the murder of little babies, so nicely labeled *abortion,* is acceptable!

"Now I'll touch on the issue of the lives of the little babies. I have suffered from abortion. A *woman* doctor so cruelly and maliciously *butchered* the life out of my baby!"

An *Ohh* came from the audience.

Lucas turned quiet, and then said, "Brothers, I want every man of us here to be *angry* – be *enraged!* – at the thought of this crime made *perfectly legal!* Our *babies!* Our *children!* – are being *slaughtered* so cruelly and in such numbers! – Our sons and daughters, brothers! The children we are pledged to raise for the Lord!"

The audience gave Lucas a standing ovation and a joyous howl. Lucas did not smile, but he was pleased; this issue, the killing of the babies, would be the issue to galvanize the voters, he could see now. The applause faded, and Lucas went on:

"Now, let's talk about pornography. I won't talk about the guys who sell the dirty movies and the dirty books and magazines. You all *know* where those guys stand. No, brothers, what worries me are illicit, promiscuous sex acts in such everyday things as advertisements, television, and music. They *show* people–unmarried–naked–crawling all over each other! And the porn crowd wants this stuff treated like it's normal and acceptable! I'm a Christian, and I *won't* take it anymore! Take that stuff *away* from us! Take that stuff *out* of public access! Take it *off* TV and ads! Close *down* the places that sell pornography! *Censor* the ads and textbooks for sexual material! Let's *use* that word, *censor!* If it displeases the civil liberties creeps who thing there's no such thing as morals, *let's do it!*"

Applause, loud and hearty, came from the audience, especially from the younger men. Lucas calmed down as he went on:

"What we are doing in this conference is to get educated and organized for political action, to make the system work for *us!* We have to know how to register voters, to lobby congressmen, to work on political campaigns, to write to congressmen and editorial pages. Certainly, our enemies are organized, and *they* learned to kick out those politicians that don't follow their line, and put in those who do! And remember I call them *enemies,* not opponents!

"In New Jersey during the Guthrie campaign, we knew that this was no ordinary political campaign, but a crusade, a holy cause for the Lord Jesus, and our enemies were those who would take Jesus away from us and our children! Only *someone* so *evil,* so full of the *Devil,* could try something like that! And if they're not knowingly working for the Devil, then they're full of pride, *full* of vanity, for thinking that they can beat the will of God! This is a *crusade,* brothers, a holy cause for Jesus, like I said and like I'll keep on saying! Let us be worthy soldiers of Jesus, like the hymn says, soldiers of the cross, and follow the great men of God, whom God in *His* wisdom, has placed in the forefront of the movement of national renewal, such as Brother Wheeland! To *not* support such men would be a great sin!"

Shouts of "Yeah! Ah-men! Preach, Dave!" echoed in the ballroom, and Lucas went on:

"The enemy says we're trying to impose our beliefs upon the rest of the population!" He stopped, inhaled, and continued:

"Well, in a sense, that's true. I'm a Christian. I tell the world that Jesus is my Savior, Lord, and Redeemer. I can think of no other way for a person to be saved and redeemed, except through Jesus. I know for a fact that he's the way, the truth, and the light, and that no man can come before the father but by Him! We're Christians, we *know* that's the truth! We read our history, too, and we know that whenever we, the United States of America, accepted the law of God through His Son Jesus, we prospered, we triumphed, we flourished as a nation! Our land was bountiful, our wars were just and victorious, our hearts were pure, our men were strong and our women chaste! God had made us the greatest land in the world!"

A roar filled the hall as the men rose in applause.

Lucas spoke again, but this time in a dull, sad tone: "But these came a time, somewhere, somehow, when we turned away from God. The Supreme Court of the United States decided that God could no longer be taught in schools. Authority was rejected, laws were violated and lawbreakers were made into heroes. Guys who should've joined their country's armed forces either ran off to Canada, or else refused to go! These guys – let's call them the *cowards, traitors,* and *weaklings* they are!"

"Yeah, let's do it!" rumbled through the audience, and Lucas went on:

"They *abandoned,* they *deserted,* their country! Why? God help us, *why?* I don't know. God forgive me, I *don't know!* Somehow, they didn't think that this country that gave birth to them was worth fighting for! They ran! They gave up! They *deserted!"*

A male voice suddenly screamed, "God, oh God, come back to us!" ending with sobs and moans.

"No, brother," replied Lucas. "It's up to *us* to return to God. It's *our* responsibility, as individuals, and as a nation. But let me go on.

"There were people in this country who kept telling us that this country was the cause of all evil in the world, that we were a wicked nation. We accepted that. We believed that. And so, we weren't supposed to love our land. And so, because we didn't love our land, we let it go down. We legalized crime, we forgave traitors and cowards who deserted their country in Viet Nam, homosexuals wave their perversion in our faces, and manhood is ridiculed and abandoned."

Lucas then blurted, "Oh, God, forgive our sins! Give us the strength, Lord to fight your fight! Let *your* way be *our* way, Lord, and *America's* way! Let us once more bring ourselves to Thy bosom!"

The ministers raged with joy, standing clapping, shouting, raising arms in prayer. Lucas went on:

"We *have* to talk about Communism." (A shout went through the audience.) "Communism is a system of tyranny that stands as a threat to our society, our freedoms, and our faith. This is an evil, atheistic doctrine, which denied the existence of a supreme being! That is what we must recognize it as, my brothers! We must pray for those who are in the bondage of Communism! We must pray for and support those nations – South Africa, Rhodesia, South Korea, all the others! Let us back these nations up if they have to take strong measures to defend themselves against Communism! Let us have leaders who will stand up against Communist aggression, and not try to deal with them! *No way* can you deal with them! They have *no* honor, *no* morality, *no* respect for the rights of other nations! Let us have no more of *presidents* and so-called *leaders* and so-called *experts* who think they can sooth this *beast,* this rabid *animal* that devours free nations and freedom! The *only* thing they fear, the *only* thing they understand, the *only* thing they know is *force!* They know only one law, the law of the jungle – the law of brute force – the law of the gun and the knife!"

"Uh-huh," muttered the ministers.

"To preserve our Christian faith," Lucas continued, "our Christian heritage as a nation, we must both support all nations threatened by Communism, and rebuild our military strength. If we don't do either one of these, our nation will fall under Communist tyrannical rule, and *then,* my brothers, we'll really have church-state separation, just like in good ol' Mother Russia!"

Applause and Lucas went on:

"But along with our military strength, my brothers, our *spiritual* strength must be built up! We must *turn back* to the ways of our forefathers, our spiritual basis of our nation! We must *return* to God, the Heavenly Father, and seek guidance from Him, and return to Jesus for salvation! Let us *fight* against all that is wrong in our society, drugs, pornography, all of the moral cancers that pervade our society! Let us fight our enemies, the feminists, the homosexuals, the libertarians and abortionists! Let us turn our face to *God, follow* Him, and fight for truth and right!"

Again, the audience applauded loudly and heartily. Then, he concluded:

"Now, I close my address, and I pray that God has given me the words and the wisdom needed to bring forth His truth for His cause, and for His people. Good-bye and God bless you all!"

The audience let loose with a thunderstorm of applause, whistles, cheers and yelps of joy, and the younger men saluted their hero with chants of "LOO-CAS! LOO-CAS!..."

Jimmy Wheeland grinned and shook Lucas' hand heavily, then took the podium again and told the ministers, "There you have him my friends, one of the great young men of God in our era. Let us pray for, and look for, many more young men like him!"

The conference continued with lectures on a variety of issues, interpreted in the light of the Gospels as the conferees understood them.

There was a panel discussion entitled "The Communist Threat and The Challenge of Christianity," on foreign policy. Taking part in the panel was the Reverend Robert Van Der Molen of the Dutch Reformed Churches in South Africa, and the Reverend Englebert Wu, of Taiwan.

Reverend Van Der Molen assured his American brethren that, yes, the racial segregation system of Apartheid was very bad and would be done away with, eventually; but it had to be done in God's good time, but meanwhile, South Africa had a bigger problem with Communists, who just happened to be active in the Anti-Apartheid movement.

Reverend Wu of Taiwan – "The real China" as they all knew – spoke of how the anti-Communist leaders throughout the world that lost their fight were strong Christians, and he dropped such names as Chiang Kai-Check and Ngo Ding Diem. Later in the conference, Brother Wu denied that he was funneling money from the governments of

Taiwan, South Korea, and South Africa into the conference – but no one asked.

Major-General Theodore Roosevelt ("Horny") Horner, U.S. Army (Retired),

lectured on the spiritual basis of military strength, and of the threat that the Soviet Union

posed to the United States, with their vastly superior number of jet fighters, long-range

bombers, and nuclear warheads. General Horner spent a whole day reading a bible,

looking for the appropriate verses, skipping at least for that day the bars and brothels that

caused him to be thrown out of the Army – although he always claimed it was because of

all those Jews in the Air Force.

Along with the speakers, there were workshops on practical political action –

fund-raising, organizing, publicity, setting up an office, and lobbying congressmen.

Lucas walked around the ballroom and the halls of the hotel, smiling, shaking

hands, chatting with other delegates. He picked up literature of the variety of groups that

set up tables – groups that were fought against the Equal Rights Amendment; evangelistic

ministries that identified the Catholic Church and the federal income tax with the Anti-

Christ; self-published authors, veterans of fascist groups at home and abroad, pushing their works concerning Blacks, Jews, the Soviet Union, and the British Intelligence system; exhibitions from the consulates of South Africa, South Korea, Chile, and Taiwan; minor-party candidates for state-legislature seats, hoping to raise money and publicity; advocates of the promotion of divine creation as a scientific theory. In his room on the fourteenth floor of the Wentworth (it had no thirteenth floor), Lucas read the materials, underlining the key parts.

Six in the evening; Lucas walked to the hotel café; he glanced out the window–*Was that?–Yes!*-Chaplain (Major) Daniel Briggs, the chaplain in the base in Texas who brought him to Jesus.

"Chaplain?" Lucas ran and called.

"David," smiled Briggs, and they hugged–his hair was even whiter and thinner than twelve years ago, but his hug and his hand-grip were still strong.

"Come on in," urged Lucas and they entered the café.

Lucas told Briggs what went on after he was discharged-his education at Garfield

Bible Institute in Pennsylvania, his marriage, his being a pastor, and the "Vote Christian" campaign last year.

"I *do* regret not being in the Viet Nam war," sighed Lucas. "I see it was a righteous cause. I was such a screw-up person then, they wouldn't have me."

"Well, you have done well for yourself," smiled Briggs. "You know you weren't all that great a soldier. 'Screw up' was one of the *nicer* things they said about you."

"Yeah," Lucas chuckled, "I try to make up for that, supporting the troops. Plus, you know, Doctor Garfield, at Garfield Bible Institute, he also, like you, talked about Billy Sunday. I try to be like Billy Sunday, be strong for Jesus."

He bent his head and said, "As a kid, in Sunday school, I'd hassle and pick on the really religious kids–steal their bibles and run around with it–the teacher couldn't do anything, it looked like." Silence, then, "I wanted so much to get away from that, not be that kind of person. Since you showed me Jesus, I, like, wanted to be a decent person. Pay attention to how I live, all that."

"Well, you did great," smiled Briggs, "I can see that. I'm proud of you, David."

They hugged, then they went their ways.

On the last day, the National Christian Political Conference voted to make itself into a permanent organization, maintaining a networking system via computers that were donated by the same computer company which helped fly Robert Van Der Molen first-class from Johannesburg. The Reverend Jimmy Wheeland was elected President of the organization; and the honorary title of "First Vice-President" went to the Reverend David Lucas.

Dan Briggs, former Army Chaplain, laid in the bed in the motel outside of Annapolis, naked with the young male Midshipman against him, smoking a cigarette, the odor of smoke and semen in the air.

Lucas was saved, thought Briggs; a real success story. All his pastoral career, Briggs preached in the Kentucky prison system and in the Army, to young men who were confused about life, who made wrong turns. This one, David Lucas, was the only one whose soul was saved. Briggs thought, *Who will save my soul?*

21

Lucas returned from Washington and the conference to Erno, in a taxi through the streets lined with fading snow. He entered the parsonage, and Christine greeted him with a "Hello, honey," a kiss, and a hug, which Lucas accepted. She had on a blue sweater over his white blouse with the blue skirt, her hair pinned back.

"How was Washington?" she asked, "did you see the Washington Monument, all that?"

"Oh, yeah, yeah, it was nice, real nice," assured Lucas, "Naw, I didn't see that stuff. Let's go to a restaurant this evening!"

At the High Top Diner, Lucas was so excited–

" – So all these preachers are gonna go out and get people registered to vote, see, and the slogan we got in 'Saved, baptized, and registered!' That's the goal we have for Christians in the elecíions in the future! This is the future of America, good, God-fearing people, people who live clean, voting, taking over the government!"

"David," Christine gently warned, "Don't let your dinner get cold."

Lucas looked down on his plate and saw his food; he wolfed down his food, straight from the teeth to the throat, bypassing the taste buds. Christine took the time to finally say, "Ellen Brockton, you know, teaches the junior-high kids in Sunday School, she's having a baby, would you want to christen it?"

Lucas shrugged and let out a "Hmmm," and kept eating.

"And Ted Walman is out of surgery for his heart," added Christine, "they'd like you to visit him."

"I'll get around to it."

22

As First Vice-President, and from his fame from the campaign for the Guthrie amendment, Lucas sought out every available platform for the NCPC. He didn't like speaking at campuses; there were so many opinions in them, including a few Marxist ones. At one meeting at Rutgers, the auditorium had a few sympathetic people, many hostile people, and a curious majority. The friendly people applauded at the appropriate times; the hostile people asked irritating questions about individual rights and respect for varieties of religious opinion; and the others just sat there.

Lucas liked syndicated television talk shows better; they went out to the nice, religious people with nice suburban or rural homes and the occasional farm, in the land known as "Middle America." The hosts of these shows were entertainers, not journalists, which made them more fun.

One of these was the "Susan Willy Country Hour," taped in Washington, DC. Susan Willy was a moderately successful country singer who found a regular syndicated series more profitable and less work.

A young woman escorted Lucas to the green room, where guests were sent to wait for their time on stage. "We'll tell you when it's five minutes before coming on, Reverend," she said. Lucas sat at the vinyl chair while the public address system played the collected works of the Norman Luboff choir. He picked through the pile of magazines on the table – *Saturday Evening Post, Grit, Yankee,* and *National Enquirer.*

At this time, Susan Willy was in her dressing room, putting on her earrings as her husband and producer, Jerome Bache, charged in. "Two minutes, we're on!" he barked.

Susan glared at Jerome, her faced pulled down; then she went into the cabinet, pulled out a bottle of peppermint schnapps, and gulped a bit of it.

"Oh, great idea!" moaned Jerome. "A preacher's coming on, and you wanna get drunk!"

"I'll say it's mouthwash," Susan shot back, "It *is* mouthwash! C'mon, let's fuck tonight, okay?"

"One minute 'till we're on," snapped Jerome.

"Not 'till you say we can fuck!" answered Susan.

"Yeah, yeah, we'll fuck," groaned Jerome, pulling her by the arm to the stage.

Susan arrived to the applause of her fans, who were in their fifties and sixties, and she sang once again her theme song, the one she always hated but sold 2.6 million copies. The set was simple–a blue cloth backdrop, with two white high-backed plastic chairs with a matching table between them. There was a commercial break, then...

"Now, my first guest is someone who stuck his neck out for what he believed in, and he's still doing so. Many of you know of him, so here he is, the Reverend David Lucas!"

As Lucas strode across the stage, the audience applauded – they *did* hear about Lucas, and they liked what they heard. His blue suit glowed radiantly, and he was so handsome and sincere – certainly Susan thought so.

Lucas looked at Susan, then at the audience–the same type of people at Wingate, he thought. *This was going to be all over the nation!* He realized. He was nervous, but he kept it under control.

"Well, David," started Susan with a smile, "why don't you tell us about yourself, and what you're doing now?"

"Well, Susan," returned Lucas, his head cocked as he smiled, "it's kind of hard to decide where to start. I have a church in New Jersey, full of some of the best people on the face of the earth, and I try to mix that in with my work with the NCPC."

"Tell us all a little about your group, the – NCPC, is that it?" questioned Susan.

"The NCPC is the National Christian Political Conference," happily lectured Lucas. "The aim of the group is to politically organize Christians, people who believe in the Bible and in Jesus Christ, and get them voting according to their Christian faith. That way, we can clean up the country, get rid of the illicit sex, pornography, and moral corruption that've been running so rampant in this country."

The audience applauded. "Looks like the audience likes what you say, David," Susan announced. "Can you do that, do you think?"

"Sure, it'll take a lot of work, but we'll *do* it," smiled Lucas. "Against us are the homosexuals, the extreme feminists, the pornographers, intellectual types who think they're smarter than God, Marxist types who've somehow wormed their way into the

183

system, and all people who deny any place for God in our society, like our schools!"

The audience again rippled with applause, and Lucas went on:

"With us are the legions of decent people who believe in values, the people who believe in the family as the most essential unit for the strength of society, who read the Bible and believe every word it says, who believe that children should respect their elders and learn from them respectfully! The list goes on! They can't be found in bars and discos picking up babes or skimming the porn shops, but they pray every morning and evening, they work for a living, they follow the instruction of society and the office, and they go to church every Sunday for a real spiritual lift!"

More applause, and Lucas happily concluded, *"That's* the people we got with us, Susan!"

"You say you have an evangelistic operation, David?" continued Susan.

"Yeah," asserted Lucas happily, "The Christian Voters Alliance was sort of transformed into the David Lucas Ministries after the election. We still have the office, staff, and mailing lists at work for the spreading of the Gospel of Jesus throughout

America."

Susan sat back and smiled, made another glance at her note cards, and asked, "What about your private life, David, can you give us a look inside yourself?"

Lucas returned, "I live the same kind of life I believe in. I have a wonderful wife, and I'm eternally grateful for her. She's beautiful and obedient, just like women are meant by God to be."

"Well, your time is up, David, and I hope you'll drop by again," concluded Susan, and they shook hands and the audience gave its' final, hearty applause. Lucas waved at them on his way off stage.

Jimmy Wheeland watched the program, liked Lucas' performance, and sent off a press release stating that Lucas expounded the ideals of the NCPC eloquently.

After the program, Susan Willy did have sex with Jerome, interspersed with smacks on her buttocks with a big police belt.

23

In October, Lucas took the train to Harrisburg, Pennsylvania, then a taxi to Gillyville, to visit the campus of Garfield Bible Institute–and to see his mentor one last time.

The Reverend Doctor R.T. Garfield followed the progress of his star pupil, David Lucas, faithfully through the years – it was the custom of the alumni to write to Doctor Garfield often and tell him how they were doing— and he lay dying in his farmhouse on the campus of the institute.

Lucas toured the campus; nothing changed much. The square brick boxes of buildings, with the signs "Classrooms" and "Library" were still there, with no other names, and nothing was ever added in ten years; Lucas almost felt like he never left. The student escorting him boasted of the now seventy-seven students in the institute, and there *could* be some expansion.

Entering the farmhouse, a nurse escorted Lucas to Garfield's bedroom, and sat by the bed, a second nurse standing by. He remembered his mentor as a lion at the pulpit, with a roaring voice proclaiming the Gospel with authority. Now, Garfield was pale, his breathing weak and raspy, his skin without color. "Brother Lucas?" he asked, barely able to turn his head.

"Yes, here I am, Doctor," Lucas replied.

"Oh, God bless you for coming here," sighed Garfield. "Brother Lucas, I heard so much about your work in New Jersey, especially that campaign against – oh, I can't mention it, it's so terrible! Even in my day, when sin was as brazen as it is now, not even *then* was there such a sin. God will judge this land as He has judged Sodom and Gomorrah for their wickedness, even His own people Israel."

"Oh, please don't say that," moaned Lucas. "Tell me there's hope!"

"Please, keep up the work you're doing, brother," pleaded Garfield as he wheezed through his breaths. "Bring America back to God." he closed his eyes, exhausted.

One of the nurses said to Lucas, "He has to rest, sir, so you have to go."

Lucas rose and walked away, out of the house and onto the campus. As he moved away, Garfield's words stuck onto his mind, and into his heart. Great prophets passed their mantels on to some protégée – Moses to Joshua, Elijah to Elisha; has Garfield passed a mantel on to Lucas, to pick up where he left off?

On the train back to Erno, Lucas put into his tape recorder the final statement:

"The Lord gives us each a duty to perform in His service. I see that the Lord has given me the task to preach His gospel to America, to speak out against all the moral evils in the nation. That is what I will continue to do as long as I live, so help me God, ah-men."

24

The following week, Lucas went back to Fieldstone High School for his class

reunion. It took place in the gymnasium of the school, with yellow and red streamers on

the yellow and red walls– the school colors. A DJ played the classics of the early sixties,

and a table was set up with cold cuts, bread for sandwiches, and punch made from fruit

juice and ginger ale.

Lucas circulated around the crowd of one hundred and twelve, graduates and their

spouses. He was the star of the show, with his fame as the promoter of the Guthrie bill

superseding the memories of the times when he and some buddies would have some

carnal fun with some of the girls in Hank Pringle's Buick.

Lucas found Hank leaning against the wall, holding a cup of punch; Hank

Pringle–Lucas' partner in screwing any girl who would have them, in small-time

shoplifting, and in terrorizing Peter Mullen. Hank wore a plaid polyester jacket over a

Hawaiian shirt – his idea of fashion. He looked tired, and he didn't shave in three days.

"So, when'd you get out, buddy?" cheered Lucas.

"About a year ago," he replied. "Did you hear a punched a woman cop?"

"Yeah, Pete Mullen told me," answered Lucas. "What're you doing now?"

"Oh, anything I can get my hands on," Hank shrugged. Lucas did not feel like pressing any further. "You hear they tore down the Jackpot Inn? Gonna put a Pizza Hut there. They already put a parking lot down."

"I see Pete Mullen's not here," stated Lucas.

"Naw, he won't show," moaned Hank. "He won't wanna be around us. You hear he invented something to turn coal into gasoline, or something? Made a fortune from it. Don't drink the punch, I put vodka in it."

"I figured you would," smiled Lucas. "Hey, ain't that Beth Orbin over there? She got fat, and she used t' be so pretty, now –"

"She got five kids," informed Hank, "and her husband's been out of work for about two years now. Welfare don't quite get enough for them. Havin' kids puts weight on a chick, you know. Knocked up one myself after gettin' out of Rahway."

At the end of Hank's monologue, Edmund Casey, the assistant principal, strode towards them, wearing his customary plaid jacket and toupee, greeting, "Well, boys, catching up on old times?"

"Yeah," Hank sighed as he moved away.

"Where you going, Henry?" stated Casey, "Don't you want to tell us about how successful you are?" Hank paused a bit, then kept moving.

Casey turned to Lucas and proclaimed, "David, I'm very proud of your work on that bill, the Guthrie bill, is it called? Anyway, at the church I go to – did I tell you I always wanted to be a minister myself? Anyway, I told them that you were one of my students, and they wanted to know more about you. I must say, I'm proud of the progress you've made in morals. I find that *usually* low-income and working-class people have no sense of ethics and morals, having, well, not being in church in such great numbers. The church really makes for respectable people, wouldn't you agree, David?"

"Well," Lucas replied, "I believe that a church must totally be dedicated to the cause of Jesus Christ, and truly live within the bosom of god in order to be effective for God."

191

Casey replied, "Yes, yes. Oh, by the way, I'm retiring after this year. Shame how the school system's gone downhill after the prayers have been removed from schools. Do you remember the Ten Commandments on every classroom wall? Hmm, this punch is pretty good."

"Yes, I remember," recalled Lucas, who violated many of the commandments.

The following Monday, Lucas was back at work in the church office. The secretaries finished transcribing the notes he made in the cassette player and organized them into chapters. All he had to do now was think of a title, and he was finished.

He read the introduction: "This is the story of my life before and after Jesus Christ, along with what I believe as a follower of Christ. I hope that this would inspire people who have sinned, as I have, to turn away from their sins and accept Jesus. I also hope that those who are Christians would be inspired to do whatever they could to transform the world for Jesus."

This reminded Lucas of the glorious battle for morality, the manly camaraderie that went into the fight for the Guthrie amendment, and the fighting song, "Stand Up, Stand Up For Jesus, Ye Soldiers Of the Cross."

That was it—the title! He grabbed some typing paper, cranked it into the typewriter, and typed:

Soldier Of The Cross

by

David Lucas

Finished! Thought Lucas. He sighed and smiled.

24

It was November 1979, one year after the defeat of the Guthrie referendum. David Lucas sat in his office in the Coventry Towers. His idea of turning CVA into an evangelistic ministry, he decided, was a brilliant one.

David Lucas Ministries, Incorporated, was mainly a media ministry. One item was the tabloid newspaper, *The Champion,* which was sold also a supermarket checkout stands, a novelty for a Christian periodical. Its managing editor had long experience working for tabloids, and he applied his talents well in *The Champion* – huge headlines, exciting stories of sin and redemption, assaults on offending persons and groups; anything bad and demeaning was printed on "secular humanists" and other "enemies of the Lord," with no time wasted on checking facts.

In the *Champion,* there was always news of missionary efforts in foreign countries; Christian schools being opened along with statistics about their superiority over public schools; Christian radio and TV stations going on the air; some or another feminist, rock performer, or campus radical from the 'sixties, who came to believe in

Jesus; attacks on feminists, gays, secular humanists (like in the clergy), and Marx and Darwin. Lucas wrote an editorial every week in *The Champion*.

Gary Hennessy, who was such a big help during the Guthrie campaign, was office manager of the ministries, and he ran it less like a loving family and more like a business that was about to go under. His nervousness about making the ministries work caused him to snap out at secretaries.

Television was another medium Lucas utilized. For an hour each Sunday, the Sunday services at Wingate were broadcasted, along with whatever extra things Lucas wanted to say from a studio made up like a bank president's office. The production facilities were from an independent production firm and paid and paid for a donation by the Corbett Broadcasting Company, as a tax write-off. The program began airing during the fall 1979 season with the title – "The David Lucas Hour" – Lucas could not think of any other title.

So much money came into the Lucas ministries, since the loss of the Guthrie amendment, Lucas did not know what to do with it. He put out a newsletter for young bible school students, titled *The Word Out,* and he encouraged them to take to the streets with the message of Jesus, urging them to form teams and speak to people in the street and hand them literature.

These thoughts of success after defeat were pleasant for Lucas as he strode down the halls of the office building and into the elevator, then down into the parking garage in the basement, finding his Olds within the grayish-yellow light. Lucas pulled a remote control from his coat pocket, turned it on, and the ignition of the car went on – no bombs. This was a gift, and a suggestion, from a sympathetic electronics dealer.

Lucas got inside the car and started the radio, and the news came on – Students in Iran charged into the U.S. embassy in Tehran and took the embassy staff hostage!

Lucas paid attention to the crisis occurring on the radio, at the same time trying to beat the traffic. He reached a red light, and then started to think about what he heard in earnest. He recalled where Iran was, and Tehran. He recalled that what he knew about Islam, which Lucas remembered as a religion that did not recognize Jesus as Savior and thus was a false religion. He recalled stories in the news about some crazy religious leader named the Ayatollah Khomeini, or something like that.

He also remembered the news about the downfall of dictators friendly to the United States–Somoza in Nicaragua, the Shah of Iran–and what his father-in-law said in his editorials: "This is the limit! In this administration we have hit *bottom!* A faithful ally has been overthrown by Communists, and we do *nothing!* Not even the half-hearted effort in *Viet Nam!* Simply because our ally's democratic system's imperfect is no reason to abandon *anybody!* Now a hostile regime is in place in Nicaragua, a short plane ride to our border, so that Soviet paratroopers could land on us! Did the liberal whiners about strong action for self-preservation have that in mind when they began screaming like frightened old women about so-called 'human rights?' You accept things as they *are* in the real world!" (Corbett said the same things about South Africa, Haiti, and the Philippines.)

25

Mike Durkin, who led the fight against the Guthrie Amendment, followed through on his promise to press the victory over the Guthrie bill. He attended every regional and national conference of every gay group he could think of, preaching his gospel of unity against the common enemy – to Durkin that common enemy was David Lucas and everybody who thought like him, including the entire NCPC. Durkin spoke to publishers of Gay magazines, Gay Methodists and Lutherans who did not split from their denominations (while the denominations wished they did), organizations of Gay political activists, police officers, dentists, and film makers.

Lucas sat in his office at the Ministries, in January 1980, reading about Durkin's activities. He folded his arms around him, bitter about the defeat of the Guthrie bill, and he felt ashamed about running away from the fags at the Pink Flamingo during the campaign. He had an idea – like with the Guthrie campaign and his street preaching, go wherever Durkin, and the other fags and feminists came together, and preach from a truck. He was ready for another showdown with the sinners, following the example of

Billy Sunday.

The showdown came in New York in March. The temperature that Monday was at fifty, and the breeze made it feel cooler. Lucas rode in a Ford pickup, and three young ministers came with him in another Ford. It was five o'clock in the evening, and the sun was phasing out into a golden sliver over the towers of Manhattan.

One of the young men asked Lucas, "Dave, would the homosexuals bother us?"

"Naw," drawled Lucas, "fags got no guts, no backbone. You stand up to them and they run like the cowards they are. Besides, God protects those who stand up for Him."

They stopped at a red light, and Lucas moaned eloquently, "Mike Durkin's gonna be speakin' at a *church* in the neighborhood! Think about it, a church helpin' the *fags!* When we take the country over, boy, we'll fix *that!"* As the truck moved at the green, the men grunted agreement.

The meeting at the church was to start at seven. At six, Lucas began speaking in the back of the truck, through the bullhorn while the people were going inside.

Lucas proclaimed, "You are in violation of the Word of God! God commands you to abandon the sin of homosexuality and accept Jesus as your Savior! Your sins will bring the wrath of God Almighty upon the country for your abomination! The nation will suffer through pain and tribulation because you will not repent! I tell you the truth, and you ridicule me and all others who tell the truth of God! In the name of God, for the salvation of your souls, turn from your rebellion and defiance of God, for your defiance you must expect to be punished..."

The people who came to attend Durkin's speech tried to ignore it. It was like the screeching on a blackboard, just annoying; then, they felt threatened, and they crowded the front steps of the church, hearing Lucas scream, "The churches that allows homosexuals to assemble is no longer a church of the Living Lord God, or of the Lord Jesus Christ! The churches must cease to allow sin! They must unite and be strong in their condemnation of this wicked sin..."

The crowd outside satisfied themselves with calling out curse words and insults at Lucas, but Durkin feared problems for the meeting-goers and martyrdom for Lucas. He maneuvered through the crowd, and the gays made way for him, calling, "Yeah, Mike, go tell him!"

Durkin marched up to Lucas, who towered over everybody from the truck, and snarled, "For God's sake, Lucas, are you crazy? You lookin' for trouble? Get out'a here *now!* You'll start a riot!"

Lucas looked down on Durkin and stated, "Durkin, if your faggots cause a riot, it's because you guys are rotten with sin! I'd like to see you try something, an' get you locked up! But –"

He turned his head at the gays at the front steps of the church – "You faggots haven't the *guts,* the *manhood,* to stand up to the teachings of the Lord Jesus! You ceased to be *men,* you turned away from the manhood God gave you!"

The crowd poured from the steps and crossed the street, grumbling and frowning. To the bible school students accompanying Lucas, this was as frightening as Hell itself. But Lucas acted like he wasn't afraid of a bunch of pansies. The only thing that kept the gays from throwing rocks was that Durkin was there, and they could not find any rocks on the street.

A siren howled. For the older gay men, this brought back nightmares of bar raids and being loaded into the paddy wagon. But this time, the police presence was more welcome – in the form of Sergeant Doreen Wade, an angelic blond whose favorite things were jazz guitar, tattoos, cheap jewelry, and other women. She jumped from the car along with the male officer with her.

Wade swaggered in her best enraged authority-figure fashion and got on the bed of the truck, her partner standing by on the street, and Wade called out, "Alright, Reverend, the show's over, so take your truck and your buddies and get out of the Village *now!"*

Lucas hated taking orders from a woman. He stated, "I have every right to be here, and I'm not leaving!"

Wade stated back, "You're creating a disturbance and provoking a riot! If you refuse to leave, I'll place you under arrest!"

Lucas turned his head back to the crowd and called through the bullhorn, "If you defy the law of God –"

Wade grabbed Lucas' coat and threw him on the roof of the cab, and Lucas saw the street fly past him. He felt the thump of the roof on his chest, and the partner snapped the cuffs on Lucas' wrists. Wade felt the material of the coat and muttered, "Nice coat, Reverend, how much it cost, four hundred?"

Someone shouted, "Gettin' turned on, Lucas?", and the crowd clapped and cheered merrily, then chanted "Jail bird! Jail bird!" as he was loaded in the back of the cruiser. Lucas aimed his eyes on Wade and muttered, "I'll remember you!"

"You better!" she snapped as they drove to the precinct.

The crowd applauded and cheered, and went inside the church. Inside, in the basement community room, Durkin told the audience, "You see the people out to get us! They don't think any rules apply to them! You see the need now to come together?"

The crowd applauded and rose to their feet.

One of Lucas' companions reached for the car phone in the cab of the truck, and he called the lawyer, telling him to get to the precinct. (This was part of Lucas' plan, for which he was proud.) After Lucas was processed and fingerprinted, the attorney, famous for representing organized crime figures, got to the precinct with the bail money, and Lucas did not even spend fifteen minutes in the lock-up.

Lucas–frowning, hands in his coat pockets, head bent down–emerged from the front door of the precinct to a chorus of reporters and camera crews, and announced, "Let all the homosexuals, feminists, pornographers, and other sinner know I'm willing to put my life on the line to bring morality back to America again! The days of Christians keeping quiet while perverts and sinners rule are over, and Christians are taking our country *back!"*

The next day, Wheeland, in his NCPC office in Washington, held a press conference condemning Lucas' "malicious arrest for preaching the truth of the Gospel to Homosexuals, showing that the rights of Christians are not respected in this country;" he further added that perhaps "Brother Lucas went a little too far and should be more careful in the future."

26

"That was an outrage!" snarled Richard Corbett as he sat at dinner with Lucas, Christine, wife Helen, son Jim, and older daughter Fran the following Sunday. "They arrested a *minister,* and let *homos* congregate! In *my* day, it worked the *other* way around!"

"So do we *have* to talk about that?" whimpered Helen as she put a forkful of ham into her mouth, chewing lightly.

"I'm not worried about it," shrugged Lucas with a smile. "I was kind of expecting it. I like to stick my neck out for Jesus. A real Christian would do that." He inhaled, let out the air, and sighed, "I *was* pretty rattled by it, though."

"But, David," moaned Christine, "you don't want to get hurt, do you?"

"No, I don't," said Lucas, smiling at his wife. "But I'm a man, and a Christian."

""Dave," Jim began to suggest, "maybe Chris's right, maybe – how long has it been since you had a vacation?"

"I don't take vacations," returned Lucas.

"Well, why don't you two go off someplace," Jim cheerfully pressed, "like

Hawaii or the Bahamas?"

"I *can't*," said Lucas, his hands pressing the table. "I have *work* to do, the church, the ministries, the campaign."

Fran, the oldest daughter, asked, "So Chris, how d' you feel?"

"Okay," she replied, quietly.

"Any kids planned for the future?" Fran asked to stimulate conversation.

Christine opened her mouth to answer, but Lucas brayed, "Sure, always! That's what a family's for, right?"

Fran kept quiet on this point, but she decided to say, "Not necessarily, Dave, I know some couples that've chosen not to have kids."

The dinner was finished, and Jim and Lucas stood to one side.

"Dave, why do you do this?" worried Jim.

"What?"

"You risk your neck with the faggots and the guys in jail," Jim explained. "You could've got yourself killed up in New York. I know you believe in what you do, but – do you have t' do this?"

"Yeah, I do," replied Lucas. "Believe it or not, I really care about the homosexuals, like I care about any other sinners. When I see a sinner, like I was, or a homo, I remember what I was before I became a Christian."

"Yeah," agreed Jim, "but Chris, she's worried sick about you. She wished you didn't have to have to run around the country. She feels lonely without you, Dave. She's said that, and I can tell from the way she acts here. She mopes around, she has the long face, she talks about you all the time, but I guess she doesn't tell you."

"No, she doesn't," said Lucas with surprise, "but I hope she understands, someday, that what I'm doing' is important to bring people to Jesus. I really would like her to accept it, someday."

That evening, Lucas considered having sex with Christine, weighed the desire for children against the sin of sex, and kept thinking about it until he fell asleep.

27

By late May, the primaries were finished, and delegates to the second national convention
of the National Christian Political Conference streamed into the Grand Ballroom of the
Wentworth Hotel.

Like the first meeting, young men in their thirties and forties constituted three-
fifths of the convention-goers, but the decisions were made by the other two-fifths, the
older men from their fifties to seventies. There was some grumbling about this; the
younger set had a hero in David Lucas.

At the opening plenum, the Reverend Jimmy Wheeland opened the session,
saying:

"Once again, brethren, we come together to begin an agenda to make sure
Christians, who have for far too long been excluded from political discussion, find their
voice in the political realm, to be sure our opinions are heard and respected. It is us, the
Christian men and women, who have founded this country, who live clean and honorable
lives, who need to get involved in the governing of our country, so that we become once

again a strong, respected, and righteous nation."

Sitting behind Wheeland was Lucas, inhaling to calm his nerves, seeing the young men seated in the ballroom; he heard the stories about the young men's complaints, and he wanted to make the organization worked.

Wheeland turned to Lucas and announced, "And now, for our keynote address, I once again introduce that brave young fighter for morality, the Reverend David Lucas."

Lucas stood, shook Wheeland's hand, and smiled at the crowd of young men– young men he respected as much as he did the older men. He began:

"There are those who would like for us in the NCPC to attack each other in public. One newspaper called this organization a dictatorship of older preachers, and that there is no influence in decision making from the lower ranks of the NCPC.

"Bickering, backbiting, we can't have that," Lucas continued, "It's not worthy of us as Christians. We are leaders of our churches, we are taught to put forward the laws of God, the ultimate lawgiver, through His Son and our Savior Jesus Christ. You cannot vote on God's laws, His laws are permanent and eternal. Those are the laws we of the

NCPC want to put back into force in this country. Call it a dictatorship if you want, but if you try to repeal God's laws and you *will* suffer the consequences."

The men sounded an "Ah-men," and Lucas went on:

"People have asked us why we Christians don't keep to ourselves. We have our *own* television programs, *our* own schools, our *own* social gatherings, our *own* institutions. But remember, Jesus told us to bring the Gospel to *every* creature! We have to bring the Gospel of Jesus to *every* person who *hasn't* heard the message. When we vote, we vote according to our Christian beliefs, which have saved us from a life of sin, and brought us to salvation under the Lord Jesus Christ. By voting Christian, we're voting for universal salvation. We're voting to bring Jesus back to our country once again. We want to vote according to what God wants for His people."

Another round of applause came from the young men, and some soft claps from the older men. Lucas went on:

"When we want to look at an issue, we turn to the Bible for guidance, just as we turn to the Bible for other matters. After we read the Bible, we make our conclusions.

And we know that the Bible isn't just some old book with ancient ideas, fit only for the time it was written. The Bible is God's infallible Word on all things, whether it's criminal justice, or national defense, or relationships between men and women."

"Ah-men," sounded again among the convention goers, and Lucas continued:

"As for our foes, the homosexuals, the humanists, and feminists, and agnostics and atheists who deny God, and who are opposed to the work we do, I must say that I *don't* hate them. I really don't. God told us to *love* our enemies. But still, they *are* our enemies. They *do* oppose our efforts to bring the laws of God back to our land. We must fight them and beat them, with all the strength God gives us. When they *are* beaten, and they give up their error, we must welcome them into the body of Christ, like the Prodigal Son. What a beautiful story, the Prodigal Son, who decides to leave his father to go out on his own, then suffers – goes down to the lowest point he could go – then realized that he was better off with his father, who welcomes him back home. The people we defeat in the upcoming elections, and the fights after that, might become someday our most loyal supporters. In the name of God, let's do that! *Ah-men!* God bless you."

The conventioneers returned "Ah-men," rose and applauded, with some whistles and calls of "Yeah, Dave, God bless you!" The older men also applauded; they were worried that the Young Turks might wrest control of *their* NCPC, but they were reassured when Lucas shook hands heavily with Jimmy Wheeland, and smiled.

The convention held workshops on issues that the NCPC was concerned about. The one on abortion included some men in Atlanta who were convicted, and did some prison time, for damaging the property of several women's health centers; that title alone, they said, proved that abortions were done there. The convicted men agreed that maybe they went a little too far, and that they could have used more diplomatic means, but they thought of all those innocent little babies being slaughtered there, they couldn't take it any more – and the nurse they beat up had no business being there.

The workshop on education discussed the promotion of private Christian schools, including tax breaks for parents sending their kids to such institutions; they also discussed the restoration of prayer in public schools, and the "monitoring" of the textbooks and library books to check their "humanist, atheist, un-Christian content", such as:

- Anything by Sinclair Lewis (Since *Elmer Gantry,* he could not be trusted with anything);
- Any works by James Baldwin, Richard Wright, Toni Morrison, or any other black authors (the thought of unhappy knee-grows unsettled them);
- *Greys' Anatomy,* until after high school, since by then the children would know all about the dirtiness of the human body;
- Any mention of Hinduism, Buddhism, Islam, and any other religion was okay, provided they were clearly proven to be false;
- Shakespeare was acceptable in some ways – *Macbeth* and *Hamlet* had great action scenes (i.e., violence), but *Othello*–about a black man married to a white woman!
- Anything by Charles Dickens – he wrote about social conditions, not good ones, and ridiculed authority figures, as well as made a fool of Scrooge, who was simply a successful entrepreneur;

- The American Revolution was to be presented as stemming from fasting and prayer by the colonists, not from any political and economic difficulties with Great Britain.

The workshop knew there were some more issues to cover, but they did not know what they would be, so the workshop on education ended its report with the phrase:

"Any other items of ungodly literature that this workshop has not covered will be decided on by the National Board of NCPC, and the state and local branches of NCPC."

The workshop on foreign and military affairs once again featured the Reverend Robert Van Der Molen of South Africa, who stated, "What should the world think of America? She's willing to deal with its enemies, the same nations who oppress free nations, including their own? But she bullies those nations, like my own, which wants and needs the friendship of America. Of course we have our problems in my country, but they're *our* problems, and only we, the people of South Africa, white and black together, without interference from foreigners, will resolve the issues confronting our nation."

General Theodore Roosevelt ("Horny") Horner also was back, and he spoke of the Communist threat in Latin America, saying, "Where there is Communist activities, there is the threat to the United States. It happened in Cuba, it happened in Nicaragua, where a *legitimate* government was over thrown by Communist guerrillas. It's happening in Guatemala and El Salvador, right under our noses. If these nations go Communist, the Soviet Union will have access to these nations as military staging areas for assaults upon the United States. Therefore, it is necessary to intervene in these nations' affairs, before it's too late, and they invade our shores." The attendees were awed by Horner's wisdom.

The workshop also discussed the issue of the military draft. The collective sentiment of everyone in the workshop was that military service made a boy into a man, building his body and his character, while women in military service were lesbians and sluts. The workshop's final report called for compulsory military service; support for all allies of the United States in their struggle against Communist subversion; and the highest possible amount of military spending.

Lucas was everywhere in the convention. He chaired the two workshops—one on education and one on foreign and military affairs—prayed the grace for lunch, and was a star at the reception for the delegates sponsored by the national office, held in the bridal suite. A DJ, clad in a green-plaid jacket, played forties' big-band music.

While the reception was going on in the bridal suite, Jimmy Wheeland was in his suite, while some of the older members of the National Board of the NCPC passed around two bottles of Jack Daniels. One man of eighty-one years proclaimed, "Never could stand the habit of drinkin'. Turns a man into a babbling fool! 'Course, a little jolt's good for you, now and then."

Another man, a more youthful seventy-five, added, "The younger guys, like Lucas, act like they wanna run the organization. I was preachin' since before they were born. Sure, it's nice to have young men take our place and keep our work goin', but they gotta wait a while 'til we teach 'em."

Friday morning was the final session of the convention. Lucas sat at the far left side of the front table, while Wheeland occupied the right side nearest the podium. Wheeland strode up to the podium and proclaimed, "This is the year that will decide the following decade of the 'eighties. I am confident that the next President of the United

States will be the one who puts forth our program to answer the most serious moral issues that our country faces. This is our opportunity to restore moral values as a factor in our public life, which has always been the preserve of the traditional, fundamental Christian church."

Then Wheeland turned to Lucas and said, "Brother Lucas, would you please lead us in the closing prayer?"

Lucas smiled, strode up to the podium, and called out, "After this prayer, I would like the convention to close with a real, sing-it-like-you-mean-it verse of 'Stand Up, Stand Up For Jesus!'" Wheeland smiled and sat down, pleased that the convention would end on an upbeat, happy note.

"Oh Lord Our God," intoned Lucas as he raised his right hand, "we ask that you guide our hearts as we make these momentous decisions that will shape the course of our country for the rest of the decade. Guide our decisions, oh Lord, and help us for it is Your guidance, oh Lord, and only so, that a nation can strive to greatness. Grant that to us, oh Lord, in Thy name, we pray, ah-men."

As he prayed, the convention sounded with cries of "Ah-men, yes, oh Lord!" and returning Lucas' closing "Ah-men." then all rose as they sang the first verse of "Stand Up, Stand Up For Jesus, Ye Soldiers Of the Cross." The convention applauded and shouted for joy.

28

Lucas arrived home at 5:00 PM. He knew that Christine was at her parent's house, and she always kept the house clean; Lucas always noticed how well she kept the house, but not to her face. Every part of his body ached; he pulled his jacket off and flopped down on the bed.

He slept until seven-thirty, then decided to call Christine. Lucas grunted as he got up from the bed, still tired, and scraped towards the phone on the dresser. He dialed Corbett's home number.

"David?" Christine began.

"Yeah, hi, I got in this afternoon."

Christine was about to ask how was Washington, but he broke in with, "Lissen, it's a little late, and I'm a little worn out from the trip, so you don't mind staying at your folk's another night, do you?"

"Oh, uh, no of course not," said Christine, feeling confused.

"Okay," Lucas concluded, "I'll pick you up tomorrow, see you." They hung up.

Lucas lay in bed, waiting to go to sleep, but he was excited about the past week. He was in the middle of some great events going on in the nation – the revival of America – and he, David Lucas, was in the lead.

People heard what Lucas had to say – cameras aimed at him – reporters asked him questions – and he recalled the time he worked in the gas station – the time he was in the Army, then in the stockade –

Was he up to the job? He worried all of a sudden. Could he lead the movement? As he lay in the bed he prayed, "Lord, help me to do the right thing, to make decisions–" he tried to think of what to say next – "to make decisions that would benefit the nation, and Your kingdom. Ah-men."

Lucas still worried, but he chose to leave it all to God, right or wrong. He then fell asleep.

29

Election Day, 1980; Lucas sat at the church office tidying up some church business. He would then go to the ministries office, then –

Should he go try to vote? Lucas worried about that. He didn't want to make a fool of himself like in 1978. He didn't recall if he ever re-registered to vote (he hadn't). So he would stay out of sight until after the voting was completed. He felt confident that Ronald Reagan would get elected, and besides, it was just his one vote, and he encouraged other Christians to go out and vote, so he didn't really have to, and also the cameras and reporters would be all over him.

There were two victory parties for the pro-Reagan forces that night in Erno – one for the Republican Party chairmen and ward leaders at the Dorita, where liquor would be served; and one for the Midland County chapter of the NCPC at the Holiday Inn.

The ballroom of the Holiday Inn was filled with men and women of various ages who worked the precincts, handed out flyers, spoke with neighbors all through the campaign, hoping their work paid off. Lucas arrived at 7:40 PM, with Christine at his side; Lucas smiling and chatting with people as he roamed around the ballroom, with a quick "Hey, how you doin', great night, huh?" adding a quick, "Hey, there," to the wife at the man's arm, with Christine tagging along like a shadow, smiling and not adding a thing to the conversation.

At eight, the polls closed, and the news specials came on the televisions that were placed around the room. The crowds became quiet as they moved in front of the TVs, one for each of the major channels–and the new cable channel CNN–absorbing the information. At the start, the news anchors were simply saying that this was a presidential election year between Jimmy Carter and Ronald Reagan. To the people in the ballroom, it was much more; a crusade, a fight of good versus evil. They worked so hand at this, but–what if they lose?

Lucas noticed a few more news crews in the back of the room, assembling the phones and cameras. As the news crews completed these tasks, Lucas jumped on a chair and announced, "Can I have your attention, please?"

The crowd was silent; the news crews knew they were witnessing more about

Lucas, who, they told each other, was "a master of public relations."

"This is the most important election this country has ever faced in a long time," proclaimed Lucas. "We should now give praise to God, who has given us the liberty which we enjoy this day." The crowd applauded.

The night went on, and the tallies came in; when the anchors announced them, people moved from the buffet tables to the TVs. One by one, states were announcing going for Ronald Reagan, and a cheer rose from the crowds at each state coming in.

Then—the networks officially declared Ronald Reagan the fortieth President of the United States. The loudest cheer of the evening rose at that announcement.

Lucas felt inspired to jump in front of everybody and say, "Can I have your attention, *please?"*

Then he declared, "This means a new beginning for our country! Once more will there be strong families as the bulwark of our society! No more will there be sin and rebellion made the law of the land! Once more will America be feared, respected, and admired among the nations of the world! No more will the flag be abused and defiled, our citizens harassed and kidnapped! America will once more be a *mighty* nation, once more a *great* nation, once more a *moral* nation, once more a *prosperous* nation!"

The crowd roared happily. Christine, forgotten in the company of so many people, just smiled in the sidelines. Her husband went on mightily:

"We who are Christians, we who accept the Lord Jesus as Savior and Lord, have an obligation now to carry out the moral program that the NCPC has formulated! We have accepted the Truth that God has given us though His Holy Bible! Now, now that we have gained the victory through God's Grace, let us never falter in our continuing the struggle against those in our society who would bring us down! Let us raise our right hands and take an oath!"

The men in the hall raised their right hands as Lucas intoned, "Oh, Lord God, Lord and Savior Jesus Christ, bless us as we carry out the work thou hast given us! Give us the strength to keep out new leader on the right path, for as Christians we must carry out the true path followers of the Way, the Truth, and the Light! In thy name, we pray, ah-men!"

The men returned with a wall-quivering *"Ah-men!"*

Lucas moved back into the crowd, hands stretched out to him, Christine smiling and gazing proudly. Lucas heard somebody say, "Reagan better come through, or he'll be out of a job!" The news crews took down everything that went on, including the raising of the right hands and the oath-taking.

That evening, Lucas and Christine got ready for bed. "Oh, honey," she said, "I'm so happy for you!" She reached out to stroke his hairy back.

Lucas jumped up and smiled, "Hey, none of *that!"*

"But, David," she pleaded, "Don't you want to celebrate?"

Lucas said, "Yeah, okay," and he laid her flat on the bed, pulled up her night dress, and went to work, and it was over and he fell asleep. Christine didn't notice anything different.

30

It was the first Sunday after the inauguration of Ronald Reagan as President of the United States; by this time, the hostages held in the US Embassy in Iran had been freed and sent home.

The Reverend David Lucas walked around the sanctuary of the church, shaking hands and greeting everyone, and glanced at the sky—a heavy gray with no clouds. Christine sat with her parents in the front pew. The choir sang the opening hymn, and Lucas stood behind the pulpit, with a good view of the crowd – he thought it was good-sized, and the video cameras in the back did not interfere much – people complained about the cables underfoot and the van taking up parking space.

The choir finished, and Lucas went to the pulpit and spoke:

"As all of you know by now, I have served in the United States Army. For that reason, I appreciate our Armed Forces, our service men, and I'm happy that we have a President who honors the military, those who risk their lives for our liberty. I didn't, shall we day, do very well there–"

A light laugh sounded from the congregation, and Lucas bent his head and smiled, then continued:

"The failure of Viet Nam obsesses me. Our great military power was not sufficient enough to prevent the spread of Communism in South East Asia. Now, in Central America, the Communists are coming on strong right beneath us.

"What we lacked in Viet Nam, my friends, was *spiritual* strength, the willingness to *stand* for what is *right*, no matter *what* the obstacle! No matter how important our military strength, my friends, and it *is* important, our *spiritual* strength is even more important. The ancient Hebrews were *always* a small group of people, but God made sure that these people won every war and beat every enemy that they came upon, so long as they followed God. When they disobeyed God, they lost their freedom and their nation. Let that be a lesson to us."

An "Ah-men" rose from the congregation, and Lucas went on:

"Now, this is what I'm getting to. What I would like to do is to conduct an evangelistic crusade tour of all the military bases of the United States in the entire world,

Army, Air Force, Navy, Marines. I want to bring the message of Jesus Christ to *all* the men in uniform, telling the plan of salvation for all. I know that from personal experience that military service is hard and strenuous, even in peacetime, but with Jesus in the hearts of our servicemen, they will be better able to endure those hardships. Plus, I hope to bring Jesus to some young man in a stockade somewhere, just as a chaplain brought Jesus to me. That way, I could turn some young man around, change the direction of his life, from Hell to Heaven. With this new administration that appreciates traditional values, we can do it!"

Two seconds of silence finished Lucas' speech, then applause rose, lasting ten seconds.

At social hour, Christine stood by her husband and said, "David, you never told me you were going away!"

Lucas smiled at his wife and said, "It's not official, but I'm going to start tomorrow."

Corbett walked over to his son-in-law and said, "Great idea, David," pumping his hand. "This is something, I'll tell you!" Other people walked over to Lucas and praised his idea.

The next day, Monday, Lucas dictated a letter to the Secretary of Defense:

Dear Sir:

I would like the privilege of conducting an evangelistic tour of United States military bases throughout the world. I admire the men of our armed forces who risk their lives to preserve our freedom, and I hope to improve their lives by bringing the message of Jesus Christ to them. If you wish to discuss the issue further with me, I will be willing to meet you at a time that is suitable to you. Thank you for your consideration.

Yours Sincerely,

David Lucas.

After sending out the letter – registered mail – Lucas wondered if there was still more he should do to bring about the tour. Maybe some friendly senator or some other official could be contacted?

Lucas also proposed the idea to the National Board of the National Christian

Political Conference; he told Wheeland and the other board members this would be a great test of the NCPC's political strength – and whether it could get through the Pentagon bureaucracy and Congress. NCPC sent computer-printed letters to all its members, and made formal and informal contact with friendly congressmen and senators.

By the end of the week, journalists were busy at work on this new move by the man now known as "God's hit man."

The opponents were also getting organized. Questions rose about an evangelistic tour of military bases – Would the rallies be right *on* the base? How would the expenses be paid? Would the military itself have a role in this?

At the office of the ministries, Lucas opened a registered letter from the United States District Court in New York. With Gary Hennessy in the room, Lucas read it out loud, clutching the letter until it crumbled: the American Civil Liberties Union had just filed a suit in federal court against the attempt by the David Lucas Ministries to conduct its Armed Forces Crusade tour, on grounds of separation of church and state. Joining in the lawsuit as *amicus curiae* would be the Committee for Civil and Human Rights–Mike Durkin's group!

"Devil, they work for the Devil!" shouted Hennessy, and when he turned he saw Lucas smiling.

"Take it easy, Gare," ordered Lucas with a smile. "We'll have our own attorney, and we'll beat 'em!"

Lucas' confidence rubbed off on Hennessy, who then smiled back.

That evening, Lucas and Christine went to the Corbett's home for dinner. Lucas chatted with Corbett in the living room, explaining the situation with the ACLU.

Corbett listened, rubbed his chin, and asked, "You know Gordon Kyle? He's one of the best corporate lawyers in the state, works out in New York, knows a lot of judges, and he's close to the administration in Washington. I have his address and phone number in my den, I'll pass it on to you."

Helen proclaimed, "The dinner's ready."

As Lucas and Corbett moved to the dining room, Lucas cheered, "I knew I'm gonna win!"

After dinner, Lucas and Corbett moved to the den, and Corbett handed Lucas the business card of Gordon Kyle, saying "Keep it, I have plenty of them. I'll call Gordon tomorrow, let him know about you."

"Thanks," agreed Lucas as he put the card in his jacket pocket. As he moved downstairs to join the others in the living room, Lucas said to himself: *I'm going to beat this. God is with me. This is a righteous cause.* He had to think like this–defeat was not acceptable.

31

Lucas and Corbett sat in the office of Gordon Kyle, in an office building in Newark. Kyle was an elegant and serious man, his hair and suit in good order as he peered at the world through silver-framed glasses. After chatting with Lucas (who insisted on being called "Dave," which shocked Kyle), they got down to business.

"The ACLU is taking this case very seriously," stated Kyle. "I've learned that Elizabeth Mallory was added to their team."

"Who?" puzzled Lucas.

"Elizabeth Mallory, the feminist attorney," replied Kyle. "She's going to map strategy and put together the brief."

"A *woman* lawyer!" sniffed Lucas, as if that was something offensive.

"Don't underestimate her," warned Kyle. "She came up the hard way in the legal game. Worked as a prison matron while attending City College, then worked as a police officer at NYU while studying law. She's a strong woman, and she'll be formidable. But don't worry," smiled Kyle, "I know most of the federal judges in the Mid-Atlantic region.

Many of them I went to school with. With the right persuasion, we could work this to our advantage. By the way, how will you pay for this?"

Lucas knew this would come up. "The money will come," he assured Kyle, "people know how important this is."

Friday night before the trial in February, Lucas got into bed. Christine, lying by his right side, gripped the pillow and watched her husband just lie there. She felt something inside her – she wanted to open up David's body to her embraces, her kisses – just to make love to him. She reached her hand over to unbutton his pajama top, and she got her hand on the top button, but Lucas opened his eyes and jerked his head to the left, at which Christine shot her hand back towards her, feeling guilty, ashamed of what she almost did. But the feeling she had, the urges…Lucas turned to his right side, wondering what the matter with her was, but feeling sure of success in federal court Monday.

32

The next Sunday, Lucas got up at six for his morning jog. Big fluffy flakes coated the neighborhood the previous night. The sidewalks were clear, but the roads still had snow packed from cars slowly driving on it. The snow glared sunlight into Lucas' eyes, and the cold air chilled his lungs. He ran around the area, past houses turned white with piled-on snow, and heard the sounds of residents scrapping it off their cars and driveways, along with the growling of cars starting with frozen motors and the squealing of tires whirling on the icy roads.

It took sixteen minutes to finish the usual two miles he ran; maybe he should try for three miles, he thought. He got home, thumped up the stairs, showered, shaved, and changed into trousers and a sweater.

When he got into the kitchen, Christine had breakfast ready – toast, fried eggs, bacon, and coffee.

"I'll be at the mall with Fran today," she said, hopefully.

Any mention of Fran irritated Lucas, but he just grunted, "Okay," then, "You want money to get stuff? Make sure it's nothing stupid."

"Thank you," agreed Christine. "What will you be doing today, honey?"

"I dunno, something," assured Lucas. "Gotta be something that needs doing." His mind searched for something to occupy his time that afternoon.

His sermon? He had the notes written down. The ministries? The church? Suggestions for Gary Hennessy? Study the Bible? That sounded good – study the Bible.

Lucas sat in the den, holding the Bible – the same copy of the Bible that he purchased after getting out of the Army in the 'sixties. Where should he start to read? It was all from God, so it didn't matter.

A quiver went through him. He worried – was he up to the task? Could he make the case for the tour in court? Could he make the tour work?

Was Lucas afraid? Was this task too big for him? He didn't want to be afraid, but – he was in the newspapers. Reporters wanted a piece of him. He didn't feel like a celebrity. He didn't feel poised and confident.

Stepping out of his desk chair, Lucas walked in front of the desk and knelt, in

236

humble submission to God. But what would he pray? All he could mutter was, "Lord, help me."

Then he thought – *Feel the fear, but go through it anyway. Don't let the fear control you.* Where did he get that thought? He wondered. From the Army? From Dr. Garfield? It had to come from God. Only God could see him through this time. A wave of comfort ran through Lucas.

Before the Sunday morning service, people flooded in, and the older members recalled how they used to come in almost one at a time. Lucas, who usually mingled with the crowd and shook hands with them, remained in a cluster of nine of the men of the church, many of whom were his loyal trusted trustees, men who could be trusted to go along with whatever Lucas proposed. This cluster met near the door inside the social room, away from the wives. Nick Pastorini, who ran the funeral home, left it just long enough to look at how many have come by 10:50. He came back with, "All packed from one wall to the other!"

"It's been like that since, oh, about a year and a half," said George Emerson, the advertising executive.

Truly, agreed the men, they were part of something big, something important, something great.

"I think the church building will have t' be expanded," worried Lucas, "but I don't want to change the building, or tear down the old church."

"Let's talk it over with Steve Nagler," suggested Emerson; Nagler was an architect who was weaned from his Lutheran church after the Guthrie campaign.

Lucas looked at his watch and said, "Let's go," and he and the men went to the door of the sanctuary. As they crossed the hallway, some of the visitors watched – *The Reverend David Lucas* was live before them! But the trustees around him looked too much like bodyguards for the admirers to come near their hero.

The first hymn was finished, and Lucas mounted the pulpit:

"Tomorrow, I find out whether or not I get to take the name of Jesus to the members of our Armed Forces. You know that this is a test of our faith verses the powers of darkness, the ACLU and the feminist crowd. I ask you here in this church, and over the television audience, to pray for our success tomorrow. That's about it from this pulpit, except that the next hymn the choir will sing will be the theme song of the Armed Forces Crusade, 'Stand Up, Stand Up For Jesus!'"

Lucas sat down and the choir rose, and sang through all the stanzas of "Stand Up, Stand Up For Jesus." They sang it with happiness in their voices, not with the usual droning that characterized their singing.

When the choir finished, a few daring souls applauded, then more and more, until it sounded like a thunderstorm. The applause faded, and Lucas resumed the pulpit for the sermon:

"When I get the Armed Forces Crusade off the ground, I'll be preaching the Gospel to men who are offering themselves, their talents, and maybe their lives, in the service of their nation. To do something like that takes a great deal of commitment, a willingness to devote all you time and energy to a cause.

"I've lived through a time when the commitment to the Christian cause and the

Christian life was so weak! And the weird thing about it all is that this was the *time* I became a Christian. You know, I often wonder if I was to become a Christian to do my part to save the Christian faith, the true, unadulterated, fundamental Gospel of Jesus Christ, from extinction.

"The Gospel, Jesus, and God take up *all* my devotion, *all* my loyalty. And since I place Christ over other things, these other things work out better. Since Christ is first in my life, I'm a better husband to my wife than if I *didn't* know Christ. No matter what else you are in the world, if you know Christ, and put Christ first in all you do, everything else works out for the best, your work, your reputation, your family, and your future.

"This commitment to the Christian way requires us to be separate from the rest of the world in our conduct. There are certain standards of conduct for a Christian to follow. But to follow such a strict moral path is easier when you accept Jesus. With Christ in your heart, you don't have any room for any temptations that destroy your faith."

Four o'clock; for Lucas the Sunday morning service and afternoon bible study were over.

He tilted back in the easy chair all the way, his body tired and weighed down. The sudden change from cold outside to warm inside added to the tiredness. He pulled out the remote and switched on the TV for a football game.

Christine glanced at the clock on the kitchen wall – she began dinner. As the ham was baking in the oven, Christine set the dining room table – plates, shakers, margarine, bread, cups and saucers. By six the whole thing was ready, and she trotted to her husband.

It took Lucas five minutes to finish his dinner, and then he flashed back to the chair in the living room, watching the end of the half-time show, taking his coffee cup with him. When the game ended, Lucas shut off the TV, newly rejuvenated, and he moved into the den.

He sat at his desk and opened his bible to Romans, then skimming the pages, stopping to read a paragraph, and then turning a page. He ended up at First Corinthians, and he got to Chapter Twelve, where Paul wrote about the differing gifts Christians had, but under one spirit. Lucas read this and thought – he read the passage so many times –

he read the Bible so many times – but this phrase stood out.

Then, as if in a flash, he remembered the trial tomorrow. He worried – what if he should lose? How can he lose? But he could! The forces of darkness were powerful in the world!

He slid off the chair and knelt at his desk, praying, "Oh Lord, my God and my strength, I pray you that you will make us victorious tomorrow against the foes of Your Son Jesus, the workers of Satan. Oh, Lord, they are so powerful in the earth, but You are the master and creator of all things. Give us the victory, so that I may have the honor of bringing the Gospel to those who offer their lives so that Thy servants may honor and worship thee. Ah-men."

He climbed back up the chair. He knew now he was going to win.

33

The day of the trial; Lucas solemnly ate breakfast, wearing his new suit – from Brooks

Brothers, a dull-grey three-piece number, one he got especially for the trial.

Christine ate daintily at her side of the table, then she said, "I hope you do well today,

honey." (She wasn't sure what her husband was doing; she was too afraid to ask.)

"Hmm," grunted Lucas as he nodded. He finished, then he said, "I'll call the cab."

He got on his coat, and Christine handed her husband his briefcase – not at all certain

what was in it – and she reached out to kiss him, but he rushed for the cab. She called out,

"Good luck, David!" he jumped into the cab, and Christine looked on – What was she

doing wrong, she wondered. Does he understand what she thinks?

Lucas sat upright in the back seat of the cab on his way to Erno Municipal Airport

for the commuter flight to New York. He now knew what was at stake in this trial; if he

won, he could take the name of Jesus to the entire armed forces of the nation. The whole

nation was hanging on to this issue. The whole nation watched this.

Then he thought – *Can I do this? What if I lose?* He felt fear of failure – but he had to go through with this.

The taxi drew closer to the airport; Lucas remembered something Doctor Garfield said in a sermon – "If you don't have anything better to occupy your mind with, think about God. Always keep your mind on God the Almighty. And to make things easier on you for doing that, keep from your eyesight anything that would distract your mind from God." Lucas lived by these words.

Elizabeth Victoria Mallory, feminist attorney, former police officer, went to her favorite hair salon, Hair Apparent, in the Village. The trial was to start at one o'clock—she worried; why so late? *Something's up, something's wrong–Kyle's up to something.* Going through the cool March morning, she arrived at the salon, and she saw a sweatered, jeaned, blond woman – Doreen Wade, who arrested Lucas last year.

They greeted each other with a kiss, and Liz pleasantly asked, "So, are you on the job, sweetheart?"

"Day off," Wade returned, "came here to be a little less butch."

The two women went inside. "All ready for Lucas?" asked Wade.

"Yeah," Liz drawled. "But I have this feeling Kyle's gonna pull something. How're you?"

"Just about t' make detective in a month," rejoiced Doreen. "I owe it to you, Liz."

"You did all the work, my dear," Liz shrugged.

"But you made it easier for the rest of us," Doreen replied. "You were the trailblazer."

Liz settled into the barber chair while the hairdresser Stefon, a slender Black man with a pointed beard, flung the cover over her from the neck down; Doreen sat on a nearby chair.

"Still living with that *Times* guy?" asked Doreen.

"Yeah, always," said Liz, "I'm pretty well settled with him."

"Still no marriage?"

"Naw, no marriage. I love him, though." Liz then turned to the hairdresser and said, "How you doin' Stefon?"

"Hanging in there," said Stefon, "I'm getting gouged by the insurance, Liz, could you look into it for me?"

"Sure," smiled Liz-she also sold insurance and real estate, for extra money.

Doreen undid her shoes and pulled off her socks and said, ""I'm worried Liz, to tell the truth. Reagan getting in there, an' the guys like Lucas, it'll be rough for gays an' women. There's gonna be assaults an' beatings, harassment, like in the old days."

"Doreen, you want a pedicure," asked Stefon, "I can get Sasha to work on you."

"Sasha, the Russian girl?" asked Liz.

"Uh-huh," replied Stefon.

"Yeah, why not?" agreed Doreen.

"Say, Dor" recalled Liz, "didn't you bust Lucas last year?"

"Yeah, I had that honor," grinned Doreen. "My lieutenant started to argue with me, whether I had grounds. But he got sense, I told him how Lucas was harassing the crowd, and they reacted to that. Lieutenant changed his mind after that. Oh, one thing," said Doreen, pulling a pamphlet out of her bag, "I just joined a fitness club, for women only. They got weights an' saunas, an' an indoor track for jogging. Interested?"

"Yeah, it sounds great," agreed Liz, "I'll visit the place. But right now I have an exercise plan. It's called sex."

Everyone in the room laughed.

Stefon finished doing Liz's hair, and as she got out of the chair, he saw the brown holster in the waistband of Liz's skirt, holding a .38 Smith and Wesson. "Once a cop, always a cop, huh, Liz?" said Stefon.

"I guess," shrugged Liz, "I'm not popular everywhere."

"Is there something more than that?" suggested Doreen.

"Yeah," sighed Liz. "I never been the way women were supposed to be, weak an' helpless an' stupid. I had'a fight for everything I believe in, like when I defend the girls on the street, an' the bars. Not everyone can defend themselves, you know. Like the Amazons, like, I'm a warrior."

Doreen grasped Liz's hand and smiled, "That's what we love about you, Liz."

It was twenty minutes before one, and a group of people—about fifty, estimated the media–crowded the front steps of the federal courthouse. In the crowd were five American flags (made in Hong Kong), and banners with the names of various churches, including one with WINGATE MEMORIAL BAPTIST CHURCH on it. They sang hymns such as, "Stand Up, Stand Up For Jesus."

David Lucas came out of the limousine, with the Ministries' Office Manager Gary Hennessy and attorney Gordon Kyle behind. Hennessy murmured into Lucas' ear, "Dave, with this crowd, maybe you need a bodyguard?"

Lucas stared at the crowd, then at the front steps leading into the courthouse. He jumped in front of the crowd of supporters and announced, "I can tell from your warm greeting this day that I need no bodyguards against the homosexuals and the atheists! I'm among friends!" The crowd roared.

At the same time, the team from the ACLU was pulling into the back entrance of the courthouse in a Chevrolet, to avoid the crowd in the front; Elizabeth Mallory sat with the two attorneys from the ACLU assigned to the case.

Barry Dubovsky was thin and bearded with a coat of brownish hair and green-brown eyes. Michael Dewitt had a deep suntan, bluish eyes, and wavy black hair, displaying the "dark Irish" background he shared with Liz Mallory. Both of these men wore dark suits and serious expressions on their faces; they had experience with cases involving dissidents, Gay men and Lesbians, and authors. "You guys be careful with Kyle," Mallory warned them, "the law is just a business for him. He once represented a real-estate developer in a case against a family hardware store, trying to portray the owner like the bad guy."

Dubovsky jotted notes on a small spiral steno pad, saying, "I'm jotting down some questions we might raise in the course of the trial."

"Yeah," nodded Dewitt, "you wanna ask, would this set a precedent for other religious bodies to hold rallies. And funding, would the military fund any of this?"

"Yeah, favoring one religion over others," agreed Dubovsky.

The media was ready for them as they emerged from the Chevrolet and entered the courthouse and up the elevator and into the chamber. They waited outside the courtroom door and there they saw Lucas and Kyle marching towards them. Kyle frowned at the media – he did his best work outside the glare of the cameras, but Lucas smiled and kept his head up.

Then – again the fear – what if he lost? What if the judge should decide *not* to allow the tour? His father-in-law spoke a lot about judges who were too lenient on criminals – and the Supreme Court banning prayer in schools – but Lucas kept up his smile.

The attorneys settled into their seats; the bailiff called, "All rise!" and he introduced the judge – the Honorable Anthony Sutton, who was descended from a long and honorable line of ward politicians. Sutton seated himself, dragged the microphone to his face, and spoke from a long yellow legal pad:

"After reading the prepared briefs, after consulting legal precedent, and after much thought" – Kyle and Sutton chatted over the issue at a French restaurant; Kyle

250

picked up the check – "I fail to see how this proposed crusade would be detrimental to the religious beliefs of others. Therefore, exercising my right of summary judgement, this court will allow the Reverend David Lucas to conduct his revival tour throughout the Armed Forces."

A loud, dull babble rumbled through the courtroom. Lucas smiled and pumped Kyle's hand, whispering, "We did it! We won!"

"I told you not to worry!" smiled Kyle.

Dubovsky and DeWitt were stunned – not even a chance to debate this thing! Liz frowned, then glanced at Lucas and Kyle.

She got up and announced, "Your Honor, it is perfectly unfair to make a decision without court proceedings! Surely you know that!"

"I have made my decision, counselor," declared Sutton, not moving.

"Then we shall appeal this decision," warned Liz.

"You may," condescended Sutton, then he said, "This court is adjourned." A bang of the gavel, and the babble resumed.

Lucas arrived at the front steps of the courthouse to witness a cheering throng, with "Praise God, hallelujah!" interspersed.

He proclaimed, "My friends, brethren in the body of Christ, the process has begun for a crusade that will bring to our brave patriotic solders the name of Jesus, and begin the revival that will shake this nation to its foundations!"

Another cheer rose from the crowd. A voice could be heard yelling, "Bless this flag, Dave, pray over it!" A man in his sixties brought to Lucas a U.S. flag. Lucas grabbed the banner and intoned, "Dear Lord, we ask You to bless this flag, symbol of our land, and all that it stands for, and we pray to be made worthy of Thy blessings. Ah-men!", and the crowd responded with "Ah-men!"

Liz, Dewitt, and Dubovsky trudged back to the elevator, conferring on what to do next.

"When we get back, let's get t' work on this appeal," said Liz. "You guys ready for a long-haul fight?"

"Sure am," Dewitt said, "my dad worked the docks, organizing for the CIO." He dipped his head a little and added, "I know he's looking down on me, and I want him to be proud of me."

Dubovsky turned to Liz and said, "Liz, I know we had our disagreements, like with criminal cases, when I was in the Public Defender's office, but I always respected you. Mike and me, we're glad you on the same side as us."

Liz smiled and said, "Thanks, guys. I have my disagreements with you too, but I'm glad to work with you. You like Italian?"

In the car with Kyle, on the plane back to Erno, and in the cab back to the parsonage, Lucas grinned and laughed. His dream came true! He beat the satanic ACLU and the evil feminist Mallory! Hey, maybe the court system worked after all!

He bounced up to the front door of the parsonage, unlocked the door, and bawled out, "Christine!"

She scampered towards him from the kitchen and worried what was wrong now – but she saw him grinning.

"We won!" he declared, "the tour's on!"

"Oh, wonderful!" she squealed as she was supposed to as she wrapped her arms around his waist. Lucas felt so good that he allowed this – women got so excited, he thought.

"Now what we gotta do," he resumed speaking, "is get together a road crew, and a schedule, and bingo, we're off!"

34

The David Lucas Armed Forces Crusade started slowly and simply. The first rallies were held in the bases in New Jersey – Fort Dix, Fort Monmouth, Picatinny Arsenal, Lakehurst, Colts Neck, and Maguire Air Force Base. Then on to the Philadelphia Naval Shipyard, Carlisle Barracks in Pennsylvania, then the Naval Academy in Annapolis, then up the Hudson to West Point.

For the road crew, Lucas placed ads in the *Champion* and other Christian periodicals and appointed Jim Corbett, his brother-in-law, as manager. Jim knew the kind of people he would need – director for television, camera crews, musicians, sound and light technicians.

Potential members of the road crew were asked such questions as, "Do you believe in a personal God? Do you accept Jesus as Lord and Savior, and Son of God? Do you smoke, drink alcohol or take narcotics? Do you have promiscuous sex?"

Lucas appointed Roy Murphy, a high school music teacher, Music Director for the tour. Murphy, happy to be away from the "stupid little demons" that he taught in the public school, accepted, hoping for – something big, something enormous, that David Lucas could provide him, if he, Murphy, would do a good job. Murphy was slender, with grey hair swept back and a mustache, giving an air of elegance. A member of the faculty of the Curtis Institute of Music, we wrote essays in scholarly music journals and directed choirs, doing both in the most arrogant, contemptuous manner.

For a singer, Lucas selected Billy Calloway—a graduate of Julliard, a native of Baltimore, and once a tepid Catholic who hung around the gospel music scene and did advertising jingles. He was excited by the prospect of working for Lucas; his feelings for Lucas extended further than hero-worship. Calloway was five-feet, six-inches tall, with a whitish, unlined face and peanut-colored hair. His steps were long and quick, and he wore blazers and tan slacks rather than suits. His smile was a flashing of his top row of teeth.

Johnnie Regan was hired as pianist for the tour; he was a couple of inches shorter than Lucas, with round arms and a round face, and big hands that glided on the keyboards. A jazz performer in clubs in Philadelphia and Southern New Jersey, he quit his cocaine habit when he found he could afford no more, and he had nothing left in his apartment to pawn for dime bags. He then unrolled and read the David Lucas pamphlet through which he snorted his coke.

Dick Michaels, the organist of Wingate Church, was hired as organist for the tour. A high-school music teacher by profession, he had a rectangular face topped with brown hair patched with gray; at the church he was known to not want to talk about his parents or what country they originated from.

Filling the space for Lucas in the pulpit of Wingate were two assistant pastors, whose names members of the congregation heard but never remembered.

The tour developed a procedure whenever it arrived in a new base. Battalion chaplains were sent letters from the Ministries announcing the arrival of Lucas, and advising them to mention it in their Sunday services. Fliers were also sent out to be placed in the lobbies of the chapels. The tour also contacted civilian churches in the area for support, and a committee of the area pastors would form and contact with the advance team, which would set up the space and time in one of the base theaters or baseball stadiums.

At every stop on the tour, inside the assembly hall, a chorus sang under the direction of Roy Murphy. The chorus was recruited, as was much of the volunteer work on the rally, from the base chapels and local civilian churches. At the rear of the theater, a television camera was on either side. The engineers and technicians for the Lucas crusade were headquartered in the projection room. The rallies were broadcast via satellite and over cable TV and stations throughout the country.

In the front lobby of the auditorium there would be a table full of literature, including Lucas' autobiography *Soldier Of The Cross,* and pamphlets written by the Reverend Lucas, which were reprints of articles he wrote in the past in the Christian press. The rest of the table had pamphlets written by Christian authors that Lucas liked, donation envelopes, decision cards which stated that the sender was a brand-new Christian, and bibles–always King James, and always for a donation.

The people who attended the rallies included young men, some in fatigues, others in civilian clothes, but all with their hair cut short. Some carried bibles or New Testaments, and cameras. Some were older-looking and better dressed-these were the officers. Many came with their wives and families. A few civilians were there, with their longer hair and by their less rigid posture and demeanor; a few of these came in Legion and VFW caps and jackets. And some just came to pass the time, to see something different from the monotony of their service far from their homes.

In the early part of the tour, Christine stayed home, since the rallies would be nearby and David could come right home. Late in November, Lucas rode home from a rally and entered the parsonage; Christine asked "How was it, honey?"

"Great as usual," he sighed. He looked at her–his wife, the woman God placed under him–and said, "Christine, the tour is going further from here, all over the world, and I want you to come with me."

Christine was shocked–to be away from her family, her friends, her familiar surroundings. "For–for how long?" she asked.

"The entire tour," he said.

"Why?" she squeaked.

"You're my wife, and I'm your husband," he said, "your place is with me, by my side."

"Yes, David, I'll do it."

Corbett and his political friends threw a party for Lucas at the ballroom of the Dorita Hotel when the tour began to move south. Men in business suits and their wives in lace and chiffon tolerated a non-alcoholic evening of roast beef and piety, with Lucas, Christine at his side, gliding through the room, receiving compliments that he was "America's greatest exemplar of traditional values, just what we need in this country."

The Reverend Jimmy Wheeland mingled among the celebrants of this tour. Ever since the court decision in favor of the Armed forces Crusade, Wheeland noticed the euphoria through the NCPC office.

"Well, Brother Lucas," cheered Wheeland, "Are you set for your nationwide tour?"

"Yes, I *am,* Brother Wheeland," smiled Lucas, as ever respectful of this senior brother in the body of Christ.

"And is this your little wife?" Wheeland smiled as he bent down to look at Christine.

"How do you do, Reverend," she blushed as she extended her hand, which Wheeland took into his larger paw.

"Well, Mrs. Lucas, are you really going to be on your husband's side during the tour? It would be truly wonderful if you showed to the world your example as a faithful, obedient Christian woman, a true helpmeet. Why don't you occasionally speak before some audiences to tell of your true Christian faith, your Christian loyalty to your husband? Or are you too bashful?"

Christine nodded her head and affirmed, "Yes, I will."

Lucas smiled, "Great idea, Brother Wheeland," and that was Christine's cue to also smile.

"Christine," Lucas added, "Why don't you go to your dad while I talk with Brother Wheeland?"

"Okay," she smiled as she trotted off into the crowd.

"Fine girl," Wheeland concluded.

"Brother Wheeland," began Lucas, "I've been hearing stories of some kind of disease going around the fag area of New York."

"Yes, I've heard something about it," agreed Wheeland

"I think we're going to hear more about it in the future," decided Lucas. "Maybe God's punishing the homos, do you think?" (He thought about the defeat of the referendum in 1978–Durkin and his fags–*Let's see them handle this!*)

"No doubt," agreed Wheeland. "God *will* always send a message to sinners no matter what."

Christine was told to go to her dad, and she would; but at this time she went off
into the phone booth outside the ballroom and dialed – collect – Fran's number in New
York.

At this time, Fran was washing the dishes from her quick dinner – she was going
out to a movie – and the phone rang. She picked it up, and she heard Christine's voice
say, "Frannie?"

"Hey, kid, how are you?" Fran returned, "What's up?"

"I'm going with David soon," said Christine, "I'm at the Dorita and they're
throwing a going-away party."

"That's nice," Fran replied.

"I'll sure be seeing parts of the world, but –" Christine mourned – "I'll miss you,
my friends. You were always – I love you, Frannie."

"I love you too, Chris," responded Fran.

"I'd like to call you up while I'm away," continued Christine. "I don't think

David would let me."

"Have you asked him?"

"No."

"Try asking him," suggested Fran, "Or you could write."

"Okay," agreed Christine.

"Anything else on your mind?" asked Fran.

"No."

"Then get back to the party and have fun," cheered Fran.

They said their good-byes, and hung up.

Two days later, the Lucas tour arrived late in the afternoon at Pensacola Naval Air base in Florida. As in every rally, Johnny Regan and Dick Michaels played their instruments, Billy Calloway sang, Christine made a brief address – the crowd *knew* she was not preaching a sermon -- and then Lucas would give his sermon.

Finally, in March 1982, the tour reached the Army base Fort Horton, Kentucky.

35

On a Monday evening in March 1982, people lined up at the base theater–the largest in Fort Horton, Kentucky–for the evangelistic meeting of the Reverend David Lucas. Posters in the lobby showed the Reverend Lucas with the words "Stand Up For Jesus! David Lucas Armed Forces Crusade for Christ!" The theater marquee read DAVID LUCAS CRUSADE.

One half-hour before the revival started, The Reverend David Lucas knelt in front of a chair, elbows on the seat, in his temporary office behind the stage of the theater. He was deep in prayer:

"Lord God," Lucas pleaded, "I beg of You to give me the strength to preach Your truth this night, with no fear of those who foolishly deny Your might and Your glory. There are so many demons out there in the world, Lord, and I know Your Son Jesus died to save us from our sins. I want, Lord, to tell as many people as I can that truth, Lord, so that they could be saved. Help me , Lord, to get this message across to the members of our Armed Forces, so that a great revival would sweep the land, Lord" –His voice picked up with volume and fervor– "and the United States of America will once more be great among the nations of the *earth*, and worthy of Thy Blessings, in Christ our Lord, ah-*men!*"

Lucas opened his eyes, inhaled, climbed to his feet, and looked in the full-length mirror; he would be on TV and he was careful about how he looked.

The rally began with the chorus singing hymns, with a piano and organ accompanying. They started with "We Are Climbing Jacob's Ladder, Soldiers Of The Cross" and continued with two others, concluding with "How Great Thou Art." People crowded in with a chatter, and the theater filled to capacity, including the blue metal folding chairs–four rows at the end and four in the front-there was barely enough room for everyone. Lucas smiled as he saw the people–usually there would be a few hundred people in each evening service. Lucas checked his Rolex watch–five minutes before eight–and he joined the others on the stage.

At eight, the base commanding general, Major General John B. Henninger, marched up to the podium in his dress-greens. His hair was short but not close, and his physique was heavy but not fat. Arriving at the podium, he began:

"I welcome you, ladies and gentlemen, to this, the first day of the David Lucas crusade here at Fort Horton, and I wish to extend a very special welcome to our civilian visitors, and I advise you to *please* follow the visitors' guidelines that you have received before entering the base.

"It is always a pleasure," Henninger droned, "to present to the young men of this base and this division such outstanding examples of honesty, decency, and patriotism, which our country needs so much in these uncertain times. Because the Reverend Lucas, who served his country just as all of you here *have* served or *are* serving your country, stands for these virtues, I feel it is only fitting to begin with the Pledge of Allegiance, to be followed by a song by Mister Billy Calloway."

Everyone stood, turned to the Flag of the United States located at stage left, and recited the Pledge of Allegiance, in a monotone, like school children in a classroom.

The organ and piano started up, and Billy Calloway stepped up to the microphone, and then sang "Stand Up, Stand Up for Jesus," in a sweet but strong operatic tenor.

At the end of the verse, Lucas jumped to the mike, startling Calloway, and announced, "All Christians stand up for the rest of the song, really *stand up* for Jesus!", and sat back down. At that, a few dozen people stood up and joined in the singing; as the song progressed, more and more people stood and sang, and when the song finished, the people who stood cheered.

Sergeant First Class Leonard Wilmont – an Airborne Ranger, identified as such by the parachute-and-wings badge on his left breast, and the RANGER flash on his left shoulder – paid attention. His body was rock-solid, and his hair was a dark coating on his head.

Wilmont heard that David Lucas brought his crusade to Fort Horton; David Lucas, veteran, a man who spoke of God and Country, a warrior of God who would not back-stab his country like so many preachers he heard about (a gang of cowards and punks wearing clerical collars, thought Wilmont), who spoke out against queers, women's libbers, degenerates, and perverts, and for doing the right and moral thing–this was what Wilmont heard about David Lucas, and he liked it.

Along with the thrill of Lucas coming to Fort Horton, Wilmont felt a hole in his life. He had tried to be as much a soldier as he could, and he did well–trainee leader in Basic at Dix, followed by Ranger training and two years in the Eighty-Second Airborne Division, where he underwent NCO school, followed by a tour in Korea–

But he still felt like he had to prove himself as a soldier. Wilmont took these frustrations out on his troops in the form of extra duty for no apparent reason, and language that was more obscene than usual. He stomped into the NCO club and yelled "Shot of J And B *now!*" at the female bartender. After a couple of glasses, Wilmont cursed the entire female sex for not freely giving him any "pussy," and of how hookers charged too much for their services. There were also obscenities about his wife and kids–a son and a daughter–for walking out on him, simply because he slapped them around, a *little.* He combated the pain of losing someone he truly loved, and the shame of abusing them–the whiskey was his heavy artillery. And now Leonard Wilmont sat straight-up in his seat in the fourth row center.

As Calloway sang, Lucas reviewed his address; he remembered what he learned from Doctor Garfield and Billy Sunday as they preached–he would hint that the audience were slackers, lukewarm, not passionate for Christ, not willing to go all out, not willing to proclaim the Gospel, say they were only Christians in name only, sinning while they thought no one was looking. He would challenge some and shame others.

Christine drifted to the podium after Calloway sat down. She wore a red dress with long sleeves and a turtleneck and hemline well below the knee; a cross was pinned near the left breast:

"I'm very pleased to see a roomful of people who want to know Jesus. David is simply the best at telling people the Good News of the birth, death, burial, and resurrection of Jesus Christ, and the saving power of Jesus from sin. David is the kind of man I've always wanted as a young girl. Every night, I would pray that I may find a man who was strong and good in body and spirit, and I found him in David Lucas. God has meant for me to be David's helper and companion to support him in all things. That is my duty as a Christian woman, and I shall never run from that responsibility.

"Fortunately for this crusade," Christine continued, "David has many supporters and helpers, Christians all over the country, and around the world, sending donations of money to help keep these meetings going. This crusade tour for our servicemen—those who defend our country, patriotic people –" Her voice quivered – "deserve nothing but the best, and that is to bring them to Jesus Christ, the Savior and Lord!"

There was applause and "Ah-mens" from the audience, in service and formerly in service.

Christine's voice quivered, but she proclaimed, "I have always, like a true Christian woman, stood beside my husband. We have had bad times, like when he would have to be away from home for a long time, to fight against unspeakable immoralities being accepted as a lifestyle –"

She paused, her throat clogging, like she was about to cry. Then she sipped from the water glass near the podium and resumed, "I knew he was doing God's work for our community and our country when he was away." Then, she turned to her husband and declared, "David, I love you so much."

That pure, innocent phrase brought furious applause, an occasional whistle, and "Praise the Lord, ah-men!" Lucas smiled and bowed his head.

"And I know that many of you girls would like a man like David, someone who is handsome and strong in body and spirit. That is my husband David. Well, I have the original, pray to God that you get one of your own."

There were titters and applause from the women in the audience–it was just *so* cute! Lucas' smile faded for a moment, then returned; he did not applaud.

"So now," concluded Christine, "here's my husband, the Reverend David Lucas!"

The crowd applauded, and there were some whistles. Lucas rose, strode up to the podium, hugged Christine as he had planned, and took his position, while Christine returned to her seat.

"Let us pray," announced Lucas, "Let every eye close, and let there be no disturbance from the audience."

As a group, the audience did so.

Lucas stretched out his right hand and prayed, "Dear God, we thank You for this opportunity today to join in fellowship with each other. May all who are present today have a relationship with Your Son, Jesus, so they may become a new being. Give them the wisdom of Solomon, the courage of Daniel, and the love of Christ, in His name, we pray, ah-men." The audience joined in saying "Ah-men," and Lucas began his sermon:

"I love speaking to servicemen, like here in Fort Horton. Guys from all around the country united in the same place for the same worthy cause, it's great that you would enter military service. This shows that someone still cares about America."

Lucas pulled the mike from the podium and stepped around the stage, saying, ""I've *been* there, in military service. I was nervous, but I knew that I *had* to go. *Some* body has to! We need men to step up and do the *man's* part, defend this country! You *still* have to do it, draft or no draft! *Morally* you have to! Yes, you can get some good benefits, but you also have great responsibilities. That's what a man does, take on responsibilities!"

The audience applauded, not very spiritedly–what was that about? Lucas' face lost its smile and looked bewildered—then had a smirk of knowing more than everyone else.

"You're with me, right?" he went on, holding on to the smirk, "you agree you're where you have to be, right? Or maybe you think you should be somewhere else, making some *big* money, right? Just sick of taking order, sick of having to always have your boots polished, sick of it all, right? You just wannna get out of it all right? You just *hate* to have someone tell you what to do, telling you how to run your life-*don't* you!"

His smile dropped off as his voice rose in volume. "You don't *want* to carry your own weight! You think you got better things to do, you just want to do your own thing and not care about anyone else! Just quit the whole thing right now! No ready as you're supposed to, to risk you lives for us, to *die* for us!"

The audience wondered what this was about. Who was he addressing this to? Could he be saying these things to *them?* And *why?*

"Well let me ask you this one thing," said Lucas, "What if *Jesus* decided to give up? What if *Jesus* decided to cop out? What if *Jesus* threw up His hands and said, 'I *quit!*

It's too *much* for me! *I-can-not-do-it!'*

"*Think* of it!" urged Lucas, "Jesus giving up on His mission and His ministry! Just giving up his ministry and going back to his carpentry business! *Think* of it! *Man,* lost, sinful *Man,* lost and burdened by Sin from the beginning, from Adam! And here comes Jesus, coming to take upon Himself all the punishments for all the sins of the human race! And we *reject* it! We *reject* it, the gift of atonement for our sins, we *reject* Jesus' offer to give His life, to *die* for our sins! We *turn away* from him!"

Then his tone was depressed and wounded as he continued, "And so Man—lost, sinful Man—continues on the path of darkness, the path of sin that he chooses, with no hope of salvation, no hope—"

Lucas felt a catching in his throat. The audience was hung in mid-air, in suspense.

"Forgive me, please," pleaded Lucas, swallowing some water from the glass, and unbuttoning his shirt collar. "Sometimes I wonder what would've happened to *me,* if Jesus gave up on me. I led a life of sin—what if Jesus *couldn't* save me? I would've fallen into sin deeper and deeper, into worse and worse sin? What if Jesus gave up on me?"

The audience paid attention; the thought of Jesus giving up–

"He *didn't* give up!" exclaimed Lucas. "He *stayed* and *fought!* He went *on* and *on* to the *finish!* He went to the Cross and *died* for our sins! He rose on the third day and trod the Earth! In *victory!* He *rose* to heaven and *sits* at the right hand of God the Father! He *lives,* He *reigns,* He *triumphs!"*

There were cheers, whistles, calls of "Ah-*men*! Praise the *Lord*! *Thank* you, Jesus!" and raising of hands to Heaven in the audience. On the stage, General Menninger sat; Christine was excited. In the audience, Wilmont was also excited. He was an Army lifer, who lived for the Army, and he was impressed with the life of the good soldier Jesus–as Lucas described. Lucas continued:

"Jesus came to the earth to bring His Gospel to Man, and to offer himself as sacrifice for our sins. Since the beginning of time, Man has sinned. Man has turned his back on God! And so *we* deserve the punishment for our sins! *We* should be on the Cross, *suffering!* In *anguish!* In *torment."*

Then Lucas mourned, "The Bible says, Romans chapter three, verse twenty-three,

'For all have sin, and fallen short of the Glory of God.' Our *sins* broke the *bridge* between God and Man! Our *entire lives* on *earth* are *filled* with sin, and the wages of sin is *Death!*"

All through his sermon, Lucas stabbed the air with his finger, waived the Bible in his right hand like a flag, and swaggered on the stage. He continued:

"Yes, I know it can be rough, your superiors can be mean, I been through it myself. But you *take* it! You go *throug*h with it! Just as it says in the Bible itself, First Peter, chapter two, verse eighteen to twenty-five, 'Servants, *be* submissive to *your* masters with all fear, not only to the good and gentle, but also to the harsh. For this *is* commendable, if because of conscience toward God one endures grief, suffering wrongfully. For what credit *is* it if, when you are beaten for your faults, you take it patiently? But when you do good and suffer, if you take it patiently, this *is* commendable before God. For to this you were called, because Christ also suffered for us, leaving us an example, that you should follow His steps: who committed no sin, not was deceit found in His mouth; who, when He was reviled, did not revile in return; when He suffered, He did not threaten, but committed *Himself* to Him who judges righteously; who Himself bore our sins in His own body on the tree, that we, having died to sins, might live for righteousness—by whose stripes you were healed. For you were like sheep going astray, but have now returned to the Shepherd and Overseer of your souls.'

"*That*," concluded Lucas, "goes for all situations you're going through, all people you're subordinate to. No matter how wrong it looks to you, no matter how difficult the person or situation is, you do what *any* good man does, and *endure* it. You *suffer through* it, and for that you gain respect and merit from man, and from God.

"Just as Jesus did *His* duty," added Lucas, "and did it to the max, so must *you* do your duty, in *all you* do, and do *that* to the max! And don't say you can *not* do it, whatever *it* happens to be! *Don't* believe in *yourself,* because you're *weak* and *helpless* without Jesus! Jesus is the only way to true happiness and salvation! When you receive Jesus as Savior and Lord, your sins are forgiven! You're a whole new being, so full of joy and peace and love for all, inside of you! Nothing is too difficult for you, and you know it, because Jesus is there for you! All obstacles are overcome, because the greatest obstacle to man's happiness and peace, *Sin,* is thrown away by Jesus! Jesus takes its place–"

His tone relaxed as he said, "And there is nothing but joy and happiness. *Hallelujah!*" and he threw his hands up into the air, jerking his head back.

There was a symphony of applause. Palms hammered on palms, and throats grew sore from joyous yelling. From the excitement and the closeness of bodies, skins were damp and steam rose. The worries of the world were not in the theater; there were just the sounds in praise of Jesus, the tears of joy, and smiles on people's faces and hearts; arms rose towards Heaven. This man on the stage, David Lucas, spoke to them with clarity and sureness in his voice, telling them–plainly, simply, and certainly–the Truth. He also gave meaning to the rough times they went through in their service.

Lucas felt his t-shirt and dress shirt stick to his skin, his body warm inside the suit, and he took off his jacket. He surveyed the crowd in front of him; the lights were dim over them, so he could not distinguish individuals from the cheering mass. He swallowed some air and resumed:

"All of you know by now how my life was like before I accepted Jesus as my Lord and Savior. I took dope! I slept with whores! I drank and brawled! And *because* of all that, I ended up in the stockade! It was *inevitable* that such a thing happened to me! I *deserved* punishment for my crimes, just as I *deserve* punishment for my sins!"

Then, calming down, he added, "It was probably the best thing, it *was* the best thing, that ever happened to me, because I met a chaplain, and he introduced me to Jesus Christ, the *Son of God,* and the *Savior* of mankind, who came to the world born of a *virgin—preached* the message of live and salvation–*died* on the Cross for our sins!"–He stretched his arms to full length–"rose on the third day! And now sits at the right hand of God the Father Almighty! He *will* return to earth one of these days, *soon,* and he *will* establish his kingdom on Earth!" pointing to the air with his long right arm, the hand still holding the bible, adding, "I *believe* that! I believe it, *each* and *every word, more* and *more* each *day!"*

Another cheer roared from the audience, with cries of "Ah-*men!* Praise the *Lord!* Hallelujah!" On the stage, Henninger sat immobile; Christine and Calloway laughed and applauded like children. Lucas moved to the podium, hands gripping the sides, grinning.

He gathered a breath of air and spoke again:

"But you don't *stop* getting problems when you accept Christ Jesus as you Savior! You-must-*witness!*-for Jesus! You must *get up!*–*Look* people in the *face!*–and *tell* them, 'God is the Supreme King, the *Supreme* ruler of Heaven and Earth, and Jesus is *His* Son and *my* Savior, who gave His *life* that *I* may be saved from my sins!'"

Lucas calmed down as he continued, "I've had to go through some difficulties, some *heat,* for my faith in Christ," He paced the stage, his bible in his right hand, his mike in the left hand and to his lips. "I've been *mocked! Laughed at! Ridiculed!* Treated like something *loathsome!* And for *what?* Just because I spoke out against *im-mor-ality!* I spoke the *Truth* of the *Bible,* about the moral principles that made America the greatest nation on the planet! And *all* the *abuse* I *took for that!*

"But I *took* it," declared Lucas. "I *took* it for Jesus the Christ, the Lord and Savior. And I *took* it for the *salvation* of the *nation!*"

A pause, then Lucas said, like a child proposing a game, "Let's chant!– Salvation for the nation! Salvation for the nation!"

The audience picked up the chant, "...Salvation for the nation! Salvation for the nation! ..." People roared through their throats, hands pounded together, sweat pouring from hot faces- "...Salvation for the nation! Salvation for the nation!..."

"Ah-*men!"* shouted Lucas with a smile, as the crowd laughed and clapped. Lucas went on:

"Remember what the Apostle Paul said, in the Letter to the Romans, chapter one, verse sixteen. 'For I am *not* ashamed of the Gospel, for it is God's power for salvation to every believer.' Your strength will come from *God* through His *Son Jesus*. When you accept Jesus, you'll have the power to deal with the world's problems, stresses, and predicaments. You'll begin to understand the Master's plan—God rules over *all* things. Things are under control, the control of God, when you come to accept Jesus as savior. Remember, his kingdom is not of this world, but in the World to Come."

Wilmont thrilled to Lucas' preaching – no hems or haws, but the Straight Truth, right from his guts. The Christian life sounded dangerous but exciting, the way Lucas described it; this was the kind of thing Wilmont trained for, accepted as part of his life, and he could not understand "candy-asses" who were not as hard-core as he was.

Lucas continued: "And you can't be like these people that's sometimes called 'Sunday Christians and weekday devils!' These are the type that put Jesus in the closet with their good suits, then go over to the video store and rent the dirty cassettes! Or go over to the bar and take in some poison! That's *wrong!* Those are the kind of people I've *preached* against, *all my life* as a Christian! To be a Christian is a twenty-four hour a *day,* seven days a week *job!* To be a Christian is to give *up* the ways of the *world,* and take on the ways of *God!* Don't follow the crowd to *Hell,* follow *Jesus* to *Heaven!* For it is the *only* way, the *only* hope for salvation! Jesus wants to enter your heart, *let Him in! That* is the challenge I give you, tonight and all through this crusade!

Lucas inhaled, and his tone became softer as he said, "You just have to say, 'Yes, Lord, yes, I *am* a sinner, and I *know* I'm weak and helpless. I *do* so need Your son Jesus to take over my life. I *want* His blood to wash away all my sins, my lies, my fears, and my hates. *Yes,* Lord, I *do* accept Jesus into my heart, and into my life, as my Savior. In His name, we pray, ah-*men!"*

Applause came again from the audience, the firm Christians beaming, their spiritual batteries recharged. The lifers, such as Wilmont, were moved by Lucas' story of the brave soldier Jesus.

Lucas nodded to the musicians; the piano and organ started the strains of "Just As I Am." At that, some young men came in front of the audience below the edge of the stage; some wore dark suits, others wore Army dress greens, and each had a bible at the ready.

Lucas coaxed, "I want you all now, all of you who accept Jesus as Savior and Liberator from sin, all of *you*, come on down up front here, and talk and pray with these prayer counselors. All of you, who have accepted Jesus already, come up and make your commitment again. Show everyone that you stand with Jesus, that you have Him as your Savior and Redeemer."

His voice was soft but urgent as he said, "Can you be sure of what might happen tomorrow? Maybe you'll be killed, with a car accident or something! Then what? Where will you go, Heaven or Hell? Don't put it off, there may *be* no next time! Come down now and accept Jesus."

The chorus began "Just As I Am," and people rose from their seats slowly, hesitating, thinking, *Should I...?,* wondering whether they should make the big decision. A few brave souls strode to the front, anxious to be saved; then the others, still not certain but taking a chance, like Wilmont.

Lucas smiled, his chest heavy with joy–more people coming to Jesus! Young men, soldiers for their country, some with their families, declared themselves for Jesus. He waved his long arm to invite more to come forward.

Wilmont walked towards a man in dress greens and four stripes, like he had, and said, "Hey, Sarge, can I speak with you?"

"Hey, sure," beamed the sergeant in green.

"I'm all—I need help—my life!" sputtered Wilmont.

The sergeant pointed to a seat and said, "Let's sit here and pray," and he nudged Wilmont. They sat and chatted, and then bowed their heads.

Lucas saw, from the corner of his eye, Christine chatting with a young woman in fatigues, a First Lieutenant's silver bar on her collar; but he kept his attention on the young man in camo in front of him.

36

Lucas' Rolex read forty minutes after ten; by that time everybody left the theater. He stood at the center of the stage, thrilled by the rally. "Thank you, Lord, for this evening," muttered Lucas in prayer.

Christine tapped over to her husband and chirped, "David, honey, that was a wonderful—"

"Chris-*tine,*" Lucas scolded, turning to her," I didn't *like* that *silly* introduction you *gave* me. 'I have the original!' You made it sound like some kind'a dirty joke!" Looming over her and aiming his finger at her, Lucas added, "This is a *Christian-evangelistic-ministry,* Christine, *not* some Vegas floor show!"

Christine held her hands to her face, her head bowed she pleaded, "I'm sorry, honey, I didn't mean–"

"And who was that *woman* who held on to you?" Lucas interrogated, "some *lesbian?*"

"Just someone who wanted to know Jesus," Christine whimpered, her eyes aimed at the floor; she quivered at the sound of the word *lesbian.*

"Well, next time, be careful about women in the military," warned Lucas, like someone who knew, "they're no good."

He then pulled out his wallet while grunting, "Better take the cab home, in fact, here's your allowance," as he pulled five twenty-dollar bills from the wallet and rammed them into Christine's small hand. "Try not to buy anything *dumb*," urged Lucas, "not that it's gonna *stop* you," and then he snickered at his joke.

"Thank you, David," apologized Christine, and then she stepped off the stage. When Lucas was alone again, he considered what a loyal little wife he had in Christine, then he moved to the back of the stage.

Christine walked to the front door of the theater, knowing she made a mistake. Wearing a light, lime-green rain jacket, she took a taxi to the base guest house. Once inside, the desk clerk said, "Mrs. Lucas? A message for you, ma'am," and he handed her a piece of paper. *Christine—call Fran,* and a phone number with the New York area code. *What could it be?*

After Christine left, Lucas met on the stage with his musical staff: Billy Calloway, Johnny Regan, Dick Michaels, and Roy Murphy. They discussed the next evening's service.

"I think Billy should sing 'The Crusader's Hymn' at the start," asserted Lucas.

A moan rose, which startled Lucas.

"Aw, *c'mon*, Dave," Calloway said, "Sure it's a nice, powerful hymn, but it's always the Army, this, and the Army, that!"

"Yeah, Dave," Regan chimed in, "I mean, man, these Army gigs are great, but when we gonna do a *civilian* crusade?"

"Johnny's right, and so's Billy," agreed Michaels, "the meetings are too military in theme. You have the Savior as some sort of *drill* sergeant! Why not make it a plain old *revival,* like *back home?"*

Lucas frowned at them—*they* disagreed with *him*? And *he*, Lucas, did God's work? He turned to Murphy and asked, "And what do you have to say, Roy?"

"They make a lot of sense," stated Murphy, "we're all musical professionals, and so you *need* to listen to us, for the good of the crusade."

Lucas faced them:

"God has inspired *me,"* he declared, "to bring *His* message to the guys in the military. We had to fight the ACLU and the atheists to do this, but we *won.* Don't you see, Jesus told us t' bring the *Gospel* to every *creature, didn't* he?"

"Dave, that's not the *point!"* pleaded Calloway.

"Well, what *is* the point?" insisted Lucas, pushing aside the chair and striding towards Calloway, being intimidating.

"All this stuff about Jesus being a soldier!" stated Regan, "Man, that's too much, that's silly! The *soldiers* don't even talk like *that!"*

"Look at the statistics!" ordered Lucas. *"Crime, drugs, divorce,* an' *alcoholism* are worse in the military that in any other part of the country! Plain Americans look *up* t' the military, it's their pride an' joy! If everybody became a Christian, in the military, enlisted men and officers, think a' the *impact* it'll have in the country!"

Calloway, Regan, Michaels, and Murphy saw that Lucas, their hero as well as their employer, was deliberately misunderstanding them. Lucas was subjecting them to a tirade.

Lucas went on, "You *know* how messed up the country *is,* with crime, inflation, Watergate, no respect around the *world* for this country! Nobody's got any *hope* for America anymore! That's why this crusade tour, to start a *revival* in America! The military's the *guts,* the *pride,* the *heroes* of America! Kids *imitate* the people they see on TV an' movies, and ninety per cent of them are boozing, doping, or queer! So we show these kids people who know Christ as savior, people they respect, examples of decent Christian living–"

From stage left, General Henninger entered the room and walked towards Lucas. "That was a fine sermon, Reverend Lucas," said Henninger as he shook Lucas' hand. "I hope the men were inspired by it."

"I'm sure they were, General," said Lucas.

"Would you and your wife like to have lunch with me tomorrow at my house?" asked Henninger.

"That'd be fine, sir, thank you." replied Lucas.

"Fine," agreed Henninger, "I'll see you at one o'clock tomorrow. I'll bring a car over to the guest house to pick you up. Good night!"

"Good night, and thanks, General. And God bless you!"

Henninger left the theater and went back to his residence (a four story mansion) in his official vehicle. There, he changed into a civilian suit and drove in his personal car, a Lincoln, to a brothel in the neighboring town–his wife was away that week.

Back at the stage, the argument went on: Murphy stepped towards Lucas and said, "I believe we should be listened to as musical professionals," in a get-it-off-my-chest tone, adding "We can't go on with the constant military theme! It makes no *sense!*"

"Oh, it doesn't, Mister Curtis-Institute-of-Music? And you, too, Mister Julliard?" Lucas laughed. "Your fancy degrees don't mean a *thing* to me! You know I can leave you dummies here an' you can *walk* back to Jersey for all I care! Just don't forget you work for *me,* and I work for *God!* So you go against me and you go against *God!*"

Lucas' face reddened, and his body stiffened; his fists tightened as if ready to duke it out with someone. Calloway, Murphy, Michaels, and Regan collapsed inside.

They lost; Lucas, right or wrong, was the boss.

Watching the looks of defeat on his music staff, Lucas relaxed, smiling; victory made him feel generous, forgiving, and he concluded, "Well, that's all, gotta go t' sleep. G'night!" and he grabbed his jacket and walked off the stage and out the exit.

Lucas inhaled the cold air, and thought: *Why can't they just do what I tell them? I AM the boss! My authority has to be respected. I don't want to kick anyone around.* Lucas got to the sidewalk towards the guest house and continued: *Too much rebelliousness in the world. The Bible condemns that.*

Lucas entered the lobby of the guest house, and felt all of a sudden weak and tired, his eyes blurring. He got out of the elevator, strode down the hall, then stopped in front of the door to his suite. He was again upset by his argument with his musical staff, forgetting the rousing sermon he gave at the revival. He didn't want to be hard on those guys–in fact, Lucas *did* think he was overdoing the military theme a bit–and he loved them like brothers. But he was right in telling them off, he thought as he leaned against the wall.

Lucas entered the suite and announced, "Christine, General Henninger's invited us for lunch tomorrow."

Christine sat on the floral-printed couch with the telephone on her lap and worry on her face. "David," she said as she rose, "my mom's had a heart attack. She's in the hospital. Could you *please* let me go see her?"

"No," said Lucas, startled, "I don't want you going around by yourself!"

"But, *David,* my *mother!"* she pleaded.

"No!" Lucas declared. "I said I don't want you going around by yourself! God only knows what'll happen t' you!"

That quieted her. Lucas smiled like a victor as he put his hands on her shoulders and asked, as if to a child, "Wouldn't your mom want you to stay with me? Huh?" Christine bobbed her head.

Lucas added, "After the crusade here, we'll go back and see your mom, okay?" in a tone of a parent soothing a child. Christine nodded again.

"David," Christine asked tiredly, "Why is this dinner so important?"

"It's *lunch,*" corrected Lucas, "and it's important because *he's* an important man. He's got influence and authority. A Christian in his position could be a great example to others, and a help to us."

As Lucas went into the bedroom, he turned and said, "When we get there, don't say anything unless spoken to. I don't want any embarrassments."

At this time, General Henninger entered the front door of Miss Sadie's House, the area's most elegant brothel. Miss Sadie herself –a tall, heavy-busted woman in a low-cut silk gown and a push-up bra–escorted him into the living room and the company of politicians, business figures, and a couple of high-rank clergymen, as well as an assortment of beautiful young women in a variety of camisoles, stockings, panties, and slips.

Seeing Henninger's frown and bowed head, Sadie asked, "Why so glum, General?"

"Ah, Sadie," moaned Henninger, "I got this *fucked-up* division I'm supposed to make work, an' the *dick*-heads in Washington don't listen to me. Plus I gotta take care of this dip-shit preacher–David Lucas, you hear 'a him? Gotta be hospitable to his ass! Oh, God, I wish I could get a real fuckin' job in Washington! I could straighten some things out!"

37

Lucas woke up at six the next morning, got into his sweat clothes, attached his pedometer, and then started his daily two-mile run; then he would get back to the guest house and lift weights. Christine still slept when he got out.

Running down the road in the chill March air, Lucas felt a light drizzle on his face. He kept up a steady, strong pace, a regular beat on the pavement–*plap-plap-plap-plap*. Through the mist, Lucas viewed the sights of the base: tanks and other vehicles of war, rows of soldiers in formation, the divisional headquarters–and the stockade.

If only I could talk to the guys in there, thought Lucas, *someone just like me could be saved.* He often visited stockades, but it was with the approval of the base commanding-general; this was in the guidelines from the Defense Department that Lucas and the crusade staff followed. Lucas respected these orders, but–*If I could talk to those guys in the stockade...*

"One, two, three, *fooour!*"

"ONE, TWO, THREE, *FOOOUR!*"

"One, two, gimme some *mooore!*"

"ONE, TWO, GIMME SOME MOOORE!"

The sound of this double-time cadence physically touched Lucas, then thrilled him, then caused him to pick up his pace. He then saw a platoon of soldiers running in formation, one guy carrying a blue infantry guideon. Lucas was back among brothers.

Christine was so upset when Lucas didn't let her go to her mother. *Women!* thought Lucas, *Spoiled children! And Christine brought up so rich!* Lucas knew he was right to not allow Christine to go home by herself; women were such easy targets.

An engine blared, and Lucas felt the air vibrate around him. He stopped and moved to one side of the road, and a big olive-drab truck roared past him, giving off diesel fumes. He stepped further away from the road, not daring to breathe right away. Waiting a couple of seconds, he inhaled. The noise of the truck faded, and Lucas got up to run again.

Then–Lucas remembered to pray for Christine's mom. He went on the side of the road, knelt, and prayed, "Dear Lord, Helen, Christine's mom, is very ill. Please Lord, bring her back to health. Ah-men." Lucas rose and resumed his run.

After running for a minute, Lucas saw a figure coming towards him, seeming a little familiar. He recalled him–Leonard Wilmont, the airborne ranger sergeant.

Wilmont stopped and said, "Hey, aren't you Rev'rend Lucas?" panting from running, sweat chilling his back and face.

"Yeah, that's right," said Lucas, also winded and sweating.

"I was at your rally last night."

"Uh-huh?"

"Jesus came t' me!" Wilmont thrilled. "I sat with one of your counselors, I prayed to God, an' I told all about my sins, an' Jesus came to me!"

"Praise God, that's just wonderful!" smiled Lucas.

"Y'know," continued Wilmont, "all the guys I serve with were sure shocked. I couldn't get along with anybody, I had fun being mean to guys who serve under me, an' how I could cuss! But–whatever it was inside me was upsetting me, it's gone!"

"That's terrific, I'm glad Jesus came to you," praised Lucas, "You'll be a great example for others."

"Uh, Rev'rend," worried Wilmont, "I gotta get back to runnin', but I'll see you at your meeting tonight!"

"Okay, great," concluded Lucas as they shook hands mightily, "I'll look for you, and God bless you!"

They went their separate ways.

Lucas was thrilled–another soul saved! *Another Christian in the world!* He would bring another person to Christ, who would bring another–

Lucas picked up speed as he got closer to the guest house. Even with his stops–to step away from the truck, to pray, and to talk with Wilmont–it took all together 14 minutes, nine seconds by his stopwatch.

37

Close to seven that morning, Chaplain (Capt.) Gregory Kirshman, the Jewish Chaplain of Fort Horton, entered the cafeteria of the base Post Exchange, and greeted the table where two other chaplains sat. He had a slender face, a suntan, and wavy reddish-brown hair.

"Come for breakfast, Greg?" asked Chaplain (Capt.) Floyd Kirby, who was ordained in the African Methodist Episcopal Church; he was walnut-colored, with a prickle of moustache on his lip.

"Naw," smiled Kirshman, "just had it, I'm getting coffee." He fixed his coffee–one spoonful of cream and no sugar–and joined his colleagues at their table.

"We're just talkin' 'bout the Lucas rally last night," said Chaplain (Major) Ben Watson, ordained Baptist. "I was there, an' I'll tell you, it–that guy was somethin' else," in the dialect of his native Kentucky. Watson was rail-thin and sunburned, with strands of tan-colored hair on his bald head.

"I couldn't go," sighed Kirby, "I was just comin' out from the field with my battalion, all I wanted t' do was sleep."

"Well, lemme tell you," grinned Watson, "Lucas had 'em all revved up for Jesus!" Like many of the base chaplains, Watson helped in set up advance work for the Lucas crusade at Fort Horton, asking people at chapel to pass around flyers and recruiting volunteers as ushers and choir singers.

"But is that the same as real religious devotion?" worried Kirby.

"Naw, it *ain't* the whole thing," shrugged Watson, "but it'll get the guys to thinking about their lives, letting Jesus in. Say, Greg, I hear y' little girl's not well."

"Just some flu," answered Kirshman, nursing his coffee and looking serious. "But she's four years old, an' it's not *'just'* flu. Debbie was up all night Monday." Kirshman inhaled and added, "I don't think I'll re-up, my time runs out in four months." Kirby and Watson nodded.

Kirby said, "Greg, you know he's having a prayer breakfast for officers, want to come?"

"Naw," grunted Kirshman, "gotta wage war on some paperwork, an' the copier jammed again."

38

After his shower, Lucas entered the bedroom and dressed. He selected a grey Armani suit, white shirt, and a blue tie. He placed his cross pin on his left lapel and put the Rolex on his left wrist. Glancing at himself in the mirror–*I'm good to go,* he decided–Lucas bellowed "Chris-*tine,* let's *go!"*

Hearing her husband's voice, Christine folded her newspaper and got up. She wore a floral-printed short-sleeved dress which was well below the knee; a frilly collar encircled the neck.

"Uh, David," Christine began as Lucas passed, "I was just reading something interesting in the paper, and–"

Lucas kept walking, and Christine thought he did not hear, but he said, "I'm listening," as he grabbed his bible and pocket notebook, and moved towards the door.

"Well, there's this poll taken by the Harris people," she added quickly as the two of them raced slowly out of the suite and down the hall, "and it said that seventy-five percent of the American people–"

They stopped at singer Billy Calloway's room. Lucas knocked, and Christine stopped talking. Calloway opened the door wearing a white tennis shirt, blue work trousers, and yellow tennis shoes. His peanut-colored hair was still damp from the shower.

"Oh, hey, Dave," greeted Calloway, looking up at Lucas with respectful nervousness, "Hey, Chris."

"Hello, Billy," started Christine, "how–"

"Hey, Bill," returned Lucas, "coming to the prayer breakfast?"

"Nope," drawled Calloway, "gotta rehearse for tonight."

"What're y' gonna sing tonight?" smiled Lucas.

Inhaling, Calloway replied, "'The Crusader's Hymn,'"

"All *right!*" cheered Lucas. Patting Calloway on the shoulder, he said, "See y' tonight?"

"Yeah," drawled Calloway again, forcing a smile.

"Okay, 'bye," chirped Lucas.

"'Bye, now, see, y', Chris."

"Bye, Billy," she replied, overwhelmed by her husband.

Calloway closed his door, and the Lucases went down the hall into the elevator while Christine continued, "As the poll said–"

"I'm listening," assured Lucas as he pressed the down button of the elevator.

Christine said, "Well, seventy-five percent of the people polled–"

The elevator opened, and they got in.

"–They've taken Jesus as their Savior!" Christine finally concluded.

"Who, in the poll?" asked Lucas.

"Yes," nodded Christine, with a feeling of *Will he be pleased?*

Lucas grinned at his wife and said, "That's great, I can use that for my sermon at the breakfast."

Christine was pleased that her husband was pleased.

They entered the official military taxi waiting in front of the guest house. As it pulled off, Christine piped, "David?"

"Yeah?"

"I wonder if I could help you in your work, you know, finding things in the paper, you know, that you could use?"

"Naw," said Lucas, shaking his head lightly, "You're my wife, that's enough for you, I keep telling you."

"But I want to help you more–" She stopped abruptly.

"You do enough, being my wife, Chris," he concluded, "don't talk about it again."

As the taxi moved through the streets of Fort Horton, Christine gazed out the window, staring at all of the exotic military vehicles, the ranks and files of men marching, the banners, and buildings. They lost their wonder for her by now. She missed home–her parents, her neighbors, her sister Fran, her friends at the church. Now, one base after the other, everyone and everything looked the same.

Lucas sat and flipped through the file cards for the sermon with the officers. He scribbled the information Christine gave him on the back of one card, stuffed the cards back into his jacket pocket, and prayed silently.

The officers club's dining room filled with men in fatigues–the officers–and their wives who hated to come to another silly event to further their husbands' careers, especially since the officers' club's food was always bad. A long table and a podium were set up in one end of the room.

Ben Watson and Floyd Kirby entered the dining room and saw their boss–Chaplain (Colonel) Douglass Boyce (Methodist), the base's ranking chaplain, a man with straight-back gray hair and a serious face–standing and chatting with the Reverend and Mrs. David Lucas, who took their seats at the long front table. Kirby and Watson slipped into a table by the window in the back, and Boyce went to the podium and spoke:

"Ladies and gentlemen," Boyce began–the audience faded into silence–"I welcome you to this breakfast and I especially welcome our guest and featured speaker, the Reverend David Lucas. Reverend Lucas has spent the last several months preaching the Word of God to servicemen all across the country, and already, the David Lucas

Armed Forces Crusade for Christ is a legend. He has inspired many with his example of change from sin to righteousness through Jesus Christ. Before we begin our breakfast, let us now pray."

Everybody stood, bowed heads and closed eyes, as Boyce prayed, "Dear God, we ask that you bless this food, that it may nourish our bodies, so that we may serve thee and our country well. In the name of Jesus, we pray, ah-men."

The crowd mumbled softly, "Ah-men," and went to the cafeteria line for their breakfast. When they got back to their seats, they attempted to eat the scrambled eggs that were tepid and greasy, along with toast to match; potatoes that had the texture and flavor of modeling clay; and they washed it down with coffee that tasted the way rubbing alcohol smelled.

Lucas ground his own breakfast within his mouth, trying to ignore the flavor of the scrambled eggs, swallowing the water to help get it down. Christine scraped a delicate forkful of egg and put it into her mouth, and instantly gave up–then Lucas stared at her and she was reminded of the lectures from childhood of the starving children of whatever country. She tried again to eat what was on her plate.

After everyone got the breakfast down, Boyce went to the podium again and announced, "It is my pleasure to introduce to all of you a man who is a great champion of God and America, the distinguished evangelist, the Reverend David Lucas."

The audience applauded as Lucas rose to the podium. He began:

"Often," he began, "whenever I appear at a rally or a crusade, people ask me, why I talk so much about the Crucifixion of the Lord Jesus Christ. They ask me, 'Aren't there other parts of the Bible that excite you?' Well, they *all* excite me, but the Crucifixion, the offering-up of the Lord Jesus on the Cross for atonement of our sins, that's *special* to me! It's special because he died for *us!* He gave his life as punishment for the sins that *we, you* and *I, committed!* And *he, Jesus,* was *pure* and *sinless!*"

His eyes watered now, and his voice clogged. He continued, "Please forgive me. It's just that whenever I think about my own sins, *my* drinking, *my* fornicating, *my* profanity–no matter how many times I speak on this, it gets to me."

Lucas gulped from a glass of water, and added: "I think also about the Crucifixion whenever I look upon you, the men of the Armed Forces of the United States, who stand ready to put you lives on the line. Like Jesus on the Cross, you are prepared to give your lives that we may live in freedom and safety. It is because of *you,* our *righteous might,* that has made this the greatest nation on the *face* of the *earth!"* thumping the podium twice.

At that, the officers applauded, some standing and smiling; Lucas reminded them about how special they were, lifting them from the dreary realm of paperwork, salary, and promotions. Lucas declared, "All praise to God Most high!", and that boosted the applause. When it faded, Lucas went on:

"Think of the Crucifixion! *Think* of the terrible, painful way Our Lord died to free us from Sin! There he is, on the Cross, naked, exposed to all the filth you can imagine!

"Jesus hangs there on the Cross, the Crown of Thorns on His head, the thorns digging into his brow!"–Lucas' face writhed with pain just thinking about it– "His *hands* and *feet* nailed to the Cross"–His own arms stretched out– "the *spikes rammed* into his *flesh* and *bone!* And the *gash* on his side, His flesh *ripped* with the sword!

"And upon all that, the *taunts!* The *insults!* He was *spit* on, he was *flogged* –" Lucas waved an invisible whip; his breathing was short and audible– *"thirty-nine times* on His *naked back!* The skin of Our *Lord being torn off!* Down to the *bone!"*

The officers and their wives–and Watson and Kirby–rubbed their necks and jaws and wriggled through this. Lucas continued:

"And after *all that!* –after *all* that *torture!* He looked down on those who were *mocking* him! Who were *beating him unmercifully!* He looked down and prayed for his tormentors. 'Father, forgive them, for they know not what they do.'

"He *said that* to *you* and *me!"* declared Lucas. *"We* were the ones who crucified him! We *wound* Jesus each and *every* time we commit a sin! *Every* time we tell a lie, *every* time we look upon a woman lustfully, *every* time we're unfaithful to our wives, *every* time we show a lack of respect for our superiors, *every* time we look at pornography, *each* and *every* time we *sin!"* – he calmed down – "is a new wound in the body of Jesus."

The officers felt a cloud of shame; few of them could say that they did not curse, or lust after women, or called their superiors wicked names behind their backs. Lucas continued:

"You know," grunted Lucas, "I had to come across some people who say that Jesus was *not* the Son of God, *not* the forgiver of sins, *not* the Savior, but some sort of crackpot or fake." He paused, letting his anger burn, "And you know where I find these types? In the *clergy!*"

Lucas waited for that to register in the minds of the audience—one male voice called out "*What?!*"

"Yes, that's right!" Lucas went on. "They say that us–*poor–gullible–naive–stupid*–followers of Jesus have bought a pack of lies and garbage! And they're *ministers!* In *pulpits!* And leading *classes* in *seminaries!* These are *men*–supposedly *men!*–with Ph.D.'s and D.D.'s , and all kinds of other degrees at the end of their names–and they get them from the finest institutions of higher learning–they get them from the lowest sewers of *atheistic filth!*"

The audience applauded and babbled in agreement. Lucas went on:

"These people–can you really call them *human?* " he demanded, and they applauded again. Lucas started up:

"They sit at the pulpits of the churches and ridicule the faith they've sworn to defend! Thank *God,* oh *thank* you, God, I went to a little bible school in Pennsylvania, and I was taught the *plain, simple, unvarnished* Word of God! It's *all* I know, and all I *want* to know!"

A murmur of agreement rose from the audience, with some claps, as Lucas continued:

"It was the *learned–men*–the *educated–men*–who *persecuted* Jesus! Right *before* them, when they asked, 'Are you the Son of God?' he replied, '*I am!*' And when they put him on the Cross, they *mocked* him! 'If you're the Son of God,' they said, 'come down from the Cross, then we'll believe you!' The *learned–men,* the *scholars,* the *intellectuals!*

"And on the crosses besides Jesus," he said, holding up his right hand, his voice loud but quivering, "were two thieves; one mocked him and said, 'Save yourself and us!' but the other one, the *other* one, said simply, 'Jesus, remember me, when you get into your kingdom.' And Jesus, in the middle of all that pain and misery, looked at the man and told him, 'This day, you'll be with me in Paradise.'"

Lucas looked slowly around the room at each and every one of the officers and added, "A *crook!* A *burglar! Definitely* not a product of the Harvard Theological Seminary! And he *knew* what Jesus was all about, while the so-called *men* of letters and academia *still* haven't figured him out!"

Calmly, plainly, Lucas said, "You and I could be either one of those two thieves, either the one who mocked him, or the one who begged to be let into Heaven. *Which—one—are—you?"* he barked.

The officers and their wives loved Lucas even more, their applause hearty. He went on:

"*That* is why the Crucifixion is so important to me! *That* is why it excites me! It's the story of *dedication,* of *sacrifice,* of giving your life for a cause! Like *you men here!* You officers, like us *ministers,* are *consecrated! Holy!* Sanctified for a holy cause, *your country!* Lord, bless these men, who offer their lives for our defense!" he announced, his arms spread wide, his head reared back.

The officers were moved by Lucas calling them sacred men, holy men. It reminded them of when they graduated from West Point or ROTC, when they were told they were different from the regular run of people in the civilian world. They forgot for a moment their cynicism about the bureaucracy of the Army, the foolish rules that could never be followed, the jockeying for promotions, the low pay they had to feed their families with. He went on:

"Jesus set an example for all of us to follow, those of us who accept him as Lord and Savior. For His Cause, Christians have *willingly! Joyfully! Risked* and *lost* their lives for the Savior!" As he inhaled, Lucas said, "Jesus died for me. I'm ready to die for Jesus."

More applause, with some whistles and standing. At the head table, Christine was upset by this pledge–one David made often, and meant it. Would some evil person, she feared, try to kill her husband? That was her fear, which she never told him. Lucas went on:

"In many nations on the face of the earth," he proclaimed, "the believers in the Lord Jesus Christ are being *persecuted!* And even when they're not being tortured or killed, they're *harassed!* They're *mocked! Ridiculed! Insulted!"*

Lucas aimed his face–grim, angry–at the audience and declared, "I am a *Christian.* I *accept* and *believe* in Jesus Christ as my Lord and Savior! I *believe* he *was* born of the Virgin Mary! I *believe* that he died on the Cross for my sins, and that he rose on the Third Day. I *believe* that He will come again on the Day of Judgment, when God will save His people and punish the wicked!

"That is what I believe, as a Christian!" proclaimed Lucas before the officers. *"That* is what I'm calling America back to, to come back to *God,* to the *laws* and *traditions* that have made America great throughout the world! And I offer *you* people here, *all* of you here, a *great* challenge. Jesus said that those who follow Him would be persecuted for His sake! That means to be *laughed at! Insulted! Mocked!"*

Lucas added, "Sometimes I think–with the state of morality going on in the world–sin and immorality being the norm–Christians could actually become *persecuted!*

Why? For being *Christians!* For opposing all the immorality that society has come to accept. *Yes, it could happen! If* it happened–*if* it became a crime to follow Jesus, would you be guilty? Would you *plead guilty?"*

"*Yes!"*

The yell came from a young artillery lieutenant–he just came from ROTC in a college in Kansas–who jerked up from his chair, staggered toward the podium, his face brimming with tears and red as fire. He fell to his knees before Lucas and sobbed, "Oh please forgive me, *please* forgive me!"

Lucas was startled at this outburst, but he bowed and knelt to the young officer, saying, "What sins do you repent of?"

"I–I got away—from God," stammered the young lieutenant tearfully, his lean body quivering. "All I do is curse and drink, and I–with women–" He stopped there.

"Do you accept Jesus as your Savior and Lord, and turn away from these things?" asked Lucas.

The lieutenant nodded heavily, still bowed with shame, and Lucas urged, "Then say it out loud, to everyone here, make your public acceptance of Jesus as your Savior."

The young man–his name tag on his left breast pocket read "Dryden"–rose up, faced his colleagues, and declared, "I accept the Lord Jesus as my Savior from sins, and I cast aside my sins. I will be a Christian and serve the Lord."

The officers and their families sat in an awed silence.

Lucas rested his hand of Dryden's shoulder and said, "And what about the rest of you here? Why don't you come up here like this man did, like a little child? Accept Jesus as your Savior, let him take your sins away from your heart. Come now."

Chaplain Boyce was impressed with Lucas' preaching, and Christine was as proud as ever of her husband–and relieved that no one tried to assassinate him. A crowd of officers went to the podium and talked with Lucas.

"Pretty dramatic," muttered Kirby to Watson. "Lucas's a terrific preacher, I'll give him that." Pausing, Kirby added, "but isn't that–well, is that just a temporary high? How'll that kid act later, when the high wears off?"

Watson said, "Say, I just had a thought. Maybe we chaplains could invite Lucas to dinner tomorrow, before his rally, and chat with him? Invite Greg also!"

"Sound good to me," shrugged Kirby pleasantly. "Let's talk it over with Boyce, maybe have it here"

After the officers and their wives left, Boyce walked to Lucas and said,

"Reverend Lucas, I found your preaching powerful and inspiring."

"Thank you," smiled Lucas.

"All of the chaplains of this base would like to invite you and your wife over for dinner, before your final rally. Would you like that?"

"Sure, that would be great," agreed Lucas. "What time?"

"We'll let you know where and when," said Boyce.

"Good, my wife and I'll be there, God bless you," agreed Lucas as he shook Boyce's hand. Then Lucas walked up to Christine, and they both walked out into the parking lot. Boyce, Kirby and Watson clustered together.

"He'll come," Boyce reported. "Where can we have it?"

"Right here's fine, sir," said Kirby, again spreading his arm wide. "We could easily reserve tables."

"And we don't need the whole room, sir," added Watson, waving his hand at the folding partition by the wall, "just half."

As they entered the military taxi, Lucas bellowed, "Well, Christine, how was it?"

"Oh, it was wonderful," smiled Christine, "Especially that young man coming up like he did." She knew he didn't use the little fact she provided, the poll she saw in the paper. She was happy for her husband, as any good wife would be—but he didn't use her little fact.

39

The Reverend and Mrs. David Lucas arrived at One O'clock that afternoon for their lunch with General Henninger. The general came down the stairs to greet them in the living room, having just finished a phone call to an off-base physician about a blood and urine test for syphilis (which proved negative).

"I'm *so* happy you came," said Henninger cheerfully as he extended his hand toward Lucas.

"Well you invited us," Lucas said smiling as he accepted the general's hand.

Henninger led the Lucases to the dining room, and they sat at the table. The table was set with silver salt and pepper shakers, three plates of fine china each with a coffee cup and saucer, and a silver knife, fork and spoon. All of this was set atop a large walnut table covered by a lace tablecloth. A maid came from the kitchen with a cart carrying a coffee pot, cream pitcher, and sugar bowl–all silver. The maid asked Henninger, "How would you like your coffee, sir?"

"Black with sugar," replied Henninger mechanically.

"Cream and sugar, please," said Lucas.

"I'll have cream and sugar also, please," added Christine.

"Christine, don't you take tea?" asked Lucas, as if a pattern had been broken.

"Uh, Oh–yes, please make that tea," said Christine, recovering from the shock of her perceived mistake.

Lucas leaned back and surveyed the dining room–the crystal chandelier, the mahogany paneling, the walnut furniture, and the thick red carpet-stating pleasantly, "This is a marvelous house, General. Simply beautiful."

"Good thing you don't have to pay for it," chirped Christine.

Lucas' neck muscles stiffened–*How many times did I tell her to keep her mouth shut?* He thought–but Henninger chuckled and thought of the Defense Department allocation that paid for all of the furniture. *He likes her joke,* thought Lucas, as his muscles relaxed.

"That's a fine, charming wife you have there, Reverend," said Henninger with a smile. "So pretty and so sweet, and *so* full of good humor."

Christine bent her head down and smiled lightly, in a shy, quaint gesture.

"Yes, God has truly blessed me with such a wonderful wife," Lucas decided to say, with a polite stretching of his lips.

"Yes, just like they used to be," continued Henninger nostalgically. "Pretty, devout, sweet. Just the kind of girl we older fellows were advised to marry."

"Yes, well, nowadays," said Lucas finding a theme to pick up on, "women are getting into so many fields–why, marriage and motherhood are almost totally neglected!" He began to speak urgently, as if some crisis was about to occur.

"Yes," that's right," nodded Henninger, finding nothing to argue about.

"Just look at the divorce rate!" urged Lucas passionately, not breaking his stride. "Look at the pornography! The free sexuality! The teen pregnancies! And they *call that freedom!"* he said, ending with a frown.

Lucas continued, "The Holy Bible has founded our laws, guided our minds and hearts, and saved millions of people from lives of crime and sin, myself included! I thank God some Army chaplain took the time with no to bring no to Jesus! My doing this tour–

"

(While Lucas spoke, Henninger glanced at the kitchen door, waiting for the food and hoping to change the subject.)

"–I'm repaying the opportunity, that some guy in the Army, Navy, Air Force, and Marine Corps could come to Jesus, the way I came to Him! I have such a burden in my heart for this country, and for the men of our Armed Forces–"

Lucas would have gone on with this monologue–the reasons for the tour was his favorite theme–but the maid came back with the cart, and on it was a huge bowl of salad, three small bowls, and small bottles of dressings. "What kind of dressing would you like on your salad, sir?"

"Bleu cheese," said the general.

"French, please," said Lucas.

"I'll have French, also," said Christine.

"Christine," said Lucas, "don't you have to watch your weight?" speaking as if something was different.

That was the first time Christine had heard that, but she said, "Oh! No dressing please."

Henninger bent his head forward, with his eyes narrowed, as he witnessed this.

After the lunch, Henninger returned to his office at division headquarters. He met a colonel from his staff in the hallway.

"How was your lunch with the Lucases, sir?" asked the colonel.

"I *never* seen such a *fucki*ng nut in *all* my *fucking* life!" snarled Henninger. "And that *wife* of his, boy, is she some dopey thing! Acts like some fucking *dog* around him! I'll be glad when this shit-ass show goes somewhere else!"

Word went out in headquarters: *Stay out of the old man's way.*

The Lucases arrived at the suite in the guest house. As soon as the door closed behind them, Lucas started, "Chris-*tine,* I *told* you! Don't say *anything, ever!* You could *embarrass* me!"

Christine was shocked, as if she had been slapped in the face. "The general liked it," she squeaked, trying to defend her actions.

"Just the same, keep quiet next time," Lucas commanded.

Bowing her head in shame, Christine asked hopefully, "David, could you let me please phone my mother in the hospital?"

"No *way,*" said Lucas quickly, shaking his head and his hands. "Too expensive. We can't have that!"

"But she's my *mother,*" pleaded Christine, "she'll *die!*" her eyes ready to tear up.

"Naw, she won't die," said Lucas, his tone used for soothing a frightened child, "Your mom's a fine Christian woman. She won't die. She'll pull through. She has before."

They hugged. Christine felt so safe and reassured. Then Lucas quickly let go and said, "I gotta get to the office."

As Lucas moved toward the door, Christine asked, "David, when this tour is over, do you think, like, we, you and I could take a vacation? I mean, we've been on the tour for so long, and we, you've never taken a vacation, and—"

"I dunno," Lucas mumbled, "We'll see after the tour," and he went out the door.

Christine raised her fists up; her head tightened—then she sighed heavily. Her head ached as she pulled off her shoes walked into the bedroom, and laid down—which she did a lot on the tour.

40

Lucas arrived at the Fort Horton tour's temporary offices, in the back of the theater, to take on the paperwork that needed his attention. Lucas, and Lucas alone, made the final decisions on all the groups and ministries he headed. "Hey, guys," Lucas called out to the people—Jim Corbett and Sylvia Duncan— inside the office..

"Dave, the latest *Time* magazine's on your desk," said Jim as he followed Lucas into his personal office

"Great," said Lucas smiling, then he surveyed his desk, looking at the stacks of letters and notes, the latest edition of *The Campion,* the day's New York *Daily News,* and the *Time* magazine. Lucas grabbed the *Time* and pried it open.

"It's on page twenty-three," said Jim.

Lucas flipped to the page and found the story on the crusade, which took up one and a half pages; the other half-page was for a lingerie ad.

"Look'a *this,* " grunted Lucas at the smut before his eyes, "Ain't *this* cute. Can't get *away* from it."

"Well, it's advertising that pays the bill," assured Jim. "Oh, the ACLU's at it again. They made an appeal to the Circuit Court in New York, to stop the tour on church-state separation grounds."

In one motion, Lucas rose and slammed the magazine on the desk. "When they gonna stop, huh?" he shouted, causing Jim to wince. "I'm trying to bring God's *word* to these guys! What's wrong with that, tell me, *tell me!"*

He brushed his hand through his hair, let the hand hit the desk with a thump, and added, "We beat 'em once, we'll beat 'em again."

Jim nodded, and left the room, closing the door behind him.

Lucas lowered his head to read the *Time* article. The story described the places the tour went to, the staff of the crusade, the crowds that attended, and praise from other evangelists–including from Jimmy Wheeland, who said, "Dave Lucas is one of America's greatest prayer warriors, and a great champion of his country, truly a great American."

There, decided Lucas. Did that sound like Wheeland didn't trust him, and was afraid of Lucas taking over the organization? Lucas was pleased to see a good picture of himself in his blue suit, addressing a multitude of soldiers in a baseball field.

As he read on, Lucas found a comment by a theology professor who was known to be a "Liberal," who said in part, "Lucas has remade Jesus into his own image. There is no endorsement of war anywhere in the Bible, and Lucas' image of Jesus as some sort of he-man, macho type is equally erroneous. Lucas' Jesus has nothing to do with the Christ who told His followers, 'Turn the other cheek.'"

Lucas slapped the magazine shut and threw it from him–to where, he did not care. He rose from his desk, his head and stomach starting to tighten. *Why'd they have to put that there?* He inhaled, heavily.

Turn the other cheek. Lucas knew that Jesus had said those words, in the Gospel of Matthew, chapter five-or four? No, definitely four. But didn't Jesus tell His followers to be strong and brave? To make a strong stand, even die, for their faith? Was "Turn the other cheek" to be taken literally, or was Jesus speaking in metaphor? Or had Jesus really said to let one's self be beaten up?

Turn the other cheek. Those words wouldn't leave Lucas' head. He needed to hear God tell him the Truth.

Straightening himself, he opened the door and ordered Sylvia, "Syl, hold all calls until, well, an hour." Sylvia nodded.

Lucas turned around, his head bowed, and stared at the red carpet. He had done this so many times–humbly, as a little child. It was the way to come to Jesus, either for the first or thousandth time. Lucas knelt on the floor, and prayed.

"Dear Jesus," he whispered, "I'm being besieged by doubt about the word of Thy Father. From the time You came to my heart, I've done all that I could for You, Lord. I've done all I could for Your cause. All my strength comes from You, Lord Jesus. Stand by me Lord, and never let me stray from Thy light and Thy word."

He stayed on his knees, waiting for God to speak to him. He felt the tension in his head and stomach easing.

Then suddenly the words came: *Put on the armor of God.*

Lucas straightened and opened his eyes. He remembered those words, from the book of Ephesians. He could almost hear them out loud. *Put on the armor of God.* Lucas jumped to his feet and reached for the Bible on his desk.

He opened the Bible, restraining himself from throwing it open, instead picking each page from the next, until he got to the book of Ephesians. There he found the words: *Put on the armor of God.* They were in chapter six, words written by the Apostle Paul to describe how a Christian should live, using the armor of the Roman soldier as a model.

Sure! Lucas could see it now. Be strong for the Lord! The battle wasn't of nations, but of God verses Satan! The battleground was the soul of every person! This–*this*–was the great battle! *Here* was the battle that the Christian was to fight! That guy in *Time,* he was so well educated, and he didn't know about *this?*

Lucas looked to Heaven, and walked to the center of the room. He went to his knees again, but all he could say was, "Thank you, God. Thank you."

He climbed to his feet and walked to the back of his desk, thinking, *Put on the armor of God,* a great idea for a sermon, all praise to God. Sitting behind the desk, he opened his copy of the *Champion.*

Christine strolled through the small PX near the guest house, looking at the magazines on the racks but not touching any, examining the cosmetics and toilet articles, and charmed by the colorful military insignia–badges of rank, ribbons, and regimental crests. She only wanted to stay a little bit, and then get back to the guest house. She just needed to get out for a while. Besides, David might go back to the house to change for tonight's meeting; sometimes he came back, and other times, staying in the office in back of the theater, he went straight to the night's meeting.

She moved a few steps down the men's toiletries aisle. Their wedding anniversary was coming up, and she wanted to get David something nice. She surveyed the racks of colognes, after shaves, shaving creams, and electric shavers. No, not an electric shaver, she decided, David already had one; but she would get him something. She has been saving money from her allowance from David.

41

The theater was full before the start of the second night of the David Lucas crusade in Fort Horton. In fifteen minutes, the rally would start, and the choir was bouncing through "Have A Little Talk With Jesus."

Among the crowd was Leonard Wilmont, the Airborne Ranger sergeant, who was still moved by his prayers the previous night. Wilmont had thought all day about his being saved. He who had been so selfish and mean was now a Christian. As a kid from eastern Texas, he had gone every Sunday with his parents to church. But he knew that a lot of the men who went to church also went to local whorehouses and beer joints, and that they went to church to deny that fact–to the community and to themselves.

Still, the preacher's sermons had stayed in Wilmont's mind, waiting for Lucas to bring them out. Wilmont decided: next paycheck, he would get a Bible. As he went to his seat, he felt better now that cussing, drinking, and dirty books were no longer part of his life. Now he planned to reconcile with his ex-wife, and try to be nicer to his son–to spend weekends with him (as much as his free time would allow) and to do all sorts of manly things with him together–to go to sports events, and tinker a little with Wilmont's Jeep Waggoner.

Rabbi Greg Kirshman, in a short tan jacket and blue slacks, quietly entered the theater, politely nodding and smiling to everyone, feeling both curious and happy— happy that his father would finally retire from the Michigan State Police, and he himself would be discharged soon—and curious about Lucas: *What's this guy like?* Kirshman felt like he had to see Lucas in action; he couldn't put it into words. Kirshman sought the most inconspicuous seat; he just wanted to watch. He found a seat in the middle of the row in from of Wilmont's and to the left.

Meanwhile, the Reverend David Lucas was in his office, praying: "Lord, help me to carry out this night's crusade, so that I may serve You–that I may bring Thy word to the men of our country, that they may know Thy way." Lucas was irritated with himself for not using the right words. "Give me, this weak vessel, the strength to do Thy work in the world, where sin abides. Ah-men."

Lucas got to his feet. There were three sharp knocks at the door, and Billy

Calloway's voice saying, "Five more minutes, Dave!"

"Yeah, I'll be there," responded Lucas, who then picked up his Bible from his desk, and walked out of the office. He sat down next to Christine, who glanced at his face, and wished she could say something, but didn't want to anger him.

Exactly at eight, Major-General John B. Henninger strode to the podium and began:

"I welcome you, ladies and gentlemen, to this the second evening of the David Lucas Crusade here at Fort Horton," Henninger ground out. "Again it is a pleasure to present to the young men of this division"–who he thought were stupid, lazy, and semi-criminal–"such a sterling example of good citizenship."

("I'm getting sick of this shit," thought Henninger.)

"To begin this evening's program, I now introduce Mister Billy Calloway–"

("What a fucking faggot!" thought Henninger.)

"–who will now sing." He sat down.

The organ and piano sounded the opening bars of "The Crusader's Hymn," and

Billy Calloway stepped to the podium. As Calloway sang "The Crusader's Hymn," he decided that the hymn was really not military; he sang of trees, meadows, sunlight, and angels, and especially the pure holy Jesus. Calloway finished the hymn and the audience applauded, some raised their hands high.

Cheers and applause came from the audience as Lucas rose and took the podium. The applause faded, and Lucas intoned, "Let us now pray. Let every head be bowed, and every eye be closed, and let there be no disturbance in the audience.

The audience fell silent. Lucas raised his right hand and prayed:

"Oh, Lord, bless this, the second evening of the Armed Forces Crusade here in Fort Horton. You have heard the applause and cheers here, Lord, let this show that these people here are ready to receive Thy Son Jesus as Lord and Savior. In His name, we pray, Ah-men."

The audience replied, "Ah-men," and Lucas spoke:

"*What*–is a Christian? Many of *you* here, who've been considering accepting Jesus as Savior and Lord, are asking that question. *How* do I live for Jesus? *How* does a

Christian act in the world? All of you here, who *are* Christians, stand up and let them see you, C'mon," he then sang, "Stand up, Stand up for Je-sus." He popped a smile.

The people stood and applauded, and someone whistled. Lucas called out, "Hallelujah!" pulling the mike from the podium, and spoke again:

"You know now that a Christian isn't *some* spaced-out, wimpy guy who's like this–" He raised his eyes to heaven, smirking, and flattened his palms together as if in prayer. Titters came from the audience, and Lucas went on:

"Christians *look* pretty much like everybody else in the world," he drawled merrily. "They also *act* just like the other people in the world– to a *point!*" He chuckled lightly as giggles came from the audience.

"Christians *live* in the world, but they're *not part* of the world," he continued. "Who *are* these crazy people?" Solid laughs came from the audience– "And *what* is it *about* them that *makes* them so special?"

Those who were already Christians felt that they were in on the joke; Lucas continued:

"A Christian," he began, "accepts Jesus Christ as his Lord and Savior. A Christian knows that he is capable of sin, that he has the *potential* for sin, no matter how supposedly *good* he is! No matter how good a person lives his life, Man is still *wicked,* Man is still *sinful.* And his only hope for salvation lies in Jesus.

"A *Christian,*" Lucas went on, "knows that Jesus is the Son of God, who came to earth and died on the Cross to redeem wicked, sinful Man! Jesus preached the Word of God, the message of redemption and forgiveness of Sin to *wicked, sinful Man!* And Jesus was crucified by *wicked, sinful Man,* and Jesus died on the Cross to wash away, with His precious blood, the sins of–" Here the audience joined him– *"wicked, sinful Man!"*

The audience applauded at this. Kirshman sat with his arms folded, observing Lucas in action. Kirshman saw that Lucas was an experienced public speaker who knew not to get excited too early–he was just building up. Lucas went on:

"A Christian *knows* that he is a sinner. *Drugs! Fornication! Lying! Murder! Stealing!* Maybe he *hasn't ever* done these things, but he knows that Man, *wicked sinful Man,* is not only *capable* of these things, he *has* done them!"

He declared, "Don't *ever believe* these people who say that Man's really good inside! That Man, with-*out* God, with-*out* Jesus, can save himself! They Say, 'God, leave Man alone, he doesn't need You anymore. He can get along well without You. You don't even *exist* anymore. You're *dead!*'"

Lucas allowed the silence to permeate the hall, and people were nervous. Then, Lucas assured, "Let me tell you something. The hottest places in Hell are *reserved* for people who say that God is unnecessary, that He is dead. You find people like that in the papers, in the electronic media, in colleges, even *pulpits!*"

His voice picked up speed and volume as he added, "And people *believe* this junk! And so they turn *away* from God, and they themselves also end up in *Hell!*"

There was booing and groans, almost of pain, and one man called out "Stand up for Jesus!" Lucas smiled, inhaled, and went on:

"So we turned away from God," mourned Lucas, his head bowed. "And for turning from God, what was the result? Crime going way up! Pornography right in our face! Our economy falling apart! America, once the champion of liberty, has become a laughing stock, so that any two-bit dictator can insult us!"

Lucas continued, "Right on the racks in the drug store, you can find pornography right in front of our children!" The TV cameras got a close-up of Lucas' face contorted with grief and pain. "All over TV, in ads–" His mind returned to the lingerie ad in *Time*.

He stopped, and let the audience shout "Ah-men! Praise God! Keep talkin', Dave!" with a shower of applause. In a shrill voice, someone could be heard blubbering "Jesus save us! Jesus save us!" It was a female staff sergeant, seized with holy fervor, crying real tears; all she could say was "Jesus save us!"

Lucas ordered into the mic, "Lou, get a shot of that!"

In the projection room, Lou Wheeler, the TV director for the Armed Forces Crusade, blandly ordered, "On three," and the camera on stage left turned to the female sergeant. She appeared on the main monitor, then on the video tape for distribution to stations around the country and on cable. Lucas said, "Praise the Lord!" The audience applauded, and the female sergeant calmed down, her body damp with sweat as she wiped away tears.

"Like I said, all this plays on our lowest desires. The Holy Bible teaches us, 'Thou-shalt-not-commit-*adultery!*'" he exclaimed, rapping the podium with each word. "The word of God *says* that! But prostitution's right out in the *open* and the cops can't seem to *do anything* about it! People are talking out loud, *bragging*, about extramarital affairs! Marriages ending in divorce! Venereal diseases, including AIDS, this new one, killing people! And *abortion–!"*

He paused for effect and breath, then mourned, "The baby, the life inside the womb of the mother, is treated like some–*garbage*–to be thrown away. The innocent victim of the mother's *wasteful lust!"*

The audience howled, sobbed, and moaned. Lucas inhaled again, and went on:

"And let's not forget *ho-mo-sex-u-al-i-ty*, shall we?" There was a groan of disgust from this mostly military crowd. Lucas drawled, "Let's talk about this gang of *niiice, nooormal–perverts!"* snapping the last word. "This gang of *degenerates! Sinners!* Yes! In case you *forgot*, homosexuality is *still* a sin, *always* has been, *always* will be!"

"Kill the faggots!" shouted a first sergeant. Many of the young men shouted and applauded.

Lucas raised his hand and proclaimed, "No, we *don't* kill them! Lou, get a shot of me on one!"

Wheeler said, "On one!", and Lucas' face was on the monitor, the frame closing in, his expression anxious and eager to speak.

Lucas declared, "I want to say something to the TV audience. If any of you are homosexuals, I *must* tell you that what you're doing is *wrong!* Your sin's become accepted by Man, but it's *still* a sin! It was homosexuality that destroyed the Greek civilization and the Roman Empire, and every other great civilization that tolerated it! But now, you have to *face* the *wrath* of *God!* You must face *AIDS,* the new plague! There's *no* cure for it, and there *never will be* a cure, because God won't allow it! God has brought *about* this disease to *punish* you for your sins! Homosexuals, what you gotta do is *abandon* this sin and *turn to Jesus! Turn to Jesus! Turn to Jesus!"*

Applause and cheers rose from the audience–thunderous clapping, shouting and yelping. Lucas stood erect and beaming; he thought about what a scare this would bring to the fags and fag-lovers. Christine smiled and clapped, as she always did whenever David said something; Calloway grinned and raised his arms to Heaven, hollering "Praise God. Thank you, Jesus!" and Henninger, for once during the entire evening, applauded with some enthusiasm, since he had no love for gays either. Regan sounded some notes on his organ, and Michaels played an arpeggio on his piano.

In the audience, Wilmont led the applause in his row, standing and calling out, "Praise the Lord, keep talkin', Dave!", guided by memories of church revivals and services back home–memories that were suppressed by his time in the Army. Wilmont also glanced at the guy two rows in front of him—Kirschman—just sitting there, arms folded, not applauding or shouting. Wilmont felt irritation in his mind—*What's this guy's problem?*

Lucas continued:

"There you have it. The results of trying to do without God! A Christian knows this. A Christian knows that God will, definitely punish those who would go against His will and His word. In the beginning Adam and Eve disobeyed God's commandments. He told them, 'Don't eat of the fruit of the tree.' As long as they obeyed that order, they were happy and life was good. But they *ate,* first Eve, then Adam! It *would* be a woman, *wouldn't* it, who sticks her nose where it didn't belong!'

The audience laughed, including the women, who appreciated the attention. Lucas resumed:

"They disobeyed God's commands, and they were *punished* for it! So man fell from grace! Man has proven to be weak and wicked, and in need of guidance. Do you need more *proof* of that?"

There was more applause and calls of "Ah-men! Yeah, praise the Lord!" The stage lights heated Lucas' face and shirt, damp with sweat, and he took off his jacket. An *"Eeeee-yow!"* came from the audience, followed by applause. Lucas folded the jacket once in half and placed it on his chair beside Christine, and Henninger sat squinting, wondering how much Lucas' suit cost. Lucas spoke again:

"Jesus, for an individual and a nation, is the only way to salvation from this mess of sin and perversion. John, chapter three, verse sixteen, says, 'For God so loved the world that he gave His only begotten son, that whosoever believeth in Him shall not perish, but have everlasting life.' That's *who-so-ever*. That's *you*. No matter what the sin, Jesus will cleanse you of it! That's why He died on the Cross, to take the sin away from you. Are you on dope or on the bottle? Jesus can save you. Are you a thief? Jesus! Are you a fornicator? Do you go out with whores? *Jesus!"*

His voice grew more excited, as did the mood of the crowd.

"Are you lonely or sad? *Jesus!"* he continued. "Are you frightened and helpless and weak? *Jesus!* Is your marriage failing? *Jesus!"*

At this point, the audience had been saying *"Jesus!"* right along with Lucas, just as he had hoped.

"Who died on the Cross for you?"

"JE-SUS!"

"Are you looking for joy and happiness?"

"JE-SUS!"

"Who wants to take your sins away?"

"JE-SUS!"

"Ah-men and ah-*men!"* He ended, and the crowd cheered, whistled, and shouted hallelujahs. Someone danced in the aisle, hugging their Bible.

Wilmont laughed and raised his hands–and still thought about the dark-haired guy in the next aisle who wasn't cheering or yelling, just sitting there—not knowing it was the base's Jewish chaplain.

Kirshman was a spectator, an outsider. He didn't feel the passion going on around him in the audience, but was impressed with Lucas' speaking. Kirshman heard people calling out, "Oh, yes, Lord Jesus, heal us," sighing and sobbing.

"Jesus changed my life!" declared Lucas. "He *changed* the life of *David Lucas! Pot-smoker! Drunk! Whore-chaser! Foulmouthed! Trouble-causing David Lucas!* And He can change the life of *anybody! You,* boozer! *You,* criminal! *You,* whore-chaser! *You,* homosexual!"

Then, calmly, simply, he said, "And you so-called 'good people!' Maybe you haven't taken any dope. Maybe you *haven't* cheated on you wife! Maybe you haven't stolen! Good for you! You haven't missed anything!"

There were light laughs from the audience, and Lucas continued, "But you need Jesus just the same, maybe more so! Satan likes to get at people who don't think they need God and Jesus. People who think they can be righteous by themselves can easily be led astray to commit sin, without their knowing it!"

Lucas spoke these words, knowing what he was talking about. Some people muttered, "Oh, yes, Lord Jesus, heal us." They sighed and sobbed.

Moving back behind the pulpit, Lucas continued, *"That* is part of being a Christian! Knowing that sin rules the world! Knowing that Jesus died on the Cross for your sins! And the replacing of sin in one's *heart* with Jesus! Have we accepted the sinfulness of the world? That we accept sin as human nature? That we accept Man's sinfulness as part of his being a human being?

"They say, 'It's human to fornicate, to go wild with sexual promiscuity!' As long as I've accepted Jesus as my Savior, I have *never* committed fornication, *never* slept with a woman besides my wife, *never* given way to lust, *never* used pornography–"

He then turned to Christine, who, during this talk about fornication, had felt her back and arm muscles tightening. Lucas stepped over to her, rested his hand warmly on her left shoulder, and said quietly, "And I remain faithful to my wife, to my marriage vows to God, to never even *think* about other women, than this little lady that God has given me, praise the Lord."

Applause rolled from the audience; Christine smiled and rested her little hand on his big hand.

Lucas smiled at Christine, strolled back to the podium, and added, "Also, narcotics, tobacco, and alcohol are accepted by the world as normal, even by those so-called *'good'* people, who don't *know* Jesus! Well, since accepting Jesus, since knowing Him as Savior, Lord, and Friend, I never *needed* that stuff that'll kill you! I have no *room* in my life for that stuff, because there's too much of *Jesus* in my life for any of that stuff! Clean living, righteous living, is the way of the Christian! And clean *speech* is clean living! I say that because when you accept Jesus, you accept a way of *living.* You accept a way of *doing,* you accept a way of *being!* And you don't bring your *mouth,* or your *soul,* into the *gutter!*

"And finally, a Christian knows," he said calmly and hopefully, "that Jesus will come again. Jesus is returning, do you *hear* me? And do you know what'll *happen* then? All the evildoers will be eliminated, wiped out from the face of the earth! *All* misery, *all* suffering, *all* pain in the earth will end!"

Then, calmly but strongly, "Wars will be no more. Jesus will set up His throne in Jerusalem, and then, and *only* then, will there be peace and happiness. The dream of the Garden of Eden will finally be fulfilled. Praise the Lord!", and there was a tidal wave of applause.

Lucas gazed at the sea of people in front of him. He was hot from the lights, and he was tired. Yet he was happy; they were all cheering Jesus. He turned around and looked at Christine, who sat with a gaze of hero worshiping on her pretty face, and Henninger, who just sat there. Lucas returned to the audience and continued, still in that strong, calm voice:

"*All* of you need to come to the Cross and wash your sins in the blood of Jesus.

No matter how big or how small the sin, Jesus will save you. That's why He died on the Cross, to save you. That's how much He *loves* you. The Gospel of John chapter three, verse sixteen, I think is simply the greatest verse in the Bible. 'For God so loved the world, that He gave His only begotten Son, that whosoever believeth in Him shall not perish, but have everlasting life.' Let us pray.

"Dear God," he prayed, "let the message of Jesus, which I have preached tonight, reach the hearts of all here. Let all souls who are thirsty for the Water of Life, let them come and drink from the well of Jesus, which never runs dry. Let all here know, as I know, the joy and peace of knowing Jesus as Savior and Lord. I pray, in the name of Jesus, ah-men."

"Ah-*men!*" the crowd returned joyfully, followed by applause and cheering. Lucas stood there grinning in his shirtsleeves, his body hot and damp. On cue, Michaels and Regan began playing "Just As I Am," and Lucas declared, "I now welcome all new Christians into the Kingdom of Heaven. If you have just–"

He was interrupted by applause and cheering, then he went on.

"If you have just accepted Jesus, *please,* come on down to speak with the prayer counselors here in front of the stage."

At that, the young men, either in dress greens or suits, all carrying Bibles, formed a line in front of the stage. The choir sang "Just As I Am," and people filled the aisles to head down front. Rabbi Kirshman stayed at his seat and waited for everybody to go down before he walked to the exits.

Wilmont saw that the dark-haired guy— Kirshman—stayed at his seat, but he wanted to shake Lucas' hand. He saw Lucas and Christine shaking hands with the soldiers and civilians crowding the stage.

"Hi, Reverend," called out Wilmont.

"Hello, again," replied Lucas cheerfully, and they shook hands.

On the stage, General Henninger went up to Lucas and said, "I'm sorry, Reverend. I have to go."

Lucas smiled and nodded, and Henninger went to his quarters to get ready to leave for Miss Sadie's brothel, thinking *Oh, God, after this shit, I need a good fuck so bad!*

Wilmont, after shaking Lucas' hand, climbed the sloping aisle, thinking about the dark-haired guy. *Looked like a Jew,* he thought, *a little weasel-faced Jew!* By the time he got out of the theater, he recalled other things from his church back home: *Jews didn't do a lick of work, didn't even turn on the lights when it got dark, but had everybody else working for them.* Wilmont grew up not having any Jews to compare these statements against.

He got outside the theater and crossed through the parking lot, swiveling his head around, trying to find the Jew son-of-a-bitch. His head felt a pressure—he had to do *something.*

He couldn't find the bastard. He jumped into his Jeep, bowing his head as if he was in pain, and slammed his fist on the dashboard.

Wilmont didn't believe in arguing with an enemy, or feeding them tea and crumpets. He was a *soldier,* an *Airborne Ranger,* hard-core to the max. And he was on the side of Jesus, and he would serve Jesus just like he served his country. He thought,

Where's a Jew around here?

After parking his Plymouth and speaking with a staff sergeant and his wife, Greg
Kirshman entered his bungalow at Officers' Row. Every house on the street looked on
the outside like every other one. Kirshman had driven this route many times daily: east on
Howitzer Street, turn onto Caisson Avenue, third house on the left. Even the kids' toys in
the yard looked the same, along with the family cars.

"So, how was it?" asked Kirshman's wife, Debbie, from the front door.

"Aw, well," he shrugged as he gave her a smooch, "Sergeant Brayden and his
wife have been talking divorce, but I spoke with them, and I think they're in no rush now.
They have a kid, they're taking him into consideration. Where's Jenny?"

"She's sleeping," Debbie stage-whispered. "She looks so cute." Barefoot, she
stood six inches shorter than her husband, with dark red hair cut at her jawline. "You
been hearing about Lucas, I guess, from the other chaplains? He worries me"

"Yeah," Kirshman nodded." Watson and Kirby spoke about him earlier. I didn't go to the Officers' Club breakfast. Not my scene anyway."

"You think he's dangerous," she suggested.

"Yeah, I guess," he agreed, upon entering. "Any coffee?" he asked as he sat in the living room. He was trying to decide what to do. Read? He was too tired to concentrate, and it was 10:30 PM.

"Sure," Debbie answered.

Kirshman pulled himself up from his chair to go to the kitchen–

A shrill crash! Kirshman spun to see glass falling on the floor, the big front window gaping open, and a wrench with a piece of paper taped to it rolling on the floor. He heard the roar of a car's engine and the screech of a tire.

Kirshman and his wife felt a flood of emotions at once–anger, confusion, fear, bewilderment, shock. They moved to stare at the wrench, which stopped rolling. There was a crying from Jenny's bedroom.

At that, Kirshman regained control. He said straightly, "Jenny!" and pointed to her room. Debbie ran to Jenny, and Kirshman barked, "Call the MPs!"

Kirshman was curious about the paper taped at the wrench's head. The paper looked like a pamphlet of some sort. He made sure not to touch it, perhaps there were fingerprints.

He saw there was something scrawled on the back of the pamphlet:

Jeu

Accept Jesus Crist or luse soul

No, not *this!* thought Kirshman. You heard about these things, but...He looked at the bottom of the pamphlet and read, "David Lucas Ministries, Inc." That guy again!

42

Lucas and Jim–Lucas' brother-in-law and manager for the tour–finished their business in the theater to prepare for the following night's service. They got their coats on, went outside, and took the base taxi.

Once they settled in the cab, Lucas sighed, "Oh, man, this tour. It's wearing me down."

"Wanna take some time off, Dave?" asked Jim, worriedly.

"I *can't* take time off," said Lucas. "What would I *do?"*

"Chris needs to spend time with you."

"I know," Lucas said. He said nothing more about the subject. "You following the news about your mom, Jim?"

"Yeah," Jim intoned.

They got to the guest house, said their good-nights, and went into their suites.

The digital clock on the night table said eleven-fifteen. Christine lay on her side of the bed, tossing and turning, fearing to close her eyes. Then, she heard a light door-slam, and some footsteps on the carpet.

"David?" she asked.

"Yeah," he answered in a tired drawl and walked, slightly hunched, into the bedroom. He took off his coat and jacket, then his tie, and laid them on a chair. On the seat of the chair, his pajamas–pale-blue cotton–were folded neatly (by Christine), and he grabbed them and walked into the bathroom to change.

Christine lay on her side of the bed and watched him stride into the bathroom. He flicked on the light, leaving the door half open. Then he undressed, not even thinking that Christine might be watching him; he was mentally and physically tired.

She hugged herself, holding on to the blanket, as she watched Lucas undress and get into his pajamas. She felt an invisible hand on her breasts, crotch, and stomach, and she found herself in a fetal position; she surveyed his back, stomach, legs, and buttocks, and she could see the shadows of the crack between his buttocks through his jockey shorts. She felt a knot between her legs, and she impulsively rubbed herself–she *had* to.

She quietly squealed–

The buzz of an electric shaver came from the bathroom. Lucas hummed "Just A Closer Walk With Thee," as he moved the shaver over his face.

Hearing the hymn, Christine stopped moving her hand, and she whispered, "Lord, I'm sorry. Please forgive me." The knot in her crotch unwound. She breathed deeply and tightly shut her eyes, her hands holding the blanket.

The buzzing stopped and Lucas emerged from the bathroom. He picked up the Bible on his night-table–his Bible for everyday use–and just held it. It felt so good in his hands. It was the Word of God, the guide to life. Just to *hold* it...

He went to his knees and prayed:

"Lord God, help me tomorrow to preach Your uncompromising Word. Make me strong in your Truth, give me the words that will bring people to the way of Your Son Jesus. In His name, ah-men." Christine prayed right along with him, silently.

Lucas moved to the bed and jerked the covers over him.

"G'night, honey," Christine purred, as she moved closer to him.

"G'night," moaned Lucas.

Christine wrapped her arm around Lucas, and kissed the back of his neck, moaning pleasantly, but Lucas muttered, "Christine, *no,* I gotta get some *sleep!"* Christine rolled over to the other side of the bed, and cried.

43

It was the last day of the David Lucas Armed Forces Crusade at Fort Horton, Kentucky. Tomorrow, the organ, piano, and the electrical and television equipment would be packed into the jet liner (donated, along with the pilots, by a major airline).

That morning, Lucas rose at six to once more perform his daily jogging ritual. He trudged along, wearing his pedometer and stopwatch, his feet going *plat-plat-plat* on asphalt, crunching on loose gravel, falling silent on grass. He sneezed – some dust got into his nostrils.

His mind was blank–nothing to think about. Christine –

He told her that they might drop back to Jersey to see her mother, just a quick side trip back, not even a whole day. Meanwhile, Jim would oversee the setup at the next stop on the tour.

Lucas jogged for about a mile, then – he felt something enter his body, like a flood of new life, the runner's fabled "second wind."

He took the second wind as a sign from God – to do what? He ran faster, feeling no discomfort, and when he got to the front door of the guest house, he checked his stop watch – 17 minutes, six seconds. His chest pounded, and his knees and the soles of his feet hurt. He endured both as he walked to the elevator and made his way to his suite.

By the time he had finished with his weights, showered, and got into his suit – this time, charcoal-gray – Christine was awake through still in bed. Lucas approached the bedroom door as she asked, "David, can I help in the office today? Please?"

"Naw, don't worry about it," he grunted over his shoulder as he got out of the suite.

Christine fell back on the mattress; maybe she could sleep a bit more? The only sounds she heard were the cars driving on the road, the mumble of the engines, and the squishing of tires on wet asphalt; it briefly rained the night before.

She was not going to sleep. She pushed the covers off her and showered, then put on her clothes – a while ruffled blouse and a paisley floral skirt. She then put on her coat, took her purse, and went outside to the PX cafeteria.

The food in the cafeteria was good, she thought, not too greasy. As she ate, she reflected: David never let her do anything for the crusade. Nothing. Why did he want her to come with him? It was about as bad as when he had gone on that campaign in '78; but at least then she had had friends and family she could be with. Now she had no one to go to; every week, it was simply a new group of strangers to meet, then, after a week's time, she would never see them again. She missed Fran and her friends back in Erno; after meeting her mom, maybe she could meet up with them?

She finished her breakfast, carried the tray to the trash can, and set the tray on top; then she went outside.

Puddles still lay on the parking lot. Fifty degrees and the sun beamed, and the wind brushed past. Christine wondered if David knew about her little rambles outside while he was at his office. This was the most adventure she had – out of the building, out in the open, the weight of her worries was off her. She scanned the other shops at the PX: the ice-cream parlor, the barber shop, the jewelry store, then inside the PX itself, showing the guard her guest ID – David wondered what she would do with it, but the base authorities gave them guest IDs as a courtesy.

Christine saw all that the PX had: the magazine rack, the stereos and TV's, the men's and women's clothes. It was all familiar to her, although the TV's on display were a good diversion for a while, playing old sitcoms and game shows.

She headed outside, feeling again liberated from the confines of four walls. *What to do now?* She wondered.

She looked at her watch – 11:32. The watch was a gift from Fran for her wedding. Maybe that was what she could give David, a watch. Did she have enough money set aside for a watch? An inscription?

Her freedom now bored her. She walked back to the guest house, taking the same way back that she had taken to get there.

She entered the suite, took off her coat and bag, and sat down – not fell, but sat like a proper lady – on the chair. She inhaled, letting her body painfully unwind, every muscle loosening. Now what would she do?

She saw a stack of magazines by the end of the couch: *Ladies Home Journal, Reader's Digest, Family Circle*. Christine got up and picked up the *Reader's Digest* that was on top of the stack. There, she found horror stories about the government entering the social and economic sector; she passed by these, as these were issues concerning men. There were reports about cancer and its treatment, adventure stories about boys caught in a deep pit, and the latest news about garlic. Christine agonized in worry about the plight of the boys and was relieved at their rescue; she was pleased at the medical breakthroughs in cancer; as for garlic – should she try to slip some to David?

Christine lowered the *Digest* on her lap, tilted her head up, and thought about it. David never said anything about her cooking, either positive or negative – or, for that matter, about any of her work around the house.

She set the *Digest* back down, and picked up one of the other magazines, which featured the adventures in macramé and needlepoint, baking a turkey, new shapes for women's hair, and stars of film and TV posing in a variety of sweaters.

She took her time with each and every article, even though she had read the same magazines four times before.

Five minutes after two, she finished the last *Family Circle,* then set it back neatly on the pile. She sat back down, letting her gaze roam around the room – until it landed on the TV.

Christine picked up the remote and turned the TV on. She pressed the channel button once, watch what was on for a bit, pressed it again, watched for a bit–then she settled on a soap opera, one she was somewhat familiar with.

Reading the magazines and watching the TV could not completely prevent those thoughts. They squirmed and wriggled to the front of her mind: *David treats me like a stupid child; David says nothing kind about me; David never lets me help out at the office or in his work; David leaves me all alone for long times.*

Christine never thought that she believed these thoughts. When they arose, she told herself: *I'm being selfish; a woman always supports her husband, no matter what he does; David loves me.*

44

Lucas arrived at his office at the base theater. The regulars – Billy Calloway, Roy Murphy, Sylvia Duncan, and Lou Wheeler – greeted Lucas as he entered.

"Who's first?" he smiled.

"Me, Dave," announced Wheeler, and they both went into Lucas' office.

As Lucas sat at his desk, Wheeler – sixty years old, with a full head of light-gray hair – warned, "Dave, I think we gotta problem with the crew."

"What kind of problem?" asked Lucas.

"Well," Wheeler drew out, "just a feeling, mainly, but I trust it, though. The guys're talking union."

Lucas sighed, let his hand *thump* on the desk, and muttered "Great, that's all we need, labor troubles. Just when we're going so great!"

"You know, if it was up to me," said Wheeler, "I'd *leave* 'em right here! Let 'em *walk* home, if they don't wanna do this kind of work!"

"No need for that, Lou," assured Lucas with a smile – he was pleased with his own sense of compromise. "Think of the fallout that would cause."

Wheeler calmed down, straightened his back and agreed, "Yeah, and we'll still need a crew. Don't worry, Dave. I know I can kid these clowns along."

Wheeler left the office, and Lucas took off his jacket and landed back on the chair. He picked up the phone, dialed, and heard a ringing on the other end that concluded with a hollow click and a woman saying, "Kyle Law Offices."

"Yes, this is the Reverend David Lucas. May I please speak with Mister Kyle?"

"Yes, sir. One moment, please."

There was another click, Lucas was put on hold, and then, Gordon Kyle's voice came on; "Yes, David?"

"Hey, Gordon, did you know the ACLU is –"

"Yes, I heard," Kyle interrupted. "But don't worry, we'll beat them again. My guess is that Liz Malory will be on their team again, and they'll try a new angle."

"Okay," muttered Lucas.

"Anything else, David?"

"Naw, not right now, Gordon. But I'll let you know."

"Fine, David, good day."

They hung up.

Lucas looked at the paperwork covering his desk. There was Hennessy's proposed budget for the next fiscal year; an application to continue the Ministries' tax exempt status in the State of New Jersey; phone messages he had to get back with; a statement from the bank that handled the Ministries' money; and letters from major contributors with suggestions for sermon topics (which Lucas read, respected, and ignored).

45

At four o'clock in the officer's club, the chaplains were prepared for their dinner with the Lucases. Greg Kirshman was still furious about the wrench and threatening message thrown through his window. The crash…Jenny…Debbie…Kirshman rubbed his forehead and clenched his teeth. Chaplain Floyd Kirby walked up to him and asked, "Gonna be okay, buddy?"

"Yeah," grunted Kirshman with a nod. "You know, I'll never quit wondering, what could have prevented this thing."

"Would it have made a difference?" stressed Kirby, leading Kirshman to the other chaplains. Then smiling, he added, "You're among brothers, Greg."

Kirshman smiled and replied, "You don't have to tell me twice, Floyd," resting his hand on Kirby's shoulder.

There was a clatter at the front door, and the sound of Boyce's voice declaring, "Good evening, Reverend and Mrs. Lucas!" as Boyce led the Reverend and Mrs. David Lucas into the dining room. Lucas was in a blue suit and red tie, and Christine was in a red turtleneck dress; both smiled as Boyce introduced them to each of the chaplains,

shaking hands with each until they reached Kirshman.

"And this is the Jewish Chaplain, Gregory Kirshman," said Boyce.

Kirshman shook Lucas' hand and stated, "How are you, Reverend? Mrs. Lucas?"

"Good evening, Chaplain," Lucas and Christine answered at the same time. Lucas

glanced swiftly at her; Christine knew she screwed up again; her head drooped.

They took their seats at the dinner table; Boyce stood and prayed the blessing:

"Dear Lord our God, we ask Your blessing on this food that it may sustain our bodies for

Thy service. In Thy name, we pray, ah-men."

The food that Boyce asked God to bless was baked chicken, baked potatoes,

onion soup, string beans, chocolate pudding with whipped cream, and coffee. As they ate

– deciding that the food was pretty good, for once – they talked:

"What effect do you think the tour will have, Brother Lucas?" asked Ben Watson.

"How do you mean, Brother Watson?" replied Lucas, glancing at Watson's name

tag.

"Well, in general," said Watson.

"In terms of people signing commitment cards, it's been very good," stated Lucas. Christine sat silently, and watched everything, giving her mind something to do, trying not to be noticed.

"Commitment cards, Reverend?" asked Kirby.

"Yes," explained Lucas. "A person signs his name on a card, writes his address, and we send him literature and study guides to help him in his new faith."

"Is that really a good way to tell if a person's really converted?" asked Kirby worriedly.

"Well," said Lucas, trying not to look foolish, "If a person isn't sincere, God would know better than I would, wouldn't He?"

"True, true," said Kirby, nodding.

Lucas wanted to say something to Kirshman–one of the People of Jesus–but Lucas kept eating; he would wait for some excuse to speak to Kirshman. Lucas glanced at Christine from the corner of his eye; she just sat there, cutting the meat daintily. Good

372

girl, thought Lucas.

"If you don't mind my saying so, Reverend," stated Chaplain (Captain) Anthony Zilkov, the Russian Orthodox chaplain—a shortish man with a round face and rectangular body— "as far as I can see it, evangelism is a little shallow in its approach."

Lucas tilted his torso forward to Zilvov and asked, "Really? How so?"

Zilkov continued, "The way I see it, Reverend, evangelism has a rather fast-food-ish quality to it. Like, all the answers to the great questions of life are packaged into neat, tidy boxes, without taking into account the great philosophical issues that have worried scholars for centuries."

"Well, Tony," Watson intervened, "you have to start with the basics first before you get into anything deeper. That's true in anything, especially religion. First a person becomes a Christian, then he works his way up to the great theologians, you know, Tillich, Augustine, Calvin –"

"That's true," agreed Lucas, believing that he had found a kindred spirit, "In fact, I never even heard of those great theologians so called, and I don't care to know anything about them."

"Never?" asked Zilkov.

"Well, I *have* heard of them," said Lucas, grinning, "but I hope you get my point. And I'll tell you something, gentlemen," beginning to make a sermon about it. "I'm a Christian, pure and simple. My beliefs are the simple truths of the Holy Bible, pure and simple." He found his catchphrase; he would use it. "And it's the pure and simple Gospel of the Lord Jesus Christ. That's the thing that will bring our nation back onto its feet. The humanists and the intellectuals can laugh about it, but the Christians will restore the pure and simple values of this land, pure meaning that the values wouldn't be changed or compromised, simple, that any idiot can understand them."

"Still," said Kenny, "nowadays the churches have to face issues that the Apostles never dreamed of, like, nuclear weapons, sexual issues, and ecumenical relations –"

Lucas raised both his hands and broke in, "Brothers, no matter what the question, Jesus is the answer! *That's* what I believe. As for ecumenical, well, I can't go along with it! Then I'd have to say that other religions are equally valid and correct, and as a

Christian, I can't accept it!"

At last, Greg Kirshman, with a small smile, chimed in: "Reverend Lucas, don't you think that people are entitled to their *own* opinions about religious beliefs?"

Boyce and the other chaplains aimed their eyes at Kirshman. Then he said, "Excuse me, please, Reverend. I'm a little shaken up about something that happened last night."

"What happened, Chaplain?" wondered Lucas with real concern.

Kirshman told the entire story, including the note written on the Lucas pamphlet.

"I'm…I'm sorry about the whole thing, Chaplain," stated Lucas sadly. "I hope you don't blame all Christians for that incident."

"No, Reverend, I don't," assured Kirshman.

Finally, Lucas had the opportunity to minister to Kirshman, and keep the conversation going; he said, "I'm sure that whoever did this got the Christian message all wrong, because the message of Jesus is one of love, not violence."

"Still," Watson stated, though Lucas wanted to keep talking, "people, that is, many Christians, tend to forget that part, that part about Love. Shame, you know, Jesus told us to preach Love, and people who say they follow Jesus can be the most hate-filled and ruthless people in the world. They can be bothersome to people when they talk about religion. They can shove their kids to Sunday School, an' the kids can get turned off."

"I believe," declared Lucas proudly, "that Christian parents have the duty to send their kids to Sunday School, whether they like it or not. Like the Bible says, 'Train up a child in the way he should go.'"

"On hearing some of your statements, Reverend," stated Kirshman, still polite, "one would consider them rather, shall we say, intolerant?"

Lucas smiled, then laughed a growing laugh. Kirshman's anger remained polite as he asked, "Did I say something funny, Reverend?"

The chaplains thought, *Oh my God, something's gonna bust*

"Please excuse me, Chaplain," replied Lucas, his laughing spasm at last out of the way, "but in all my career as a minister, I've had that thrown at me. I've been called a bigot, narrow-minded, intolerant. I'm just saying what the Bible says, and I'll keep saying it. I know I'm being persecuted for my work and my faith."

"Persecuted, Reverend?" asked Kirshman.

"Yes, I *am,*" replied Lucas. "Jesus said that those who follow Him would endure persecution. Not just from a government, but the world–people insulting and ridiculing those who follow Him."

Boyce worried that this dinner party would fall apart. He smiled and happily announced, "Brothers, Mrs. Lucas –" this was the first time had anybody noticed Christine – "I can see that we have differences, but happily we can come together in a spirit of brotherhood."

"I agree. I agree completely," said Lucas, smiling, not suspecting anything going wrong, "but still, I'm a Christian, and so I have to believe in the rightness and truth of my faith, and that all other religions are false."

"But, Reverend Lucas," began Kirshman, still not showing his anger, "you must understand that what you call false religions aren't false to the people who believe in them. Can't you accept that?"

"No!" Lucas chuckled, "Jesus told us, 'I am the Way, and the Truth, and the Light, no man can come before the Father but by Me.'"

Lucas sprang to his feet. Boyce and the other chaplains felt like Lucas had gone out of control. Christine felt like David was doing something wrong, but she could not identify what it was.

"We don't deny the link between Christians and Jews," Lucas announced joyously, "but really, our Savior Jesus is the fulfillment of all the prophecies of the Old Testament!"

Kirshman pulled himself to his feet and muttered, "Excuse me, I have to go," and he stepped from the table.

Lucas smiled and continued, "Chaplain Kirshman, as a Christian, I've always been supportive of your people and Israel." Kirshman headed for the closet as Lucas added, "All the prophecies have been fulfilled and Jesus is soon to return! But the Jews out of foolishness have rejected Him as the Messiah–" he followed Kirshman to the closet– "but God did not reject the Jews, and someday the Jews will learn that Jesus really *is* the Messiah that you've been waiting for so long!"

Kirshman spun to Lucas and snarled, "Reverend Lucas, I don't agree one bit with you beliefs, but I would *never* force my beliefs on you! Why in God's name are you trying to do that to me?"

"Because it's *the truth!*" Lucas shot back, still smiling and still not believing that Kirshman still had not gotten the message. "You know, Chaplain, your people would have had a lot better time's it if you accepted Jesus in the first place!"

"You *are* a bigot, Lucas! You saying that guy that terrorized my family was some sort of holy man?"

"Oh, boy, some people are so stupid, you gotta knock them on the head to wake them up!" barked Lucas with a grin, right in Kirshman's face. Lucas turned to Christine and ordered, "Come on, Christine, we're going!" as he stepped to the door. Christine was getting up, but he snapped "Come *on!*"

She joined her husband at the door, and they left, leaving the chaplains in bewildered silence.

Boyce walked over to Kirshman, who droned tiredly, "Are you angry at me, sir?"

"No, Kirshman," sighed Boyce. "I'm amazed that he could be an evangelist."
They had a fraternal hug.

"How'd they let him on this tour?" worried Kirby?

"The real question is why," added Kirshman.

As the Lucases climbed into the military taxi, Christine whimpered, "David, I
don't feel well, I guess it was the food. Could you please drop me off at the guest house
tonight so I can take a nap?"

"Yeah, okay," Lucas grunted.

When they got to the guest house, Christine got out of the car and entered the
guest house. Lucas watched her get inside, then the car drove off.

Christine really didn't feel well, but the food had nothing to do with it. She had
seen her husband being insulting and acting rude. How did his actions match her image of
him as her husband? All the way back to the room, the same thoughts kept coming back:
David treats me like a stupid child. He ignores me. He won't let me do anything. I've

been a good wife to him, and he doesn't appreciate it.

But this time, she could not, and would not, try to think of anything to counteract those thoughts.

She went inside the suite, switched on the light, and found an envelope. Seeing the words *Western Union* and *Mailgram* on it, Christine set down her hand bag and opened the telegram:

We regret to inform you of the death of your mother, Mrs. Helen Hoyle Corbett, at 3:37 p.m., of a heart ailment.

Crossland Memorial Hospital.

Christine read this, and started crying. Then she wept in earnest, crumbling up the paper in her fist, sobbing loudly and shrilly, looking around, for something, someone, anyone, anything. She fell into a chair, crying out, "I can't! I can't!"

46

This was the third and final evening of the David Lucas crusade in Fort Horton. Leonard Wilmont swaggered down the aisle and sat in the fifth row, by the aisle; he wanted to be closer to the action. It all came back to him, everything that the church back home had taught him: love of God, love of Country, the country's English heritage, as opposed to the foreign papist people and ideas–and the *Jews!*–coming from Europe. Lucas' preaching brought out Wilmont's religious background, which brought out the beliefs his church members had shared, along with the big picnics the local Klan klavern held every June. Wilmont thanked God that the Reverend Lucas had shown him the way.

The choir, directed by Roy Murphy, sang, "The Garden," with accompanying music from Johnny Regan's piano and Dick Michael's organ. The song sounded sweetly over the dull rumbling of the crowd as people took their seats.

Backstage, the Reverend David Lucas paced, his Gucci shoes sounding *clack-clack-clack* on the cement floor. He was angry – about the Jew chaplain that had attacked him, and about Christine not being by his side, like she should be. *Liberation, my butt,* thought Lucas, *I work on all this, I get insulted, and she takes a nap! Women have it so easy!*

He paused his thoughts to receive a message from an aide to General Henninger. The general sent apologies to Lucas that he could not come; he would not be able to attend the rally, as he had important staff work to attend to (but the aide did not say that the "work" was with the staff of the brothel).

As Lucas watched from backstage, the evening's performance pleased him – the choir, the preparations, and the music were all were in top form. But he was still angry. Billy Calloway tapped Lucas' shoulder. "Dave, what's wrong?" he asked kindly.

"Ah, Christine's sick, and the dinner went all wrong!" muttered Lucas.

"Just listen to the music," recommended Calloway. "Music can heal so many things."

Lucas stopped pacing and listened to the choir and the musicians perform "The Garden", and its lyrics describing strolling in the cool spring morning with Jesus and the joy that stroll brought. Lucas' head and stomach unwound; Jesus was with him.

Christine lay on the bed. The clock on the nightstand read exactly 8:00. She knew that the crusade was about to begin.

Already, she had accepted the fact that her mother was dead. David had told her that her mother would not die. But she had.

All of her feelings about David were negative. She cooked and cleaned for him, had risked her life to bring forth a baby, had stood by him in his work–enduring his absences and putting up with his scolding when she said something. She did not hate David; she just did not want to be around him.

She sat on the edge of the bed. She rested her face in her hands. The money...

She remembered the money she was saving in her purse, for a gift for their anniversary. Then she remembered that whenever David gave her money, he would say, "Just don't buy anything stupid." So she had saved the money – for him. She went into her purse and looked through its folds: two hundred dollars.

Guilt crept in. Was she being ungrateful to David? She sat down to think it over.

The guilt passed.

She picked up the phone, and as she dialed and waited, she wondered if Fran had gotten word of Mom's death too…

Fran had indeed received a mailgram at her apartment. When she had finished reading it, she asked the young man who she had earlier invited over that night to please go back home. Fran sat down to sort her thoughts. Her phone rang, and as she answered she heard the voice of her little sister saying, "Frannie?"

"Oh, Chris," sighed Fran in relief.

"Did you hear?"

"Yeah," replied Fran, "how do you feel?"

"Bad," Christine replied. "Fran, I can't live with David any more. But I don't know where to go."

"You know you can stay with me. But did you have a fight or something?"

"No," Christine groaned, "but he said that Mom wouldn't die. He wouldn't let me speak to her on the phone. I wanted to talk to her!" She recounted the dinner with the chaplains, heaved a sigh, "Could you really put me up for…well, until I get things straightened out?"

"Sure," reassured Fran, "Y'got money t'get up here?"

"Yes, I do," replied Christine. "I saved it to get a present for David. Some present, huh?"

"How you getting up here?"

"By bus. There's always a bus station on every base."

"Yeah, and busses coming to New York end up in the Port Authority," added Fran. "I'll wait for you up there."

"Okay, right. Bye."

"Bye."

Christine packed her suitcases, and then, as she put on her long coat, she remembered: David. She had to leave a note for him. She had read enough novels to know that when a wife walked out on her husband, she left a note – and her wedding ring. She found the yellow crumpled paper on which the mailgram was written, and wrote on the back of it:

David, I'm leaving you. I can't live with you anymore. I'm going to stay with Fran.

She could not think of anything else. She left the paper on the bed, pulled the wedding ring off her finger, and the golden cross pin she wore for the crusade from her dress, and placed them on the note.

She then opened the door and dragged the two suitcases out into the hall, her arms aching up to the shoulders, and then she closed the door. She went down to the ground floor, and then dragged the bags to the front door, glancing at the desk clerk. Would he recognize her? But as Christine lugged the suitcases, the clerk did not raise her head from the phone she was speaking into.

She got outside, and a cab, dropping off its passenger, pulled to the curb. The driver, a sixty-year-old former policeman, asked, "Where to, ma'am?" punctuating the sentence with a smile.

"The bus station," replied Christine. "Could you please –"

"Help with your bags?" concluded the driver. "No problem!" He got out, opened the trunk, put the bags in the trunk, slammed the trunk shut, and opened the door for Christine.

"Thank you," she said as she entered the vehicle. The cabbie got in, and pulled the car from the curb.

"Were you visiting someone here on the base?" asked the driver.

"Oh, why, yes," said Christine.

"Yeah, I get a lot of people visiting their loved ones here."

They passed by the theater where the rally was being held, the words DAVID LUCAS CRUSADE on the marquis. "You see this?" asked the cabbie nicely.

"Oh, well, not really," answered Christine, feeling bad about lying. But was she lying? She wondered...

After a three-minute drive, they arrived at the bus station, which was in the same building as the taxi office. She handed the driver the fare, and he said, "I'll help bring your bags in."

"Oh, thank you very much," she replied.

"Part'a the job, ma'am," he said with a shrug.

At the ticket window, the cashier, a heavy woman with pale yellow hair asked. "Yes, ma'am?"

"I'd like a ticket to New York, please," Christine requested.

"Certainly. Will that be one way or round trip?"

At that question, Christine realized that a line had to be crossed. "One way, please."

The cashier left, and after some clicking noises, returned to the window with a ticket. Christine paid.

The cashier said, "The next bus leaves at 11:10. Will you need some help with your bags?"

"Yes, thank you," replied Christine.

After leaving her bags in the clerk's keeping, Christine settled in one of the room's curving plastic chairs.

She looked at the clock over the ticket counter – 8:14. David would be starting his sermon now.

47

At the flick of Roy Murphy's wrist at exactly 8:00 PM, the choir finished singing. Murphy stepped from the choir to the podium; this was a last minute change of plans, as General Henninger was not around, having to tend to his "business." Yet this often happened, so Murphy was prepared:

"Welcome, brethren in the heart of Christ," Murphy proclaimed in his usual florid style – while a few of the other staffers wondered when Murphy had last taken a vacation – "to this, the final day in this holy tabernacle, the David Lucas Armed Forces Crusade for Christ. Every stop we make on the tour, every hall, every field we assemble in, no matter what its purpose in the secular world, is hallowed ground."

Lucas sat at the stage next to Murphey, and still felt a weight in his guts. The Jew chaplain, the other idiot chaplains, Mallory, Christine not on his side, the ACLU…His face felt heavy, and he was grimacing. He pressed his fingers together. He was on holy ground, like Murphy had said, and he was ready for battle. He might work this in his sermon.

Applause rose as Lucas got to his feet and approached the podium. Silently, he gazed out at the audience and heard a faint murmur. The lights were dim over them, and all he could see was a blur of bodies.

"Let us pray," he began. "Dear Lord our God, we seek Thy grace and guidance. We beseech Thee, oh Lord, that You would come in our midst, and show us the way, through Thy son, Jesus, in whose name we pray, ah-men."

The audience repeated "Ah-men," and Lucas rested his battle-worn bible beside the podium.

"From the book of Ephesians," he announced, "I read the sixth chapter, verses ten through seventeen. 'Finally, my brethren, be strong in the Lord, and in the power of His might. Put on the armor of God, that ye may be able to stand against the whiles of the Devil. For we wrestle not against flesh and blood, but against principalities, against powers, against the rulers of the darkness of this world, against spiritual wickedness in high places. Wherefore, take unto you the whole armor of God, that ye may be able to withstand in the evil day, and having done, to stand. Stand, therefore, having your loins girt about with truth, and having on the breastplate of righteousness; and your feet shod with the preparation of the Gospel of peace; above all, taking the shield of faith, wherewith ye shall be able to quench the fiery darts of the wicked; and take the helmet of salvation, and the sword of the spirit, which is the word of God.'"

Lucas closed the Bible, stepped away from the podium, and stated, "Christians are in a state of war. *Always.*" He paused – it was a great dramatic effect – and added, "There are forces at work that would seek to destroy the faith of people who have no hope but in Jesus. And do you know where the worst of these forces are? You can find them in *churches!* Yes, you heard right! In *churches!"*

His voice began to rise as he said, "The reason for the downslide of morals in this country was *be-cause* of the *un-willing-ness* of the *churches* to take a *stand* for *Jesus!* To tell the world that Jesus *lives* and Jesus *saves!* To tell the good news of the salvation of souls through the *shed-blood-*of *Jesus!* They can't bring themselves to *do* that!"

Lucas thought to the forces arrayed against him: the chaplains in the dinner; Mallory challenging him and his work; Durkin and the rest of the fags; Christine not with him now, at the stage, being weak like all women were. He continued:

"The Christian has to face enemies of the spirit–doubt, fear, and temptation. The early Christians had to face these things, but not the things we have to face now, such as drugs, pornography, and sexual promiscuity! But *still,* the words of Paul the Apostle ring true! 'Put on the armor of God!' And when you put on the armor of God, you *will win* over the forces of darkness, and *win* in the war of the spirit!"

A loud "ah-men" and some applause. Wilmont was pleased at this description of Jesus; he enjoyed the talk about the struggle of the spirit between God and Satan, and took the side of Jesus to win. Wilmont listened to Lucas and liked this idea of Jesus as a great warrior – not the candy-ass peacenik he had heard about since the 'Sixties. This was a Jesus he could go along with!

Lucas was not satisfied; the reaction of the audience had been visceral, but he sensed something was missing. He felt it in his gut. He waited – another dramatic pause. Then he prayed: "Oh Lord and Savior Jesus Christ, it is You alone we seek in our hour of need. We are surrounded by evil temptations, people and things that would cause us to stray from Thy righteousness."

He spoke slowly, letting them all hear every word: "Be Thou always there, Lord Jesus, to guide and protect us, to give us the strength for Thy cause. In this world we face all sorts of iniquity and darkness–"

At this, a young black PFC felt his skin tingle, and he grimaced, rubbing his face.

"And by Thy grace and light, may we see that Thou art the Way, the Truth, and the Light!" he said quietly, "In Thy name, we pray, ah-men."

Applause rose, higher and higher. Palms slammed together, throats went sore from shouting praise. Wilmont laughed and thrilled at the good old-fashioned prayer straight from the camp meeting. Lucas too felt at peace with himself. He went on:

"As the chapter says, "taking the shield of faith, wherewith ye shall be able to quench the fiery darts of the wicked, and take the helmet of salvation, and the sword of the spirit which is the word of God.' We Christians are *always* under attack! Time and time *again* the Devil hits us with his weapons of slander, doubt, innuendo, and lies!"

He raised his Bible up with his right hand and proclaimed, "But we have in our hands the sword of the spirit, which is the word of God! We're going on the offensive with the Holy Spirit, and we're gonna *attack* sin and darkness with the sword of the Lord, this Holy Bible, and we *will* smite these enemies of Christ absolutely, and we *will* gain the victory for our Lord and Savior Jesus Christ!"

The audience howled and yelped with joy. Lucas sang into the mic, "Amazing grace, how sweet the sound, that saved a wretch like me, I once was lost but now am found, was blind but now I see."

Another tidal wave of applause and cheers rose from the audience, some of the crowd standing. From behind him, Lucas heard the claps and yells of the men working for him – Murphy, Calloway, Regan, and Michaels. Lucas felt over heated, so he took off his jacket and said, "Getting to work now," and the audience again raged joyously. He went on:

"Like the song says, '*Onward*, Christian Soldiers,' *not* backwards! *Preach* the Gospel to every creature! Tell *everyone* about the saving, healing power of Jesus! How He died on the cross for our sins! How He rose on the third day, and rose to Heaven, and of His return! How!–"

He stopped, then continued in a soft, low voice, "How He saved a low-down, drunken, pot-smoking excuse of a soldier, and made him a minister of the Holy Gospel, an evangelist, a bearer of God's message! That's right! *God* has given *me, Dave Lucas,* the *honor* of preaching His message to *you*, the defenders of our nation!"

The audience screamed, shouted, waved, and called out, "Thank you, Jesus! Praise God! Hallelujah!" Lucas went on:

"If someone did not attack the forces of sin, some of us would not have heard of the Gospel, the words of Jesus." He paused, looking like he had had a revelation. "If a chaplain didn't come to the stockade when I was a guest there –" he paused again to let then appreciate the nice gallows humor– "I would *never* have heard the Gospel of Jesus, would *never* have changed from the doping, whoring, whiskey-drinking no-good punk I *was,* to being a minister of the Holy Gospel, standing before you now! For that I love You, Jesus, forever and ever, *ah-men!"*

Again, applause from the audience and a waving of hands. Lucas loosened his tie and unbuttoned his shirt collar, and went on:

"Wherever I go, in my church in New Jersey, the Armed Forces Crusade, and in the civilian crusades I've done on the street, *some-one* always thinks he can insult, harass, and mock the faith of Christian like you and me!" As he spoke, he recalled Kirshman doubting that Christians were still persecuted. "The *world* is *not* a safe place for Christians. Like the old hymn says, 'This world is not my home, I'm just a-passin' through!'"

The crowd muttered a collective "Uh-huh" and Lucas continued:

"I'm *not* ashamed of the Gospel, and I'm *not* ashamed to proclaim it, and I'm *not* afraid to put my life on the line for it, for the cause of Christ and the Gospel!"

He then took a more conversational tone: "You know that *so* many Christians have given their lives for Jesus. They did that rather than give up their faith. They knew their reward for their faith was in Heaven. In Russia – you remember Russia? The Soviet Union? The great beacon of hope for the world?"

The audience had a great laugh, and Lucas added, "In Russia, they're arrested for proclaiming the Gospel! You can even get *killed* for it! They do it *differently* in *this* country!"

His voice rose: "They call you a *nut*! A *weirdo!* A *screwball*! They *mock* you and our Lord Jesus! But some day, *some day,* you may have to put your *own* life on the line for Jesus! Like me, there's always someone out to *kill* me! Yes, they want to *kill* me, for my *faith!* Well, here I am! *Kill* me if you wanna, but you'll *never* kill Jesus! C'mon, you dirty atheist murderer, *here I am!"*

The audience fell silent, thinking, *Someone's going to kill Dave!* They expected a gunshot somewhere. The MPs, who were bored, woke up and grabbed their 45's. The men behind Lucas glanced at each other: *Has Dave gone crazy?* Lucas stood still, arms hanging loosely, face shiny and slick with perspiration, his shirt sticking to his body.

It took a couple of seconds for everyone to realize that no one was about to kill Lucas, after which began a trickle, then a river, then a flood of applause. Lucas felt tired; he had done enough for that evening. Looking at Regan and Michaels, Lucas nodded, and they played the opening notes of "Just As I Am." The young men from the audience, wearing suits and dress greens, strode to their places in front of the stage.

At that, Lucas announced, "Now, this is the time to make your acquaintance with Jesus. The prayer counselors are here, ready to help you into the Christian life. Or maybe you somehow strayed from Jesus. That's okay, he wants to meet you again. Come now and accept Jesus."

Then, the choir sang "Just As I am," and half the audience eased down the aisle. Wilmont stayed at his seat, waiting for the crowds to pass by before exiting. Before being a Christian, he would have shoved people away, muttering, "Get the fuck out the way!" Now, he was a Christian, and he was nice and polite and respectful to people.

By 10:40 PM, the theater was empty. David Lucas was on the empty stage, janitors sweeping the debris away. Lucas' lungs hurt, his arms hurt, his eyes burned and his skin was still wet with sweat. He was pleased with the way the evening, and the tour in Fort Horton, had gone. He slipped on his suit jacket and strolled to the guest house.

He entered their suite and closed the door behind him. The bedroom light was lit: *What could she be doing?* He wondered. He found the bed undisturbed, not even a wrinkle, and a piece of paper–the Mailgram–with the wedding ring and cross pendant in on it. "What the –" muttered Lucas, as he read the note.

Lucas panicked, a tension striking him, feeling pressure behind his eyes, as if he was about to cry. He ran into the living room, swiveling around. *Christine! Where's Christine?* He raced to the elevator, punched on the buttons furiously, and hammered down the stairs, across the lobby, and out the front door – just in time to see the bus to New York, with Christine inside, drive past.

Christine stared out the tinted window, watching David rush out the house to scan the base in terror. She felt…nothing. He could not see her because of the tint.

Lucas felt drained, empty. It sank in: Christine had walked out on him. His head lowered as he entered the building. Brother-in-law Jim ran at him, his face twisted with worry, and said, "Dave, something just happened—"

"Jim, Christine just ran away!" said Lucas.

"Dave, my mom's died!"

"Why would she do that?"

"I need some time off!"

"Time off for what?"

"My mom died!"

The news of his mother-in-law's death was a new shock to Lucas. "Is this real?" he asked.

"Yeah," Jim replied as he showed his copy of the Mailgram.

Lucas unfolded the Mailgram, read it like it was a message from God, and muttered, "Maybe this..." He left the sentence hanging there.

"Okay," Lucas announced in a low, dull, voice, "The crusade's suspended for a while, until this thing's settled."

They went back to their separate rooms. Lucas was weary, his body weighing on him. It was getting close to midnight, too late to do anything that day. *Christine,* muttered Lucas. *Oh, Lord, help me!*

Lucas pulled the belt, hissing, from his waist, folding it once. *She walked out on me. After all I did for her, the little slut!*

He swatted the bed with the belt–one, two, three times–then stopped and shouted, "Christine! Wait'll I get my hands on you, bitch!"

Lucas heard a thudding in the hallway, and Jim dashed into the room, demanding, "What's the matter, Dave?"

Lucas looked at Jim and barked, "What are you, stupid? My dear loving wife's walked out on me!"

"She's also my sister!" snapped Jim. They stood facing each other, then Jim added, "Dave, don't you ever try to harm her, understand?"

Lucas just stared at Jim, then, backing down, he calmed down and said, "Jim, I'm sorry. I'm just upset. Forgive me." They shared a manly hug.

Jim walked out, himself calming down—he recalled Dave had a temper—and Lucas collapsed on the bed, falling fast asleep from weariness. No one was there to hear his thrashing and moaning, his calling out Christine's name while using words he had not used in years –"fuck," "shit," and "cunt." Then he howled in his sleep, as if in pain, calling out, "Christine! Where are you?"

Christine sat in her seat in the bus, the heater blowing hot air on her ankles, the engine of the bus emitting a dull hum. She sat stiffly and nervously, fearful of the other people on the bus. She was glad to be away from David, but what about the future? The safety of her marriage was gone.

48

Fran leaned against the stairwell at the bus depot of the Port Authority building, waiting for the Nashville bus with Christine on board. A guy in an orange sweat shirt over a black t-shirt stared at her and fondled his crotch; Fran looked around for a cop to walk towards if this creep came toward her, but she didn't want to leave before Christine arrived.

The poor kid, Fran thought. She always needed someone hovering over her, telling her what to do; first Dad and Mom, then Dave. Her sister was like a lost child.

It was 6:43 AM; Fran straightened when she saw a bus pull into the spot where the bus from Nashville was to arrive. Fran walked to the depot's door and saw Christine exit, wearing a wool overcoat even though it was in the low 'sixties.

Fran called out "Chrissie!"

"Frannie!" she replied, and they hugged.

"Welcome to New York, stranger!" said Fran, grinning. "Need help with the bag?"

"No, I'm okay," she replied nervously, but Fran helped her with the big, heavy suitcase, and loaded it into the trunk of her Toyota.

"Thanks a lot, Fran, really," said Christine wearily. "I hope I won't be a burden to you, Fran."

"Naw, don't worry," assured Fran as they entered the car and drove off.

"Don't you have to work tomorrow?" asked Christine worriedly.

"Most of my work I do at home," Fran replied.

"I don't know what happened," Christine began wearily, slowly. "Once the telegram came, everything between David and me just ended. It was like there was nothing between us in the first place."

"If you feel like crying, it's okay," advised Fran.

"I don't," calmly replied Christine. "I don't feel anything for David anymore. I don't hate him or love him."

They stopped at a red light and Fran asked, "Are you scared?"

"Why?"

"You just flew the coop, broke into the world on your own," Fran explained. "Dad won't help, and David's out of the picture. I'll give you as much help as I can, though."

"Have you heard anything about Mom's funeral, the time and location?" asked Christine.

"Don't know," said Fran with a shrug. "Most likely it'll be Pastorini's." They parked and Fran said, "Here's my humble abode."

The humble abode was a three-story brownstone in the Village. They entered the building and entered Fran's apartment on the second floor.

"This is a nice place," remarked Christine.

"Tired?" asked Fran.

"Oh, yeah, very!"

"You can sleep on the sofa, I'll get it," said Fran as she began pulling out the bed from the sofa. Christine changed into a flannel gown, got into and she fell asleep instantly.

Christine stayed in bed until a little after eleven. She woke up, her mind much clearer, and she could see the details of Fran's apartment – most notably the plants in brass pots, which Fran watered carefully, and the orange and black cat patrolling the floor. The cat jumped onto Christine and snuggled next to her on the sofa.

"Hey," smiled Fran, coming in from the small kitchen. "I see you met Dusty. How you feel?"

"I had this dream," softly recalled Christine, "I was – it was dark, and these arms squeezed me, and I struggled but I couldn't break free. Then I saw David's face, and he was smiling. He was enjoying seeing me wrapped up like that."

"I called the hospital," said Fran as she sat on a side chair, brushing the lint from her bare feet. "The funeral *is* at Pastorini's. The viewing's on Monday and the service is Tuesday."

"Dad'll know by now I left," said Christine anxiously. Then she said, "Fran, were you ever angry at me?"

"For what?"

"Did you ever resent me? About how the folks seemed to favor me? Always watching me all the time, trying to make me what they thought was good?"

"Naw," said Fran, shurgging. "They were part of another time. You hungry?"

"Yeah, a little."

They went the apartment and into a café Fran favored in the Village, the Cup of Love. Once inside, Fran called out happily, "Hey, Lily!"

Lily was the owner of the café, a Greek woman with long black hair and a long purple dress. She smiled widely and hugged Fran, saying, "Frannie! How are you?"

"Fine, Lil, fine," she agreed as she added, "this is my sister, Christine."

Christine was a little nervous about new people, but this woman in purple was warm and friendly. She and Fran sat at a table.

"So, what would you like?" asked Lily.

"I'll have the tuna salad," said Fran.

"Uh, me too," nodded Christine.

After Lily left, Fran began, "Well, hon, what're your plans?"

"Plans?"

"Yeah, with your life."

"I know I can't go back to David."

"Does that mean a divorce?"

Divorce. Christine had learned, from church and her marriage, divorce was both immoral and socially unacceptable. Nobody divorced, even though the couple could not stand each other; the gossip could spread widely.

"Couldn't I just not go back?" asked Christine.

"Not that easy, Chris," Fran warned. "There are legal things involved. A divorce will mean a clean break, and a new start."

Christine nodded, knowing that what her sister said made sense. "David will fight like mad to prevent a divorce. I know that much about him."

"Then you need someone who'll fight like mad for *you*," Fran said, resting her elbows on the table. "Liz Mallory's the only name I can think of."

Christine was mildly shocked at the mention of that name. She recalled David having spoken the name in anger. "Why her?" she wondered aloud.

"I know her," Fran replied. "She handled a case where a client refused to pay me."

"But what about payment?" asked Christine.

"I'm sure we can work something out," assured Fran. "Besides, your future's at stake."

On the shelves, the office of Elizabeth Mallory had leather-bound books – statutes of the City and State of New York, Supreme Court decisions – that blended with the robin's-egg blue carpet, and the curtains opened to let light in. Liz's desk was made from plain oak with a glass top. Behind the desk was a teddy bear from her boyfriend.

Liz leaned at her desk facing Christine and said, "Sure, I'll take your case. But I gotta warn you, I'm sure David will hire Gordon Kyle for this. Kyle's going to say that there's no grounds for divorce."

"I have to try anyway," Christine said flatly, "but, please, Miss Mallory –"

"*Liz,* honey," she assured.

"Please, Liz, don't say the divorce isn't possible."

"I didn't say impossible, just difficult," assured Liz. "I know Kyle, and I can be sure he'll pull something."

"Still, I'm going to fight it," stated Christine.

"How close were you to David?" asked Liz.

"What do you mean?" asked Christine with concern.

"How often did you make love?" Liz knew this could be a delicate issue, but she believed in being straightforward. "Honey, you can trust me," she said, smiling, and then she added, "We're all women here." Christine smiled at that.

"Every time he wanted sex, I was scared," Christine recalled, feeling a strange sort of self-confidence. "He'd just, well, jump on me, and when he was finished he'd fall asleep. Ever since he lost that campaign in New Jersey, though, he was too busy to do it, too preoccupied."

"Lousy sex, not too good grounds for divorce," Fran said, and they all laughed.

"Don't believe it," replied Liz. "But again, don't think it'll be easy."

"As long as David isn't around, I feel safe," Christine said.

49

The press releases came out: the David Lucas Armed Forces Crusade for Christ was suspended until further notice, due to family problems. The tour's crew– the camera crews and musicians–were told to wait for word of when the tour would resume. When the news media asked what for comment, the Ministries' Office Manager Gary Hennessy answered with a resounding "No comment!"

Meanwhile, David Lucas sat in the living room of the parsonage in Erno, New Jersey. He looked again at the article in *The New York Times,* headlined, "Wife of David Lucas Sues For Divorce, Citing Irreconcilable Differences."

Lucas read the article again:

"The wife of New Jersey evangelist David Lucas sued in Newark County Common Pleas Court yesterday for divorce from her husband, citing irreconcilable differences...

"Mrs. Lucas, the former Christine Corbett, has retained the services of Elizabeth Mallory, Esq., who has gained prominence in handling legal matters for feminist groups.

Rev. Lucas has been conducting a worldwide evangelistic tour of U.S. military installations.

"When asked about her decision to divorce her husband, Mrs. Lucas said, 'I don't feel that I can live anymore with my husband. He treated me like a child incapable of intelligent thought or independent action. He has not conducted himself in a matter fitting a Minister of the Gospel, a profession that I hold in high esteem.'"

What happened? thought Lucas. What could he have done wrong in his marriage? He took care of her, provided for her, and she had walked out on him. Why? She always obeyed him, cooked for him, took care of the house, kept herself pretty for him. He liked that – and she had *seemed* grateful.

Mallory again! She had prompted Christine to say that stuff. *The feminists! That was it!* decided Lucas. They got to his own *wife!* They were evil, the feminists! He knew that, but he had no idea –

The phone rang, and he grabbed it. It was Colonel Paul Essington, an Army public-relations officer who was the Pentagon's liaison to the Lucas Ministries for the

Armed Forces Crusade. He was a thin-faced man who, Lucas was pleased to know, was active in a Christian fellowship for officers at an evangelical church in Arlington.

"Good evening, Reverend," said Essington pleasantly.

"Oh, uh, hello, Colonel," said Lucas, off balance.

"I've heard of your troubles with your marriage," said Essington, "and I'm happy to let you know that we're all praying for you and your wife."

"Yes, thank you, Colonel," said Lucas, sighing.

"The reason I called, Reverend," began Essington in an official tone, "is that the White House has taken a great interest in your crusade. The administration was wondering if you would be interested in a private-sector, private-citizen foreign policy initiative."

"Yes, go on," said Lucas gravely.

"The administration," added Essington, "is seeking to organize private citizens and groups to do two things. First, to pressure Congress to support the administration's policy in Central America to prevent further pro-Soviet incursions in the region. You know, Reverend, that Congress doesn't really understand the situation down there, the threat to legitimate, allied governments."

"Uh, hum," agreed Lucas. "Go on."

"Then, second," said Essington, "the Nicaraguan resistance forces, the so-called Contras, need material assistance–such things as food, clothing, medical supplies, and so on. In this private program, Reverend, the resistance movement would continue to hold together and fight the Sandinista regime, giving continued hope for the movement, until Congress gives its full support for the resistance."

"Yes, I heard talk about this," said Lucas, "Christian groups chipping in on this. There was even a conference about this in Washington about this. Wasn't there?"

"Yes, there was," said Essington. "I was at that meeting. Reverend Jimmy Wheeland was a guest speaker, and he spoke well about the project."

"This sounds very good, Colonel. I would like to be active in this, but I have to take care of the Crusade, and my problems. Please keep me posted, okay?"

"Will do, Reverend," Essington replied, and they made their good-byes and hung up.

Lucas sighed. The work of evangelizing had to go on. He had to get Christine back, then resume the tour. *Why, Christine? Why?*

The phone rang again, and Lucas grabbed the receiver. "Hello?"

"Brother Lucas," said the voice. It sounded familiar.

"Yes, who is this?"

"Jimmy Wheeland."

Lucas' heart jumped. "Oh, Brother Wheeland, how nice of you to call."

"I've heard about your problems, Brother, concerning your wife."

"Oh, yes, Brother, it's…I can't describe it."

"What do you think is responsible for this, do you know?"

"It's the feminists, no doubt," said Lucas. "How did they get to her? She was never interested in that sort of stuff."

"Well, Brother," replied Wheeland, "I'll have a prayer for you and your wife in my program this Sunday and every Sunday this goes on. This, as you know, is a fight for the family unit. God wants the family to be preserved."

"Yes, Brother, He does."

"Do you need anything else, Brother?" asked Wheeland.

"I don't think so," said Lucas, "but I'll let you know." Then he had a flash idea – "Wait!" He straightened up in the couch and said, "We can–the NCPC–we can begin a campaign against divorce! We can tell the public of the dangers to women that divorce can bring! And to the kids!"

"Hm, yes, I agree," said Wheeland thoughtfully. "We have to discourage couples from divorcing, for the sake of society and our children. I'll bring it up with the board and keep you informed on how far we go."

"Great!" said Lucas smiling, and they made their good-byes.

As Lucas hung up the phone, he realized: this was a test from God. God was allowing David Lucas to suffer through a trial, an ordeal, to make him a better man. God did that, Lucas knew. He caused Job to suffer terrible ordeals to test his faith, to challenge him, to see if he would hold on to his faith. Pain, suffering, misery, they were gifts from God.

Lucas knelt on the floor, and got ready to pray, but he didn't know what to pray. He pulled open one of the Bible he always carried; he needed something, some word, from God. He aimed his eyes down at the Bible, praying that God would guide him. He found himself reading the tenth chapter of Second Kings: "And Ahab had seventy sons in Samaria. And Jehu wrote letter, and sent to Samaria, unto the rulers of Jezreel, to the elders, and to them that brought Ahab's children..."

That told Lucas nothing he needed to hear at that time, so he let the pages fly backwards to the book of Isaiah: "Ah, sinful nation, a people laden with iniquity, a seed of evil doers, children that are corrupters: they have forsaken the Lord, they have provoked the Holy One of Israel unto anger, they are gone away backward...

"Zion shall be redeemed with judgement, and her converts with righteousness.

"And the destruction of the transgressors and of the sinners shall be together, and they that forsake the Lord shall be consumed."

Lucas was thrilled at the words he had just read. The evil and wicked shall be punished. God would bring His wrath on those who transgress against God. The feminists, the atheists, the homos and the preachers who said it was okay to sin, the destroyers of the families in America – God knew who they were, and He had their number.

Excited at this rediscovery of that passage of scripture, Lucas flipped the pages forward to Second Timothy, chapter three:

". . .all that will live in Jesus Christ shall suffer persecution.

"But evil men and seducers shall wax worse and worse, deceiving, and being deceived. . .

"All scripture is given by inspiration of God, and is profitable for doctrine, for reproof, for correction. . ."

Lucas had read this before, but he was reading it again, but with a new appreciation. It made sense now: God would protect those who love and worship Him, and also reproach and chastise their ungodly ways.

Lucas closed the Bible and got to his feet. Then he walked to the middle of the den. So much turmoil, *so much. . .This, all this*, thought Lucas, *on me!* He knelt on the floor again, his hands clasped, and muttered, "Lord, save my marriage." That was all he could say. He squeezed his eyes shut, as if in pain. He repeated, "Lord, save my marriage."

Then the thought came: *God will save my marriage!* He heard the words: *Accept. Believe. Obey. Love, honor, and obey. Trust and obey, for there's no other way, to be happy in Jesus but to trust and obey.*

He felt better now, and rising to his feet, He then realized that his show was on. He turned the TV on and found himself back in Fort Horton, on the third day of his crusade there. He was pleased with his performance.

50

The funeral of Helen Hoyle Corbett, held at Nick Pastorini's funeral home, was a major

social event. Helen was dressed in a formal gown of blue silk that matched the faint tint

of her finely-styled hair and her turquoise earrings. The casket was of polished bronze

and ringed by a huge collection of flowers.

The Pastorini funeral home resembled a stately old southern mansion, a classical

structure with a wide parking lot in front. The mourners for Helen Corbett gathered in the

largest room, with its pews, white stucco walls, and (presumably) marble trim. Helen's

eyes were shut and the make-up made her look like a mannequin. Many of the women

who passed by the coffin remarked about how nice her wardrobe and accessories were.

In the front row sat Richard Corbett, as his friends and business acquaintances

offered condolences. He did not cry, not now, and not when he first heard of his wife's

death, after taping an editorial supporting more defense spending ("When it comes to the

defense of this country, no amount is enough!" he proclaimed.). He had heard the news,

and sighed: it was over. Then, hearing the news of Christine leaving David, Corbett had shouted, "How could she?" Then he inhaled, and sat at his desk to write notes for an editorial in favor of cutting funding for Community Legal Services.

David Lucas entered the room, walked up to Corbett and shook his hand. "How're you doing, Richard?" asked Lucas.

"Bad times all around," Corbett replied tiredly. "The FCC's on me again. Plus I hear that someone in the company's trying to set up a union. So how are you, David?"

"Okay," said Lucas shrugging. "Have you heard anything about Christine?" he asked.

"Not that much," said Corbett with a sigh.

Lucas settled into a seat, and muttered, "She's my wife, Richard, and I'm gonna get her back. I swear to *God!*" he pledged, clenching his fist. Then he looked at Corbett and asked, "Would you like to pray, Richard?"

"No, why?" asked Richard.

Francine Corbett and Christine Corbett-Lucas stepped into the cool dignity of the funeral home. They wore the finest dresses they had – Christine in a ruffled white blouse and red-checkered dress, Fran in blue and black. Christine saw people staring at her; she knew what they were thinking: *Why would she do this? She was always a good girl.*

Lucas and Richard Corbett, sitting in the front row, looked at the two women passing– Corbett just looking, Lucas angry. Lucas jerked toward Christine and muttered, "Christine, what *is* it with you?"

Christine was nervous about David being here. Her stomach tightened, her eyes widened, and her breathing became thin. He was about to grab her by the arm when Fran pushed his hand away and said "Get *back!*" Christine stepped away.

"Stay out of this. Fran, she's my wife!" commanded Lucas.

"Not anymore!" snapped Fran.

Lucas winced at this. Christine said quietly, "David, please just let me see my mother and let me go."

Lucas stared at her, then he returned to his seat next to Corbett.

Fran and Christine turned toward the casket, and gazed at the lifeless form of their mother.

"What would she think of this? With David?" asked Christine.

"Doesn't matter now, anymore," said Fran, sighing. "You know, it's funny. I never could get along with Mom when she was around, but now, well, it seems strange, like something's missing, and you know it won't come back."

"I realize now I was angry at her. Only I didn't know it at the time," said Christine. "I didn't think you were allowed to be angry at your parents. Now I know that parents aren't always right."

Lucas was recovering his feelings of anger and superiority now that he had stepped away from the two women. "That's some nerve of them," he complained, "Them coming here!"

"Why, it *is* her mother," Corbett replied.

"Richard, I'd appreciate it if you'd try to talk to her and straighten her out."

"No," Corbett drawled.

51

After the funeral, Lucas reached New York and the Manhattan Arms Hotel. One of the smaller meeting rooms of the hotel was being used for a press conference. Lucas walked through the assembly of journalists, not making any attempt at banter. He swaggered through the crowd to a raised podium, and then he pulled a sheet of yellow legal paper containing his notes.

Lucas looked at the sheet. The script on the paper looked a little fuzzy, and just looking at it hurt his eyes and brain. He squinted, tilted forward, and read the statement:

"My wife, the former Christine Corbett, has performed an act of disrespect toward the marriage vow and to the institution of marriage itself. I received word that she has retained the services of Elizabeth Mallory–a notorious feminist and enemy of moral values–to assist her in obtaining a divorce. I maintain that no person who believes in the Lord Jesus Christ or the family can ever accept a divorce. Therefore, I will obtain the finest possible legal services I can, and with the help of God, I will save my marriage, and the marriages of others."

As he spoke, cameras flashed and clicked. Lucas paused for breath and continued:

"I made my decision to go high-profile with this case because I have always believed in the sanctity of the family as long as I have been a Christian. I am fighting as much for all Christian families as I am for my own. By doing this, I'm continuing my fight to restore traditional values."

There came a babble from the journalists and hands were raised for questions. Dale Herbertson of the *Times,* a thinning-haired young man, asked, "Mr. Lucas, can you ascertain why your wife is seeking divorce, that is, on what grounds?"

"I have no idea why she would do such a thing," said Lucas with a shrug, his eyes relieved from the burden of reading.

Bill Loman of the *Daily News,* a man with a round face and black hair, asked, "Mr. Lucas, if indeed you do prevent this divorce, do you believe your wife will return to you?"

"Absolutely," snapped Lucas. "In my experience, whenever I make a strong stand, the opposition gives in easily. I expect that my wife will cease her foolish rebellion. My Christian faith has made me strong in the face of all enemies of Christ, and divorce is one of those enemies."

Again, Herbertson of the *Times*: "Reverend Lucas, a report has come out of Fort Horton, Kentucky, where your latest rallies took place. A sergeant there was arrested for anti-Semitic vandalism on the base, and the sergeant, named Wilmont, cited your influence. Any comment?"

Lucas stared at Herbertson, said, "No more questions," and he stalked off the podium and out of the room.

Lucas dragged himself to his suite in the Manhattan Arms–he would stay there for the night–dead tired. He entered is room, took off his jacket, and sat on the bed. He kept thinking. He tried to think of somebody to talk too. His mother!

"Oh, Ma," he moaned, "how could this happen to me? I tried, I really tried to be a good Christian husband! How could she *do* this?"

"Maybe *you* thought you were a good husband," Grace counseled him irritably, "but you always talked about her like she had no brains! Cripes, when you talked about her, you sounded just like your father."

At that, Charlie Lucas scrapped his feet into the kitchen, groaning, "Goddammit, I cut myself shaving again! Told you we needed a new color TV, but like the dumb bitch you are, you had to buy *food!* Why didn't yuh tell me about the game this evening? Once in your life, wake up!"

"Your son, *your son,* the *minister,* is on the phone!" Grace replied. "You want to speak to him?"

Charlie muttered, "Who's he humping this time, some greaseball cunt?" and drug his feet away.

"What was that?" asked Lucas.

"Your father," Grace replied. "They let your father retire early at the phone company. He's been yelling and cussing at everybody. I'm handling his pension and disability, the court declared him incompetent."

52

The day of the trial; Lucas emerged from the parsonage and headed towards the limo. Jim
Corbett and attorney Gordon Kyle were already inside. The limo cruised out of Erno and
toward Newark as Lucas announced, "I sent a message to the congregation at Wingate.
They'll rally at the courthouse steps."

"Why didn't you tell me, Dave?" asked Jim.

"Sorry, buddy," replied Lucas guiltily. "This divorce thing, it's been getting to
me. I'm all caught up in it."

"Dave, when was the last time you, well, took some time off?" asked Jim.

"I don't take vacations," Lucas pronounced plainly, in a *that's that!* tone.

"Why, it'll be good for you, Dave," Jim added, "especially–"

"No," Lucas concluded. "I don't take vacations. I work. I *always* work! I don't
waste a day! I don't care about resting. I have a job to do."

"I think Jim has a point," Kyle agreed. "What's so wrong with being a little kind
to yourself? It does wonders for your work afterwards."

"The world *isn't* kind," replied Lucas. "Suffering is part of life! Life is suffering and pain and torment! I *accept* that! I want *everybody else* to accept that! I especially want *Christine* to accept it as part of being a Christian woman!"

Kyle had to ask, "David, you seem to be making a political statement with this divorce, what with all this publicity. Divorces are pretty routine."

"I'm fighting for my family, for the traditional family!" snarled Lucas, emotion quivering in his voice. Then he exclaimed, "I *can't fail!* I *can't!* If I do, the faggots'll say – they'll have a field day with this divorce! I can't fail! It's for the *family!*" His face turned red, and rage radiated from him like heat. Then he said, "I'm a *man,* a *Christian man!* I *got'a* get her back!"

Jim and Kyle glanced at each other.

Liz Mallory drove Christine, Fran, and Linda Coyle, Liz's secretary—a youngish redhead in glasses— all the way from New York to Newark. As they arrived at the courthouse, they saw a crowd of people gathered at the vast courthouse steps, two dozen strong. They carried signs saying such things as "Save the family," "Divorce is a sin," "No homos in our schools." There was one long banner, red with yellow letters, saying WINGATE MEMORIAL BAPTIST CHURCH, ERNO, NJ.

Christine's heart fell. These were people she had grown up with, who she had known for the longest time. One woman in particular – a class mate, a woman she had loved like a sister – said, "I knew her, and she was *never* worth anything!"

Fran, sitting next to Christine in the back seat, saw her sister's distress and said, "You upset, kid?"

"They turned against me," Christine mourned. "I thought they were my friends and neighbors, but it's like they never knew me before."

"Don't worry, hon," assured Liz, "I'm prepared for something like this."

"You knew David would do something like this. Didn't you, Liz?" asked Christine.

"I've handled divorce cases before, and they can be pretty vicious," recalled Liz, "and David's a pretty well-known guy, I knew events involving famous people attract crowds."

As they spoke, Liz pulled the car toward the side entrance, and they got out. A sheriff's deputy came out, guided them inside the building, and asked, "You alright, Counsellor?"

"Fine, just keep those people on the front steps," answered Liz, pointing her thumb toward the courthouse steps, "I'll keep using this entrance."

The deputy nodded quickly, and five other deputies came to observe the crowd as it sang "Blessed Assurance" and "Onward, Christian Soldiers."

"You arranged this, Liz," asked Christine, "all these officers around?"

"Yeah, I spoke with the sheriff's office, asked them to watch the crowd," explained Liz. "As an attorney, I'm an officer of the court, and a former cop, too. That helps."

The four women walked down the hall and into the elevator, and emerged at the second floor. Christine felt a quivering in her stomach and said, "Liz, please keep David away from me."

Liz saw that Christine was nervous and asked, "You afraid he'll kidnap you or something?"

"Well…" drawled Christine.

"Don't worry. He won't do anything in public, in the courtroom," assured Liz.

Lucas, Jim, and Kyle, were already in the courtroom, seated at the defendant's table. The courtroom filled with spectators and Lucas supporters. *Good*, thought Lucas, *she might be intimidated.* The news media was in the back, and Lucas heard the clicks and buzzes of cameras and recorders. He folded his hands on the table, closed his eyes, and turned his mind toward God. Kyle dug into his briefcase and pulled out notes, while Jim rubbed his chin in anticipation of…something.

As Liz, Christine, Fran, and Linda entered the courtroom, they glanced at Kyle's table – Christine worriedly, Liz coldly, and Fran curiously. Lucas' supporters grumbled angrily at the unfaithful woman, hussy, and trollop who had walked out on her loving husband.

One woman, in her late sixties, rose and screamed, "Submit to thy husband in the name of the Lord Jesus! Thou hast committed fornication and thou shalt suffer torments in Hell!"

"Myrna! Sit down and don't make a fool of yourself!" barked the man sitting next to her.

Lucas finally turned and watched the enemy come up the courtroom aisle. Kyle glanced at his learned opponent. "Christine!" Lucas snapped as he leapt to his feet, but Kyle raised his hand, hushing Lucas, and gently pulled him down. Frowning, Liz glared at Lucas, while Christine gave her husband a quick glance. Jim looked at his little sister, as if to communicate, "I'm sorry about all this," but he said nothing; he knew what David would say if he did: "What's your problem, you some sort of faggot?"

Once the plaintiff's team was seated, the bailiff proclaimed, "All *rise!* This court is now in session, the Honorable Walter Spanelli presiding!" The Honorable Walter Spanelli strode into the courtroom, and after an introduction, he said to Liz, "Counselor, you may proceed."

Liz rose and began, "Your Honor, we ask that you grant the divorce requested by

Mrs. Lucas on the basis of irreconcilable differences. Mrs. Lucas is not willing to live anymore with her husband, and she asks for no alimony, just her independence." She sat down.

Kyle rose and spoke: "Your Honor, my client, the Reverend David Lucas, begs that you preserve his marriage. As a Minister of the Gospel, Reverend Lucas highly prizes the sanctity of the family unit and the honor of the marriage vow. There really is nothing wrong between them, Your Honor, so I ask you to save their marriage and let them work out any issues between them." He sat down, exchanging winks with Lucas.

Spanelli announced, "Miss Mallory, you may call your first witness."

"Mrs. Christine-Marie-Corbett-Lucas," stated Liz, and Christine rose, walked to the stand, took the oath administered by the bailiff, and sat down.

"Mrs. Lucas," began Liz, "would you please begin by explaining the nature of you relationship with your husband?"

Christine began, "As his wife, I felt it was my duty as a Christian woman to obey and serve him as he ordered. That was what I believed I was to do. If there were any problems, I thought it was my fault. If ever I was angry, I tried to avoid being angry, to, you know, stop the anger. I felt guilty for being angry at him."

"For what reasons were you angry at him?

"He would tell me to be quiet when people were around, and he yelled at me when I said anything. I know they weren't bad things but"– she sighed – "he wanted me to keep quiet."

"Was this often?"

"Yes. He never gave me anything to do while on the crusade except once in a while I would speak to the audience on my role as a Christian wife."

"Did you ask to do this public speaking?"

"No, he asked me to do this, and I didn't protest, because I felt obligated to do it, and it gave me something to do."

"When you weren't speaking,' continued Liz, "what did you do?"

"I would either stay at the hotel room and read magazines and watch TV, or else I'd sneak out and walk around not far from the hotel."

"Did he know you were doing this?"

"I didn't tell him what I was doing all day."

"Did he ask?"

"No."

"When he got home, what did he talk about?"

"His work, what he was doing during the day."

All this was new to Lucas. Mallory put her up to it.

Liz continued, "Would you tell us, please, Mrs. Lucas, the time when you were pregnant?"

"No!" snapped Lucas, jumping up. "That was – my baby was killed! By some evil woman doctor!"

"Mr. Lucas!" proclaimed Judge Spanelli *"Please* cease these outbursts!"

Kyle rose grandly and said, "With all due respect to the dignity of the court, Your Honor, I believe that Mr. Lucas is justified in his desire not to relive such a painful experience. Therefore, I must formally object to this line of questioning."

Liz, ready for this, replied, "I wish to demonstrate, Your Honor, the nature of the marriage between Mr. and Mrs. Lucas, how he really felt about her, and where his priorities were at that time, which included a referendum campaign against homosexuals, the results of which upset him."

Spanelli looked at Kyle, then Lucas, then Liz. "I will allow the questioning to continue," he announced.

"Thank you, Your Honor," said Liz, then she turned toward Christine, who told of her pregnancy, of how David had been away on the referendum campaign, of her heart attack, and of how David had broken down and cried in the hospital room.

Lucas bowed his head, resting it on his folded hands, breathing in short spurts. *The murder of his baby…*His eyes pressed shut, as if he was in pain.

"You say, Mrs. Lucas," Liz went on, "that he wept when you asked about how the referendum went?"

"Yes."

"How do you think he felt at the time of the abortion?"

"I feel as if he was more concerned about the failure of his campaign than with my welfare," Christine answered plainly. "I still do."

Lucas kept his head down, fighting inside himself with the thoughts – *She's telling the truth* was at war with *That's wrong, I love her.* Liz glanced at Lucas and Kyle from the corner of her eye, gauging the effect of the testimony, reading the body language. Kyle, in the meantime, was studying Christine's testimony, analyzing it for weak spots.

Liz continued, "Did you ever discuss any of these things with your husband?"

"I would try to," replied Christine, "but I'd be too frightened."

"Why were you frightened?"

"I was afraid of him, and I didn't feel I should tell him things he wouldn't want to hear. As I said, I believed that I was to obey my husband and follow him in all things."

"What was the point when you decided you had had enough?"

"It was when David and I had a dinner with the chaplains at Fort Horton," Christine said, and she described how David antagonized Chaplain Kirshman.

"Do you love your husband?"

"I *thought* I loved him," said Christine, "but I can't say that I do anymore. I don't hate him, but I feel nothing for him. I thought I was supposed to love him, since I was married to him."

Liz knew this would be a touchy subject, but she had to ask, "What kind of sex life did the two of you have?"

Christine's throat tightened at that; she breathed deeply and said, "I got no pleasure from it. None whatsoever. In the past few years, David was all caught up in his work, and so we had no sex."

"About when did this occur? When did you stop having sex?"

"About the time I had the heart attack and the abortion."

"How do you think he felt after that?"

"He said nothing to me about the abortion. I heard him talk about it to my father, but not to me."

"Do you have any children, Mrs. Lucas?" asked Liz.

"No."

"Did he say often that he wanted children?"

"He never said anything about having children after the abortion. Before that, he spoke of us having good Christian children to bring up in God's way."

"For how long have you been married, Mrs. Lucas?"

Christine checked her memory, and then said, "We got married in 1973, so it would be nine years."

"Considering the length of your marriage, Mrs. Lucas," Liz went on, "does it not seen strange that you haven't had any children?"

"Yes, it does."

Lucas started to twitch nervously. He felt like his manhood was in question. He whispered to Kyle, "Do something, object!"

"On what grounds?" hissed Kyle.

"Do you have any idea, why, Mrs. Lucas," continued Liz, "in spite of all the sex you had until a few years ago, you never had children?"

"Objection," grandly stated Kyle, and Lucas heaved a sigh.

Liz twitched her shoulder in a shrug, then asked, "Mrs. Lucas, do you want any alimony from your husband?"

"Not at all," proclaimed Christine. "I believe that I'm capable of earning a living on my own. I'm undergoing job counseling to determine what kind of occupation would be best for me."

"No more questions, Your Honor," said Liz as she resumed her seat and Kyle rose. Lucas thought *Get 'im, boy!* Christine was ready for Kyle's questions.

"Mrs. Lucas," Kyle began, "Miss Mallory told you to say those things, did she not?"

"The words and feelings are my own, Mr. Kyle," returned Christine quietly.

"Does it not make you feel ashamed, Mrs. Lucas, that you walked out on your husband?" Kyle proclaimed, trying to sound like a mighty prophet.

"I regret that I did not confront my husband with my disagreement," Christine continued in her monotone voice. "But it's done, and it can't be undone."

"Mrs. Lucas," Kyle continued the pressure, not letting up, "Your husband cared for you, he provided for your needs, and you just walked away from him! Do you feel proud of yourself?"

Lucas sat with a small smile, expecting her to break down and cry on the stand.

"I'm sorry you put it in those terms, Mr. Kyle," answered Christine. "I'm not his property, I'm not his slave. Even if David spent a million dollars on me, I'm still not his property. Like David, I value the traditional family unit, but I realize now that there has to be respect between the two parties involved, and that respect is part of the love between the two partners. A marriage without respect, Mr. Kyle, should not keep going."

Christine's voice was confident and clear. Liz smiled at her client standing up for herself, and Fran enjoyed the new-found maturity of her little sister.

Kyle was caught off-guard by Christine's speech, but his face did not show it. He knew he had to withdraw and plan strategy for the next assault, so he concluded with, "No more questions, Your Honor."

"You may step down, Mrs. Lucas," stated the judge, and Christine was greeted with hand squeezing from Fran and a pat from Liz as she sat.

"Is that all?" hissed Lucas.

Kyle glanced at his client, then proclaimed, "I call to the stand the Reverend David Lucas!"

Lucas rose and he strode to the stand. *At last*, he thought. He took the oath, and sat.

"Reverend Lucas," Kyle began, "How would you describe yourself as a husband?"

Lucas replied with sureness, "I know that I was a very good husband. I follow the Bible as my guide, and it tells me how I should conduct myself as a man and as a husband."

"Have you ever physically abused your wife, Reverend?"

"Never."

"Ever said an irate word to her?"

"Only when she deserved it."

"Do you believe that you are superior to your wife simply because you're a man?"

"No, not superior," answered Lucas, "but I believe that God has placed me at the head of my wife. She's to obey me, and I am to care for her out of love."

Lucas made occasional glances at Liz as he spoke. He hoped she was getting annoyed, but she stayed cool.

"Thank you, Reverend," Kyle concluded, and he moved to his seat and said, "Your witness, Ms. Mallory."

Liz began, "Mr. Lucas, you truly believe that the wife should subordinate herself to the husband?"

"That's what it says in the Bible," assured Lucas.

"If your wife were to express an opinion, Mr. Lucas, would you consider it?"

"Yes, but the final decision would be mine," replied Lucas. "That is part of my function as the head of the household."

"Are you serious about that statement, Mr. Lucas?"

"I'm *completely* serious," sneered Lucas.

Liz knew she would get into an unnecessary argument with Lucas, so she went on with, "How do you get these beliefs, Mr. Lucas?"

"My Christian belief, my faith in the Lord Jesus and the Bible," replied Lucas proudly. "Before I met Jesus, I looked on women as sexual playthings, and now that I *am* a Christian man and husband, I see it as my duty to honor and protect them."

"Did you know what your wife was thinking and feeling, as she expressed them on the stand?"

"Ms. Mallory, you told her to say those things."

"What do you think your wife thinks about you?" asked Liz.

"She loves me as much as I love her," returned Lucas with confidence.

"So, Mr. Lucas, why do you think she walked out on you, if she loves you so much?" pressed Liz.

"She was just upset at the death of her mother," Lucas stated like an expert. "She wasn't thinking straight."

"Well, Mr. Lucas," Liz went on, "the shock of her mother's death has worn off, and she's still pushing for this divorce."

"She doesn't want it," insisted Lucas calmly, "and I won't allow it."

"Let me guess," Liz asked. "You assume that because you won't accept it, because you are so determined and stubborn about this marriage, that you will have your way, correct?"

"Precisely," said Lucas with a smirk. "I have been around brave and determined men in the Armed Forces Crusade who are the best America has to offer, and who know that the way to success is to never take the easy way out, to never give in!"

Liz stated, "Getting back to previous testimony, Mr. Lucas, you said that I was putting words into your wife's mouth. Don't you think she has a mind of her own?"

"I have found Christine to be rather like a child in many ways," replied Lucas.

"Could you please go into more detail, Mr. Lucas, about your wife being like a child?"

"Nothing more to say," Lucas answered, smiling.

"Is that how you expect your wife to be, Mr. Lucas?" Liz asked, putting the pressure on Lucas. "Do you want her to depend on you and not have any self-reliance?"

"I believe that God has placed the man at the head of the woman, both in and out of marriage," declared Lucas. "I follow the Holy Bible, and nothing else, and many of the ills of society and the world in general could be traced to the fact that there is no guidance, no order, no control –"

"Then you won't mind if I ask you to control your tirade, Mr. Lucas!" snapped Liz.

Lucas got quiet. Kyle – whom Lucas had made eye contact with for a second – had no grounds for objection.

Liz inhaled, exhaled, and then continued, "Mr. Lucas, have you ever told Mrs. Lucas what you feel about her?"

"She knows what I feel about her," Lucas responded, no longer smiling.

"Have you told her verbally?"

"I don't have to tell her," he replied plainly.

"How could she know what you think of her if you don't tell her?"

"Well. . ." Lucas drawled, looking for something to say, and then he decided: "We lived long enough together to know what we're thinking!"

Liz went on, "Did she ever offer to assist you in your evangelistic work?"

"Uh. . ." Two seconds of silence. "Yes."

"Did you let her?"

"No!" exclaimed Lucas. Then calmly, he repeated himself. "No."

"Why not?"

"She's my *wife,*" he answered, as if he had responded to the question.

"Now about the time your wife was pregnant, and you were engaged in the referendum campaign," Liz stated, "she had a heart attack, and to save her, she had to have an abortion. Do you understand the necessity of the abortion at the time?"

"It was due to the cruelty and viciousness of a woman doctor!" said Lucas, raging.

"Mr. Lucas!" snapped Liz again, "kindly refrain from any tirade!" Then she asked, "Did the doctor not tell you about the heart attack?"

"Yes, she did."

"And?"

"I still see that as no reason to kill a poor, helpless, little baby," Lucas concluded.

"Even at the risk of your wife's life?" hinted Liz.

"Yes." It fell easily from Lucas' lips.

"Thank you, Mr. Lucas," concluded Liz. "No more questions for now. Maybe latter."

Lucas went back to the plaintiff's table. Judge Spanelli proclaimed, "Court will resume at the same time tomorrow." A knock of the gavel, and the courtroom broke into babbles.

Lucas, Kyle, and Jim were the first to go down the aisle and out the door. The press went after them as the trio raced toward the front door and the supporters outside.

Some of the media people said to each other, "Let's get Mallory," and they moved toward Liz, Christine, Fran, and Linda. Christine quivered inside as she saw the microphones and cameras aimed at her.

"Ms. Mallory," one young man asked, "What do you think your chances of winning are?"

"I'm quite certain that any fair-minded judge would agree to this divorce," stated Liz plainly. "We have shown that Mr. Lucas has failed to fulfill the emotional needs of his wife, and that this marriage should not go on. That is all I have to say." They walked out the courtroom door, accompanied by a deputy.

Once they had gotten out of the courtroom, the deputy muttered into Liz's ear, "Watch out for Spanelli. He's bad news. He'll do anything for a vote." The four women got out the side entrance and into Liz's Cadillac, and moved out.

The crowd of Lucas supporters remained on the front steps of the courthouse during the trial. They cheered as Lucas, with Kyle and Jim behind, walked from the door to face them.

"Thank you, my friends, for coming to my aid," Lucas announced to his supporters. "I'm not just trying to save my *own* marriage! I'm fighting for the old-fashioned family, the very foundation of civilization itself! Only if the family survives will we survive as a society! Pray for me as I fight the good, noble fight!"

The crowd yelled with joyous anger and opened a path for Lucas, Kyle, and Jim, and the three men entered the limo.

As the limo pulled from the curb, Kyle confessed, "I was a little worried back there, David, when she was questioning you."

"What's wrong, Gordon?" wondered Lucas.

"I don't think you looked so good on the stand, and the media might pick up on that," Kyle warned. "Don't underestimate Liz Mallory just because she's a woman. She's a very through cross-examiner, and she handles the media like a pro."

"I don't think it's a winner, Dave," Jim warned grimly. "What if the judge *does* grant the divorce?"

"I'll win. Don't worry," said Lucas, smiling, although he didn't feel so confident inside.

Kyle stated, "I'm going back to my office, to plot strategy for tomorrow."

"I'm going straight home," sighed Jim, "see how Dad is doing."

"Yeah, okay," approved Lucas.

53

At Four PM, Judge Walter Spanelli, his robe off, dialed the Newark office of Gordon Kyle, Esq., who was planning for the next day's session.

"Good afternoon, Counselor," began Spanelli brightly.

"Good afternoon, Your Honor," responded Kyle respectfully. "How may I help you?"

"Let me begin, Mr. Kyle," started Spanelli, "by saying that I truly admire your client, Reverend Lucas, and all of his work to uphold the traditional values of the nation."

"Yes?"

"And let me also say, Mr. Kyle, I've heard of some things about Ms. Mallory, the kind of loud-mouth bitch she is."

"Yes," said Kyle, "but why are you calling me?"

"Counselor, I'll come right to the point," stated Spanelli. "I've seen the kind of people supporting Reverend Lucas this morning. Those are the kind of fine, upstanding people I would love to be around, you know, in the circles I travel in."

Kyle knew what was coming; dealing with politicians in the state for the longest time, he had heard it all before–a favorable ruling in exchange for future favors. Kyle responded, "Yes, he has a lot of respect in such circles, and I can assure you, your honor, that Reverend Lucas never forgets a favor."

"Of course," warned Spanelli, "I can't appear to be partial, or else I'd be disbarred. You understand, Mr. Kyle? And I'd appreciate it if Reverend Lucas refrain from any outbursts in my court."

"Of course," agreed Kyle. "I'll convey your respects to Reverend Lucas."

"Yes, please do, Mr. Kyle, and thank you."

"Thank you, Your Honor."

They hung up.

Lucas sat at the linoleum-topped table in the kitchen of the parsonage, eating Chinese take-out and reading the Bible, his left hand propping up his forehead, trying once again to make sense of what was going on. *Hadn't I been a good husband?* He kept thinking. *What did I do wrong? I've done nothing wrong.*

The white phone on the wall rang. Lucas grabbed it and said, "Hello?"

"Gordon, here, David," said Kyle, "and I have *good* news." He told Lucas of the call from Spanelli.

"Oh, yeah?" said Lucas, smiling. "That's beautiful, that's just terrific! God bless you, Gordon!" and he hung up.

Back in Fran's apartment, she and Christine sat at the couch, chatting before going to bed.

"I feel a lot better, now, Frannie," said Christine with a sigh.

"You see now, you got people on your side," Fran replied.

"It's strange," said Christine. "Now that I'm away from David, I can see how he was. It's as if his ministry was all he cared about. I knew it was important to him, but he ignored me, took it for granted that I should go along. Like that set of encyclopedias you sent us as a wedding present?"

"Yeah?"

"He kept them in his den, and he never let me inside his den. You see I called it *his* den, not *the* den or *our* den?"

Fran put her arm around her sister's shoulders and assured her. "There are a lot of people who love, but don't know how to show it right. Maybe David *did* love you, but he couldn't communicate it. It was the same with Mom and Dad. They loved each other, but they acted like they were stuck with each other, like they had nowhere else to go."

"Still," said Christine, "I realize now that if you love a person, you have to let them know."

The tea kettle was steaming, and Fran said, "Let's have some tea, then it's off to bed for us."

The phone rang, and Fran answered, "Hello?"

The voice on the other end said, "Frannie?"

"Jimmy?"

"Yeah."

Fran was surprised; Jim had been working for David for a while. She asked, "How are you?"

"Okay," said Jim, then he said, "I just want to let you know I love you and Chris, and I want what's best for her. But I can't go against Dave, see, I have to stick with him."

"Want to speak to Chris?"

"Yeah."

Christine got on and said, "Hi, Jimmy." A brief pause, then she said, "Thanks for calling me."

At the same time, David Lucas had laid in his bed. Already, he won, and he knew it. His marriage was saved, his wife would come back to him, and they would be a happy Christian couple. As he slept, he dreamed that Christine was floating back to him, her arms outstretched.

54

The next morning, Lucas emerged from the front door of the parsonage, and a crowd awaited him outside, cheering, waving, and applauding. "We're with you, Dave!' called out a happy male voice. Lucas smiled widely, waved, and walked toward the limo with Kyle and Jim inside.

Before entering, Lucas turned and joyously proclaimed, "With your prayers and good wishes, I know I'll win my wife back!", and then he opened the car door and got in.

In the limo, Kyle and Jim were waiting. As Lucas closed the door, Kyle said, "Dave, you remember Reverend Van Der Molen, from South Africa?"

"Sure, he spoke at the opening meeting of the NCPC," recalled Lucas.

"Well, he wanted to get in touch with you about a project he's been working on. He and a lot of other ministers are forming a radio station near Cape Town to preach the Gospel to all of Africa in all the continent's languages. The South African government's supporting this effort, providing news and commentary from the government, along with some seed money to start up with. Oh, and the government is letting them use a transmitter and a building for the station. Reverend Van Der Molen wanted me to ask you if you'd help promote the station here in the States, and get other fundamentalist clergy to get involved."

"I'll do it!" Lucas stated, quickly and happily.

"Wait, let's be careful about this, Dave," cautioned Kyle. "If your connection with the South African government becomes known, you could lose your credibility as an evangelist."

"Gordon, I don't care why the government is doing this," Lucas said, smiling. "In this country, I need permission from the courts to preach to servicemen, here in the land of the free, so-called. The government of South Africa's going to help aid religious activity, and I *like* that!"

"David," warned Kyle, "we might be accused of doing propaganda work for the South African government rather than preaching. You *know* how unpopular the South African government is."

"Yeah, I know," said Lucas. "I don't care, though. People just don't know the real story. That's all! Christians, I think, ought to get behind South Africa! You did some lobbying for the South African government, Gordon, so you can help on that score!"

"Of course," agreed Kyle. "I have plenty of connections in South Africa. But you understand I'm giving some words of caution. We have to do this the right way." Lucas nodded and smiled.

On the highway to Newark, Liz Mallory drove Linda Coyle, Christine Corbett-Lucas, and Fran Corbett in her Cadillac. Christine noticed Liz frowning.

"Liz, what's wrong?" worried Christine.

"I had an argument with my boyfriend," explained Liz. "Nothing serious."

"Will things be all right?"

"Sure," said Liz. "We have these little disagreements now and then. We accept them as part of the relationship we have. We love each other enough not to let them destroy our relationship. They even help, because they get out the bad blood and they don't keep things bottled up and cause troubles later."

"David and I never argued," recalled Christine. "Now that I think about it, he argued and I just accepted what he said."

"Even if it was against you?" asked Liz.

"Yes, I'm afraid so," said Christine. "I thought it would be selfish of me to assert myself, to not go along with him or accept what he said."

They arrived at the courthouse in Newark, and again Lucas' supporters crowded the front steps, singing hymns and waving placards and Bibles. And again, Liz and her passengers pulled up to the back, entered the courthouse, and headed up the elevator and into the courtroom.

Lucas, Jim, and Kyle were already at their table, talking and grinning, acting and sounding a little too confident. Reporters asked each other, "Did Kyle get another judge?" As Liz, Christine, Fran, and Linda entered, Liz heard the reporters talking, and she frowned. The media crowded around them, and Christine shivered a little as the lights and cameras were aimed at her.

The bailiff announced the arrival of the Honorable Walter Spanelli, who took the bench and glanced at Kyle with a smile. Liz thought, *Uh oh, Kyle did it again.* Christine squeezed Liz's hand fearfully under the table. Spanelli announced:

"I have reached a verdict in this case. I have been very concerned about the collapse of the family unit and the resulting juvenile crime, drug abuse, and other problems stemming from broken marriages. The Reverend David Lucas strikes me as a man dedicated to the family as a vital social unit, and I believe that he is capable of resolving the problems facing his marriage.

"Therefore, after due consideration, I will *not* grant the divorce."

There was a commotion in the courtroom. Lucas, Kyle, and Jim looked as each other and grinned, and Lucas told Kyle, "We'll never abandon this guy!"

Christine gasped, suddenly feeling weak. Liz turned to her guessing that what she feared was true.

"I *can't* go back, I *can't!*" muttered Christine.

"Don't worry, Hon. We'll still fight it," assured Liz, and she got up and announced, "Your Honor, we wish to make it known that we will appeal this decision."

The room quieted down, and Spanelli announced, "So noted! Case dismissed!"

and he banged the gavel and strode out of the courtroom.

The commotion resumed, and Christine stood and muttered again, "I *won't* go back, I *won't!*"

Lucas, grinning, shook Kyle's hand. Jim nodded and smiled, and cast a glance at Christine, seeing her look of work and fear.

Lucas turned to claim his prize, smiling, "Christine!"

Christine walked over to his quickly.

Like in the dream, she's returning to me, thought Lucas.

She swung her open right hand to the left side of his face, making a *plap!* An *oooh* rose from the crowd as she warned, "David, no matter what that judge says, we're *through!*" Lucas' face burned, his eyes and mouth wide open, as the four women walked quickly out the door. The cameras caught all of it.

The four women strode to the elevators. When they got in, Liz said smiling, "Chris, I'm proud of you, honey," and Linda smiled and patted Christine's shoulder.

"You stood up for yourself, kid. That was great!" said Fran, cheerfully.

"I feel so good, I can't explain it," Christine smiled widely. The elevator arrived, and they went in.

The elevator stopped at the bottom floor, and they got out.

Liz said to Christine, "Well, my dear, in front of all those people, you slapped David Lucas. You declared your independence, with the news media looking on."

"I feel weird, but good,' said Christine, smiling. "I really don't feel bound by the judge's order. I've never done anything like that in my life."

"You get more practice, kid," said Fran smiling too, and they walked to the car.

The courtroom was empty, except for David Lucas, Gordon Kyle, and Jim Corbett. Lucas leaned on the counsel table, the slap still burning his face.

What happened? He wondered. He had won the case – the judge denied the divorce – but his wife wasn't with him.

"Dave, we have to go now," advised Jim.

As if pulled by strings, Lucas walked with Kyle and Jim out of the courtroom and into the elevator. When they got in, Lucas muttered, "I won this case. She'll always be my wife. I'll have no one else, ever!" Then they got out of the elevator and went out of the court house's front door.

His supporters applauded and yelled praise when they saw Lucas. He smiled at their faith and support; he forgot that Christine was not still with him. He spoke cheerfully to the crowd: "My brothers and sisters in Jesus, I thank you again and again for your prayers and steadfast faith! My marriage is saved, and may every marriage be happy and blessed by God!"

The crowd yelled their praise again. With the cameras on for the six o'clock news, the crowd surrounded Lucas and Kyle and sang, "Stand Up, Stand Up For Jesus, Ye Soldiers of the Cross," and they entered the limo.

Lucas' smile drooped. He won the case. As the limo moved down the road, Lucas looked outside the window and saw a person walk by–long blond hair, body reed-thin, shirt open to show a hairless chest–and he shouted through the glass, "Are you a man?

Are you a Woman? Make up your mind!" He sat back and shouted, "Where's Christine?"

THE END

Made in the USA
Middletown, DE
16 September 2021